She found herself trembling as the great iron monster drew nearer to them, and Seagrave, kind and thoughtful for her, slipped his hand within her arm.

"You mustn't forget me, little ladybird," he said wistfully.

"Oh, I won't forget you ever," said Fraley earnestly, "and I'm so glad I have one friend. I'm very grateful to you for what you have done for me."

The train had come up beside them now and passengers were beginning to board. Seagrave suddenly stooped and kissed her gravely, reverently on the forehead.

"Good-by, little sister. You've done a lot for me, I think. Here, get on in this car. Good-by, my little ladybird."

She stood an instant trembling, and then the train began to move, and Seagrave walked alongside, tipping his hat to her, and waving his hand. Then he was gone out of her sight.

Would she ever see him again?

Grace
LIVINGSTON HILL

LADYBIRD

LIVING BOOKS®
Tyndale House Publishers, Inc.
Wheaton, Illinois

This Tyndale House book
by Grace Livingston Hill
contains the complete text
of the original hardcover edition.
NOT ONE WORD
HAS BEEN OMITTED.

Living Books is a registered trademark of Tyndale House
Publishers, Inc.

Library of Congress Catalog Card Number 92-60097
ISBN 0-8423-2081-4

Printed in the United States of America

99 98 97 96
 9   8   7   6   5   4   3   2

FRALEY MacPherson stood in the open door of the cabin, looking out across the mountains. The peace of the morning was shining on them and the world looked clean and new made after the storm of the night before. She gave a little wistful sigh, her heart swelling with longing, and joy in the beauty, and a wish that life were all like that beauty spread out so wondrously before her.

For a moment she reveled in the Spring tints of the foliage, the tender buds of the trees like dots of coral over their tops, the pale green of the little new leaves, the deep darkness of the stalwart pines, that seemed like great plumy backgrounds for the more delicate tracery of the other trees that were getting their new season's foliage. Her glance swept every familiar point in the landscape, from the dim purple mountains in the distance, as far as eye could reach, with the high light of snow on the peaks, to the nearer ones, gaunt with rocks or furred with the tender green of the trees; then down to the foothills, and the valley below.

There was one place, off to the right, where her eyes never lingered. It was the way to the settlement, miles beyond, the trail that led past a sheer precipice, where her father had fallen to his death five months before. She always had to suppress a little shudder as she glanced past the ominous yawning cavern, that crept, it seemed to her sensitive gaze, nearer and nearer to the trail each month. It was the one spot in all the glorious panorama that spoiled the picture if she let herself see it, not only because of that terrible memory, but also because it was the way the men of the household came and went to and from the far off world.

Peace, and contentment came into Fraley's life only when the men of the household were gone somewhere into the world. Peace and contentment fled when they returned, terror and dismay remained.

The girl was good to look upon as she stood in the doorway, the sunshine on her golden hair that curled into a thousand ripples and caught the gleams of light till she looked like a piece of the morning herself.

Her eyes were bits of the sky, and the soft flush that came and went in her cheeks was like a wild mountain flower. She looked like a young flower herself as she stood there in her little faded shapeless frock, one bare foot poised on the toe behind the other bare heel—pretty feet, never cramped by shoes that were too tight for her, seldom covered by any shoe at all.

Her arms were round and smooth and white, one raised and resting against the door frame. The whole graceful little wild sweet figure, drenched with the morning and gazing into life, a fit subject for some great artist's brush.

Something of all this came into the weary mind of the dying woman who lay on the cot across the room and watched her, and a weak tear trickled down her pallid cheek.

Fraley's eyes were resting on a soft cloud now, that

nested in the hollow of a mountain just below its peak. She had eyes that could see heavenly things in clouds, and she loved to watch them as they trailed a glorious panorama among the peaks and decked themselves in the colors of the morning; or the blaze of white noon; or the vivid glory of the sunset. This cloud she was watching now had wreathed itself about until she saw in it a lovely mother, holding a little child in her arms. She smiled dreamily as the cloud mother smiled down at the little leaping babe in her arms, that, even as she watched, sank back into sleep, and became a soft billow of white upon the mountain. How the mother looked down and loved it, the little billow of cloud baby in her arms!

"Fraley!"

The voice was very weak, but the girl, anxious, startled, her smile fading quickly into alarm, turned with a start back to the sordid room and life with its steadily advancing sorrow that had been drawing nearer every hour now for tortuous days.

"Fraley."

The girl was at her mother's side in an instant, kneeling beside the crude cot.

"Yes, Mother?" There was pain in her voice, and a forced cheer. "You want some fresh water?"

"No, dear! Sit down close—I must tell you something—"

"Oh, don't talk, Mother!" protested the girl anxiously, "It always makes you cough so."

"I must!—Fraley—the time—is—going fast—now— It's almost run out."

"Oh, don't, Mother! You were better last night. You haven't coughed so much this morning. I asked that strange man last night to get word to a doctor. He promised. Maybe he will come before night!"

"No, Fraley, child! It's too late! No doctor can cure

me. Listen child—Don't let's waste words—Every minute is precious—I must tell you something—I ought to have told you before—Come close—I can't speak—so—loud."

The girl stayed her tears, and leaned close to the beloved lips, a wild fear growing in her eyes. Persistently she had tried to hide from herself the fact that this beloved mother, her only beloved in all the world, was going from her; tried not to think what her lot would be when she was gone.

Persistently now she put the thought from her and tried bravely to listen.

"Fraley—when I'm gone—you—can't stay here."

Fraley nodded, as if that had long been a settled fact between them.

"I hoped—I hoped—I always hoped I'd get strength to go with you and get away—somehow—only I never—did. I never found a way—nor money enough for us both—even for one—"

"Don't, Mother!" moaned the girl with a little quick catch in her breath—"don't *apologize*. As if I didn't know what you've been through. Just tell me what you want me to know, and don't bother with the rest. I *understand*."

The feeble hand pressed the girl's strong one, and the pale lips tried to smile.

"Dear child!" she murmured, then struggled through a spell of coughing, lay panting a moment, and struggled on.

"There isn't enough—yet—not even for you—" she panted.

"I don't need money," scorned the young voice. "I can take care of myself."

"Oh, my dear!" sighed the woman, and then girded herself to go on.

"There's only fifteen dollars. It's in—three little gold fives. Never mind how I got it. I sold the heifer they thought went astray—to that stranger that rode up here two months ago. I had to bear a beating—but it gave me the last five. The first I brought out here to the wilderness with me and the second I got from the man who came here the day your father was killed. I—sold my wedding ring to him—but that was all he would give—"

"Oh, Mother! You oughtn't to talk," pleaded the girl, as the mother struggled with another fit of coughing.

"I must, dear! Don't hinder now—the time is so short!"

"Then tell it quick, Mother, and let's be over with it," cried the girl, lifting the sick woman's head tenderly and helping her to sip a little water from a tin cup that stood on a bench by the cot.

"It's here"—she pressed her hand over her heart, "sewed in the cloth—You must rip it out. Put it in the little clean bag I made for it, and tie it around your waist. If Brand Carter should lay his hands on it once you'd never see it again! Twice—he's tried to see if I had anything—once when he thought I was asleep. He suspected, I think. Take it now, Fraley, and fix it out of sight around your waist. Here, take the knife and rip the stitches—quick— You can't always tell if one of the men might come back! Go look down the mountain before you begin. Hurry!"

In a panic the girl sprang to the door, and gazed in the direction of the trail, but the morning simmered on in beauty, and not a human came in sight. A wild bird soared, smote the morning with his song—smote her young heart with sorrow. Oh, why did that bird have to sing now?

She sprang back and deftly cut the stitches. Through blinding tears she sewed the coins into the bit of girdle

5

her mother had crudely made from a cotton salt bag—most of their clothing was made from bags, flour and salt and sometimes cotton sugar bags—and solemnly girded herself with it as her mother bade her.

"Now, Fraley," said the mother, when this was done to her satisfaction, "You're to guard that night and day. It won't be long till I'm gone. And you're not to think you must spend any of it on—me—on burying—or l-like that—"

A sob from Fraley stopped her, and she laid a wasted hand upon the bright rough head that was buried in the flimsy bed cover.

"I know—little girl—Mother's little girl! That's hard—but—that's a *command!* Understand, Fraley? It's Mother's last wish!"

The girl choked out an assent.

"And you're not to stay for *anything* like that. It wouldn't be *safe!* Oh, I ought—to have got you out of here long ago! Only I—didn't see the way clear—I couldn't let you go—without me—You—were so young—!"

"I know, Mother dear, I know!" sobbed the girl, trying to smile bravely through her tears. "I wouldn't have gone—you know—not without you!"

"Well, I should have gone—we should have gone together long ago and found a nice place in the wilderness, if there wasn't any other way, a place where they would never think to look, where we could die together. That would have been better than this—than leaving you *here* all alone. You—all—alone!"

"Mother, don't blame yourself! Please! I can't bear it!"

A wild rabbit scurried across the silence in front of the cabin and a hawk in the sky circled great shadows that moved over the spot of sunshine on the cabin floor. Fraley with ears attuned to the slightest sound in her wide silent world, sprang up and darted to the door to survey the wilderness, then came back reassured.

"It's no one," she said, laying her firm young hand on the cold brow, "Now, Mother, can't you rest a little? You've talked too much."

"No, No!" protested the sick woman, "The time is going! I must finish! Fraley, go look behind the loose board under your bed. There's a bag there! Bring it! I want to show you! Quick!"

Fraley came back with a bundle of gray woolen cloth which she examined wonderingly.

"I made it from your father's old coat," explained the mother eagerly. "It's some worn, and there's a hole or two I had to darn, but it will be better than nothing."

"But what is it for, Mother?" asked the girl puzzled.

"It's a travelling bag for you when you start. It's all packed. See! I washed and mended your other things, and made a little best dress for you out of my old black satin one that had been put away in the hole under the floor since before you were born. It may not be in fashion now—but it's the best I could do. I cut it out when you were asleep, and sewed it while you gathered wood for the fire."

"Oh, Mother! And you so sick."

"I loved to do it, dear—I'd always thought—how some day—maybe I'd get where I could buy you— pretty things—maybe some day a white—wedding— dress! But now—!"

"Oh, Mother!" burst forth the girl with uncontrollable tears, "I shan't ever need a wedding dress! I don't *want* a wedding dress! I hate men! I hate the sight of them all. My father never made you happy! All the men around here only curse and get drunk and swear. I shall never get married—!"

"I'm sorry, dear child, you should never have known

all—this—sin, this terror—Oh, I dreamed I'd get you out of this—into a clean world some day! But I've failed—! There *are* good men—!"

Fraley set her lips, but said nothing. She doubted that there were good men.

"Fraley, we must hurry! My strength—is—going—fast."

"Don't talk Mother! Please."

"But I must! Look in the bag, child. I've put the old Book there! It's almost worn out, but I've sewed it in a cloth cover. Fraley—you'll stick to the old Book?"

"Yes, Mother, I promise. I'll never let anybody take it from me!"

"But if it should be lost—or stolen—Fraley, you've much of it in your heart. You'll never forsake it, Fraley?"

"Never, Mother. I promise!" said the girl solemnly.

"Well, then I'm satisfied!" sighed the mother, closing her eyes. "Now, child, hide the bag again! Everything is there I could give you. Even your father's picture and mine when we were married, and a few papers I've kept. Put them away, and come back—I want to tell you—what I've never told you before!"

Fraley obeyed trembling at what revelation might be coming.

"Come closer, child, I'm—short—of breath—again—And—I—must tell—I should have told—before—!"

Fraley nestled close, and held her mother's cold hand in hers.

"Child, I did a wrong and foolish thing—when I was a girl! I had a good home—I've never talked—much about it! I couldn't bear to! My heart was breaking for it—all the—time!"

Fraley held her mother's hand closer in sympathy.

"Child, I ran away from that home and got married.

I've never seen—nor heard—from any of—my own—since—"

There was a great sob like a gasp at the end of the words!

"Oh, Mother!" gasped the girl in wonder and sorrow, "Oh, Mother—if you'd only told me—I might have helped you more!"

"Fraley—darling—you have been everything! You have been wonderful! You have—been—my world—my life—! Oh, if I could take you with me where I am going—now! But—you'll *come?* You'll be *sure* and—come?"

"Yes, I'll come! That will be *everything*—for me, Mother!"

"But I—must—hurry on."

"Mother—did you have—" the girl hesitated, almost shyly, "Did you have a Mother like you? You told me once my grandmother was dead. Was she dead—when—you went?"

"Yes, child. She had been gone a year. You—think I would not have gone—if she—had been there? Well—perhaps—I do not know. I was young—and headstrong. Even before she went she warned me against Angus MacPherson. But I did not heed! Perhaps she worried herself into the grave about me. While she lived—I did not go with him—*much!* But—she knew where my heart—was turning! I was mad with impatience to be out—like other girls!"

Fraley listened as to a fairy story. *Her mother*, young and wild like that!

"Angus was young and handsome. He had dark curls, and a cleft in his chin—and he was very much—in love—with me—then—! No, child, you mustn't look like—*that!* You mustn't think—hard of *him!* He was—all right—always—till he took to drink—!"

"He didn't have to drink, Mother!" said the fierce young voice. "He must have known what drink was."

"Well—child—it came little by little! You don't understand. He never meant—to be like that—not when he started—He—was always wild and independent. He didn't care what folks thought—of him—but—he wasn't bad! Not bad! And when he came and told me he was in a hole—someone had framed him up to a life in the penitentiary—to cover a gang's doings—and that there wasn't any thing for him—but to—disappear—forever—I believed him! I believe him—yet, Fraley! He didn't do the robbing, nor he didn't forge the check—there's all the papers in the bag there to prove it! But he wouldn't go back—on one fellow—who had been—innocent! If he got free, and told the truth—the other boy—would have to bear it—and he had a sick old mother. He was like that, Fraley—your father was—he wouldn't go back on some one who had been—his friend!"

"But he went back *on you!*" said the fierce young voice again. "He brought you out away from everybody that loved you—and then—he treated you—!" the girl's voice broke in a sob of indignation.

"Not then, child—" pleaded the mother's voice. "He was tender and loving, but he put it up to me! It was either go with him then—or—never see him—again! Fraley—I—loved him—!"

"Don't mind me, Mother!" said the girl struggling for control of her feelings. She could remember the cruel blows he had given the frail mother. She could remember so many things!

"It was the drink that did it," pleaded the mother, reading the thoughts of the sensitive girl and struggling for breath as a paroxysm of coughing seized her.

The old dog trotted in from his wanderings after the

cow, snuffed around the cot lovingly and lay down with a soft thud of his paws on the bare floor. Fraley put the tin cup of water to her mother's lips again, and after a time she rallied:

"I—must—hurry!" she gasped as she lay back on the pillow. "I can't stand many more—like—that!"

"I wish you wouldn't," begged the girl, "What difference will it make? I love you—anyway—and I don't care anything about all the rest. It's you—you, I want. I can't bear to see you suffer!"

"No, child," the feeble hand lifted just the slightest in protest, "let—me—finish!"

Fraley's answer was a soft hand on the thin gray hair around her mother's temples.

"Go on, Mother dear!" she breathed softly.

"My father was a stern man, especially since my mother's death—" the sick woman whispered the story with the greatest difficulty. "He had said—if I—married—Angus—I need never—come back!"

The old dog heaved a deep sigh as if he, too, were listening.

The sick woman paused for breath, then went on, her words very low.

"That night I slipped out—of the house—when he—was asleep! We were married in a little out of the way church—I pasted the marriage certificate and license—into the Bible—you'll find—it—" she paused as if her task were almost done, then hurried on.

"When—we got out here—we found—this was a place of—outlaws."

"Outlaws!" said Fraley, startled—"What does that mean?"

"It means—that every man for miles around—has committed some crime—and is afraid—to go back—where he—came from."

Fraley turned her startled eyes toward the open door and her faraway mountains.

"Was—my—father—?" she faltered at last.

"No! No! I told you he was innocent—"

"Why didn't he get away then?"

"He couldn't—child—even if he had had money—which he hadn't—not a cent! The men here wouldn't let him go. They would have shot us all first! Your father—knew too much! There were—too many—notorious criminals on this mountain. There—wouldn't have been—a chance for the three of us— You see—we didn't find it all out—not till after you came. You were five months old—the day—your father—told me!"

A chill hand seemed to be clutching the girl's throat as she stared unseeingly at the spot of sunshine on the floor beside the old brown dog.

"We tried—to think of some way—but your father—knew too much. He'd been out with the other men—rustling cattle—He'd have been implicated with them in their crime—of course. At first he didn't understand—at first he thought it was cattle that belonged to them. He was green, you know, and didn't understand! The man who brought him out here had made great promises. He had expected to go back rich—some day. I had thought how proud I would be to show my father I had been right about Angus. I thought he would—be a—successful man, and we would go home—rich!"

The old dog stirred and snapped at a bug that crept in the doorway and the sick woman looked around with a start.

"It's all right, Mother, no one is coming," said the girl with a furtive look out the door.

The mother struggled on with her story.

"When your father—found out, when he saw he too had been stealing, and there was no hope—to get away—it seemed he just gave up—and let go. He said we had to live—and there was no other—way. He had always been wild—you know—and it seemed as though—he kind of got used to things—and fitted right in with the others after a while. When I cried and blamed him—then he took to drinking hard—and after—that—he didn't care, though sometimes he was—very fond—of you. But when he got liquor, then he didn't care!"

"Drinking didn't make it any better!" said the fierce young voice.

"No—It didn't," went on the dreary voice—"No—and then he brought the men—here! I couldn't help it—I tried. But I saw they had some kind—of a hold—on him! He was *afraid*—!"

The dog made a quick dash out the door after a rabbit that had shot by, and the woman stopped and looked up sharply.

"Listen!" she said, gripping the firm young hand in an icy clasp, "I must say the rest quick!" She was half lifted from her pillow with her frightened eyes turned toward the door, "I might go—or they might come—any minute now. Listen! I had a brother. He went to New York. He was Robert Fraley. You—must go—to him! It's all written down in the cover of the Bible—under the cloth I sewed over it. You—must find him! He—loved—me. Angus—had people too—but they were—ashamed of him! They were rich—but it's all written down. You must get out of here at once. Promise me! I—can't—die—till—you promise!"

"I promise!"

"Promise—you—won't wait—not even—for any—burying!"

"But, Mother—!"

"No 'but' Fraley! They'll bury me deep all right, don't

worry! They'll want me out of their sight—and mind!
Many's the time—I've told them—before your father
went—what I thought of them! I told them—about the
wrath of God!—Oh—I know—they've had me in their
power—since—I was—sick! I—had to shut up! But—
when I'm gone—they'll take it out on you! Fraley, my
girl—they can't hurt—my dead body. No matter what
happens—God will know—how to find it—again—at
the resurrection. But they can do—terrible things—to
you, my baby! You're safer—dead—than here alive, if it
comes—to that! Now promise me! Promise!"

Fraley choked back the racking sobs that came to her
throat, and promised. The woman sank back and closed
her eyes. It seemed she hardly breathed. The girl thought
she was asleep and kept quite still, but after a time the
stillness frightened her, and she lifted her trembling hand
and touched the cold cheek. Her mother opened her
eyes.

"I've been—praying!" she murmured, "I've—put
you—in *His* care!"

There was a flicker of a smile on the tired lips, and the
cold hand made a feeble attempt at a pressure on the
warm vivid one it held.

After that she seemed to sleep again.

The girl, worn with sorrow and apprehension, sank in
her cramped position on the floor into a troubled sleep
herself, and the old dog, padding softly back from the
hunt with delicate tread slunk silently down near her,
closing sad eyes, and sighing.

Tired out, the girl slept on, past the noon hour, into
the afternoon, never knowing when the cold hand grew
moist with death damp, never seeing the shadow that
crept over the loved face, the faint breaths, slow, and
farther between, as the dying soul slipped nearer to the
brink.

The dog, hungry, patient, sighed and sighed again, closed his eyes and waited, understanding perhaps what was passing in the old cabin, his dog heart aching with those he loved.

The shadows were changing on the mountain tops, and the long rays of the setting sun were flinging across the cabin floor, laying warm fingers on the old brown dog, bright fingers on the gold of the girl's hair, and a glory of another world on the face of the passing soul. Suddenly the dying eyes opened and with a gasp the woman clutched at the young relaxed hand that lay in hers.

"Fraley—! Child—! The old Bible!" The words were almost inarticulate except to loving ears, but the girl started awake and put her warm young arm about her mother.

"Yes, Mother! I'll keep it! I'll always keep it! I'll not forget! I'll never let anyone take it from me!"

Her words seemed to pierce the dying ears, and a smile trembled feebly on the white lips. For a long moment she lay in Fraley's young arms, as if content, like a nestling child. Then, with superhuman strength the dying woman lifted herself, and a light broke into her face, a light that made her look young and glad and well again, as her child could never remember her having looked:

"He's *come* for me!" she cried joyously as if it were an honor she had not expected, and then, her eyes still looking up as if hearing a communication—"He's going to keep *you* safe! Good-by! Till—you come!"

With the smile still on her lips she was gone! The girl, stunned, dazed with her sorrow, yet understanding that the great mystery of passing was over, laid her back on the flabby pillow and gazed on the face so changed, so rested in spite of its frailty, its wornness; that face already taking on itself the look of a closed and uninhabited dwelling. She watched the glory fade into stillness of death, wrote it down, as it were, in her secret heart, to recall all through her life, and then, as sometimes when she had watched the sunset dropping behind the mountain and all the world grow dark, she knew it was over, and she sank down on her knees beside all that remained that was dear to her in the great world, and broke into heart-broken sobs.

The dog came and whined about her, nosing her face and licking her hands, but she did not feel him. Her heart seemed crushed within her. All that had passed between herself and her mother during that long, terrible, beautiful parting, had faded for the time, and she was throbbing with one fearful thought. She was gone, gone, gone beyond recall! For the moment there was no future, nothing to do but to lie, broken, and cry out her terrible pain. It seemed as though the pent-up torrent of her sorrow, now that it had fallen upon her, had obliterated everything else.

Then, suddenly, a low, menacing growl beside her startled her back to the present. She lifted her face and turned quick, frightened eyes toward the neglected watch she had been keeping, and her heart stood still. There in the door, silhouetted dark against the blood-red light of the setting sun, stood Brand Carter, her mother's enemy—and hers!

2

IT was incredible that a girl could have grown to Fraley's years in this wilderness, this mountain fastness of wickedness, so fine and sweet and unsoiled as this girl was. Nobody but God would ever know at what expense to herself the mother had been able to guard her all her years, especially the last few months since her father died.

Like the matchless beauty of the little white flower that grows in the darkness of a coal pit and, protected by some miraculous quality with which its petals are endowed that will not retain the soil, lifts its starry whiteness amid the smut, so the child had grown into loveliness, unstained.

And now the frail hand that had shut her from the gaze of unholy eyes more times than she would ever know, the strong soul that in a weak body had protected her from dangers unspeakable, was gone; cold, silent, still, it could no more protect her. The time that her mother had warned her against had come, and caught her unaware! She had been merely weeping!

She sprang to her feet in a terror she had never felt before. There had been times in the past when she had been deathly frightened, but never like this. Her very heart stood still, and would not beat. Her breath hurt her in her lungs, her eyes seemed bursting as she gazed, her mind would not function. He had come. It was too late! It was useless to flee!

Then with sudden realization she glanced toward the silent form on the cot beside her, with an instinct to protect her who could no longer protect herself. But the majesty in that dead face brought the realization that the dead need no protection. She caught her breath in one quick gasp and tried to think.

But even that glance had been enough to break the spell that rested on the room. The man's eyes went to the dead face too, and with an oath he made a move to come forward.

The old dog gave a low growl and sprang with fangs exposed, but a cruel boot caught him midway, and sent him sprawling outside the door, where for a second, he lay stunned by the well-aimed blow.

"Ugh! Croaked at last!" said the man, coming close to the cot, peering down at the dead face, lifting a waxen eyelid roughly, and glaring into the dead eye, "Well, she took long enough about it!"

Then he turned to the trembling girl, who, with enraged eyes, watched him.

"Now, young 'un, *you* git out and milk the cow and git us a good supper. The men are coming, and we're hungry. See? Now, *git!*"

He seized her in a rough grip and flung her through the door, almost into the arms of another man who had just sprung from his horse and was coming toward the cabin. He was a young man with an evil face and lustful eyes. Pierce, they called him, Pierce Boyden, lately come to the wilderness. Fraley hated him, and feared him.

"Here, you—Pierce, come in here! We gotta get rid of this old woman! Give us a hand!"

Then, turning to the other three men who drove up he gave his orders.

"Pete, you stand there with your gun and watch that girl while she milks that cow and gits us some grub. Whist, you and Babe get your shovels and be quick about it."

Fraley darted around the house to where the cow stood waiting to be milked. Every word that was spoken stung its terrible meaning into her frightened soul. Scarcely knowing what she did she went at the task, a task from which her mother had saved her as long as she could. The angry voice of Brand rang out from the house where he was going about, roughly shoving a chair across the floor, flinging the old tin cup against the wall in his anger. She shuddered as she thought of what the men were doing. Her precious mother!

The tears that had been flowing seemed to sting backward in her eyes. Her cheeks scorched dry, her heart came choking to her throat. Her hands were numb and could scarcely hold the pail in place. The milk was going everywhere.

The voice of Brand, drunker than usual, sailed out into the twilight from the open doorway:

"You, Pete! Stay there till I come back. If she starts to run shoot her in the feet, then she can't go fur!"

He laughed a terrible haw, haw, and then she could hear the awful procession going down the mountain!

She knew what they were doing. She could hear the ring of a shovel against a rock. It seemed that every clod they turned fell across her quivering heart.

Pete, with his gun, stood guard at the corner of the house. Pete, the silent one with the terrible leering eyes of hate. Pete who never smiled—not even when he was drunk. And now he was drunk! Oh, why had she lost her senses? Why had she not gone before they came, as her mother had meant her to do?

The old dog hobbled to her and began to lick the tears from her face, and she felt comforted, and less afraid. She whispered to him to lie down and he obeyed her, sneaking into a shadow behind the cow.

Pete stalked nearer and gruffly bade her make haste. She managed to finish her milking, though her hands still felt more dead than live, and stumbled into the house. The old dog slunk after her, and hid in the bushes near the door. The shadows were growing long and deep on the grass, and on the mountains across the dark valley, where they had taken—No!—it was not her mother! Merely the worn-out dress with which she was done! Hadn't Mother tried to make her understand that?

She tried to take a deep breath and hold her shoulders up as she marched about the room, tried not to see the empty space where the cot had stood. Tried not to think, tried just to get the supper, and get the men to eating. There were hungry now, and they would not bother her till they were fed, if she fed them quickly.

She started the coffee boiling, and put some salt meat on to cook. She fried a great skillet of potatoes, and mixed up the crude corn bread. The familiar duties seemed to take her hours, and all the while her heart was listening in terror for the sound of returning feet. Pete had come into the house and was sitting in the corner with his gun aimed toward her. She shuddered when she looked at him, not so much because of the gun as because of the cunning look in his eyes, and once—as she glanced up because she could not keep her eyes away from his shadowy corner—he laughed, a horrid cackle, almost demoniacal. Pete, who never even smiled! It was as if he had her in his power. As if he were gloating over it. She would rather Brand had left almost any of the men than Pete. There was something about him that did not seem quite human.

Feverishly she worked, her head throbbing with her haste, setting out the old table with the tin plates, the cracked cups. She could hear the men's voices. They were coming back up the mountain now. They were singing one of those terrible songs about hanging somebody by the roadside, the one that had always made her mother turn pale.

Fraley sprang to the stove and broke eggs into the hot fat beside the meat. She would give them such a supper as would make them forget her for the moment.

The corn bread was ready, smoking hot on the table as the men came noisily in. Brand watched her as he towered above the rest, his evil eyes gloating, she thought, with the same look that had been in Pete's eyes. She brought the coffee pot and set the frying pan with its sizzling meat and eggs in the middle of the table, and the men, with drunken satisfaction, sat down and drew up their chairs. They were joking among themselves about their task just completed, in words that froze her heart with sorrow and horror. But she was glad to have their attention for the moment taken from herself.

They were all busy with the first mouthfuls now—like hungry wolves, too busy to spring.

She turned stealthily and her foot touched something. It was the old tin cup that Brand had kicked away in his anger. With quick instinct she stooped and picked it up. She might need it. Some bits of dry bread that were on the shelf as she passed she swept into it, and hiding the cup in the scant gathers of her cotton dress, she made a stealthy movement toward the door of the room that had been her refuge from the terrors of the world ever since she could remember.

The men did not notice her. They were eating.

Silently, as unobtrusively as she could move, she glided to the door and slipped within. They had not seemed to notice she was gone. She pushed the bolt quickly. It was a large bolt, and her mother had kept it well oiled so that it would move quickly and silently if need be. There was a bar, too, that slipped across the bottom of the door. That too, her mother had cunningly, crudely, arranged. Probably it would not endure long in a united attack, but it was a brief hindrance at least. If she only dared draw the old trunk across the door! But that would make a noise.

Stealthily she moved in the dark little room that was scarcely larger than a closet. With fingers weak with fear she lifted the loose board beneath the cot and pulled out the woolen bag. Suppressing the quick sob at thought of her mother, she opened the flap of the bag and stowed away the tin cup and bread, then, standing on tip toe, she lifted the bag to the little high window over the bed and pushed it softly over the sill. As it fell she listened breathlessly. What if the men should hear it drop, or Larcha the old dog should begin to bark, and the men should go out to look around!

Softly she took down the old coat that had hung on a peg in the wall ever since her father died, and put it on. The men were talking loudly now. Two of them seemed to be fighting over something that a third had said. It would perhaps come to blows. It often did. She welcomed the noise. It would cover her going. But as she stepped upon her little bed her heart suddenly froze in her breast! What was this terrible thing they were saying? It was about herself they were fighting. They were saying unspeakably awful things. For an instant she seemed paralyzed and could not move. Then fear set her free, and she was stung into action. It was not an easy matter to climb from the creaky little cot to the high narrow window sill above without making a particle of noise, and she was trembling in every nerve.

The window was barely large enough to let her slenderness through, and it required skill to swing outside, cling to the window sill and then drop with catlike softness to the ground, but it was not the first time she had accomplished it. There had been other times of stress in the little cabin when her mother had sent her away in a hurry to a refuge she had, out in the open, and that experience helped her now. But there was no time to pause and be cautious, for at any moment the men might discover her absence and call for her. Then they would rush outside to hunt her down, and death itself would be better than life!

With the awful words of the men ringing in her ears she dropped from the window, praying that she might not make a false landing. Her head seemed dizzy and there was a beating in her throat. For an instant her body felt too heavy to rise up, and she lay quite still where she had dropped, holding her breath and listening.

The old dog came softly whining and licking her face as if he understood she was in trouble and new panic seized her. She hushed him into quiet, picked up her bag and slung it over her shoulder by its strap, then, her hand upon the dog's head, she moved like a small shadow across the ground, her bare feet making no sound, her heart beating so wildly that it seemed as if it could be heard a mile away.

It was not toward the trail she directed her steps, and she did not look back to the awful pass where the precipice was, nor down the valley where they had carried her precious mother's form. Into the wilderness where there was no trail, into the darkness she went.

Like a voice there silently stole into her heart a phrase

from the words she had learned for her mother, sitting morning after morning in the cabin door in the sunshine, learning her lesson out of the old Book, the only book she had, or huddled in a blanket when the weather was cold and the fire was low, learning, learning, always learning beautiful words to repeat to her mother. It was the only school she had ever known and she loved to study, and to repeat the words she had learned; pleased to be able to say them perfectly, often asking what they meant, but only half comprehending what her mother tried to tell her. Now suddenly it seemed that these words had taken on new, wide meaning.

"He knoweth—the way—that I take. He knoweth the way—He knoweth—"

As she stole along cautiously, her accustomed feet finding the pathway in the dark, her heart fearful, her eyes looking back in dread, the words began to come like an accompaniment to her silent going, and their meaning beat itself into her soul.

Suddenly, back through the clear stillness of the starlit night came a sharp cracking sound, a snap and a sound of rending wood, then a kind of roar of evil bursting from the door of the cabin. Casting a frightened look back she could see the light from the cabin door which was flung wide now, could hear the men's voices calling her angrily, shouting imprecations, swearing a tumult of angry menace. It put new terror into her going, new tremblings into her limbs. She hastened her uncertain steps blindly on toward an old tree that had been her refuge before in times of alarm, her arms outstretched to feel for obstructions in her path as she fled down the side of the mountain.

She could hear the clatter of hoofs now, ringing out on the crisp night air, as the horses crossed the slab of rock that cropped out a little way from the house. Yes, some of them at least, were coming this way. She had hoped they would search the trail first, but it seemed they were taking no chances. They would be upon her very soon and her limbs were trembling until she felt they would crumple under her! Her feet were so uncertain as they stepped! Her heart was beating so that it seemed as if it would choke her. Weakly she snatched at a young sapling and swung herself up to a cleft place in a great rock she knew so well. If she could only make it now, and reach the foot of the old tree!

Breathlessly on she climbed, not pausing now to look back, and at last she reached it.

As she swung herself up in the branches she remembered the old dog who had followed her. Where was he? Had he gone back? Much as she loved him, and wanted his company on her journey, she realized now that she should have shut him in the cow shed where he could not have followed her. Now, if he lingered at the foot of the rock, he would give away her hiding place to the enemy!

For an instant she paused, but the ring of horses' hoofs on the rock-strewn path she had just left warned her that she had no time to spare. They were hot-foot on her track. Possibly it was Pete, and it might be he had searched out her haunt. Pete had a way of appearing at the shack of late when everybody thought he had gone afar. Pete might have seen her going or coming to her tree.

The thought sent the blood hurrying through her veins with feverish rapidity. Her hands almost refused to hold on to the branches, so frightened was she. She tried to think. If this tree was no longer a refuge, where could she go? It was too late to go back, to hope to get down this sheer rock on the other side and make the valley before she would be heard, even though the dark did hide her. It would be folly. She would be dashed to pieces in the dark, for the way down the precipitous incline was dangerous even in the daytime when one could pick and choose a cranny for a footing, step by step. It was a long and slow and fearsome descent. To make it in the dark, and in haste, would be impossible. To go back to where she had begun to descend to this rock would be to meet the enemy face to face. There was nothing for it but to climb to the topmost limbs and wait. Yet, if it was Pete, and he should find her, he would not hesitate to cut down the tree! She would be at his mercy!

In terror she climbed to heights she had never ventured before, till she clung at the very top of the great tree, enveloped in its resinous plumes. Even in the light of day it would have been hardly discoverable that the tree was inhabited, so thick were the branches. It had been Fraley's playhouse in her childhood and her refuge in many a time of fear. But she had always guarded her goings so that she thought no one but her mother knew of her whereabouts. Now, however, in this, her most trying crisis, she began to wonder whether, perhaps, some of the men might not recently have spied upon her.

Clinging to the old pine, her arms about its rough trunk, her feet curled into the crotch of the slender branch upon which her weight rested, the woolen bag her mother had made dragging heavily from her shoulder, she waited, her heart beating wildly.

If it had been daytime she could have almost looked into the eyes of her pursuer, though his horse's feet traveled ground far above where the tree stood, for the tree top was almost on a level with him. But she could see nothing now but the black night ahead of her and a high line of dim starry sky far above the mountain. But she knew by the sound that her pursuers were almost opposite her, and that a moment more would tell her whether they had discovered her trail, for now if they guessed where she was they would turn abruptly down the mountain toward her. And, Oh, what had become of Larcha, the old dog? If he only would have sense enough not to whine!

Suddenly a sound broke on her startled ear, like the hurtling of some heavy object through small branches and dry sticks, a rush, a menacing growl, followed by curses, and the sound of a plunging horse, rearing and stumbling on the slippery hillside.

Instantly her forest-trained ears understood. It was almost as if she could see what was being enacted before her in the dark. Old Larcha, the dog, had tried to help. He had cunningly stolen above the trail where the enemy was coming, and at the right instant had plunged down upon the horse and his rider, had dared to attack in defense of the girl he loved, had been intelligent enough to try to mislead her pursuer into making chase higher up the mountain, and so covering her hiding place.

Instantly she knew, now, even if she had not heard the rough curses, that it was Pete who rode that horse. Larcha had always shown deep dislike to him, and fear in his presence. It had been a joke among the men to send Larcha to Pete and hear him growl. And Pete had been cruel to the dog, kicking him brutally whenever opportunity offered, throwing stones at him without provocation, pointing the gun at him. The dog would always hide when he came around. Fraley had often noticed how the hair would rise on the brown back, and how the dog would lift his upper lip and show his teeth whenever the man came in sight. He would always disappear, hiding for hours together, till his enemy had left the place. Larcha had cause of his own, now, to fight her pursuer. Yet Fraley knew he would have done this even without the personal cause. Since she was a little child Larcha had been her one playmate, and comrade whenever she strayed away from her mother. Larcha was all the friend she had left in the world. And now that friend was offering up himself for her. For Fraley had little doubt what Pete would do to the dog. The answer to her fear came sharp and quick in a shot that rang out over the mountain, followed by the dull thud of a body falling on the ground and rolling a few paces.

Then into the night came the sound of curses, and of other horses riding, and cries.

A sharp little light shot out from the rider of the horse, and twinkled over the ground till it focused on a dark, huddled object at the foot of a tree. Pete had recently come from a surreptitious visit to the outside world, and had brought back with him a number of these strange little flashlights. Yes, there was no question but that her pursuer was Pete, and that, if he wanted to, he would shoot her as readily as he had shot Larcha. At least he would shoot to disable, perhaps not to kill.

The other horses were coming on, Brand's big roan stumbling with his lame foot, and two others. They would surround her now. Oh, if she could only be sure they would kill her. The awful words she had heard the men speak a few moments before still rang, menacing, in her ears.

One of the horses caught his foot in a root, and stumbling, began to slide down a steep place. His rider was evidently thrown forward. There was a sound of struggling and more curses as the horse righted himself and the drunken rider remounted.

A consultation in low tones followed. Fraley could catch a word now and then. Pete was laughing that awful cackle of triumph, telling of Larcha's attack and finish. She held her breath and clung to the tree with arms that were numb with tensity, expecting momently that the wicked little flashlight would play upon her face and reveal her to her enemies.

Then she heard Brand cry out:

"Which way did the dog come? Up there? We'll soon have her then. She can't make time up hill. All set?"

The four horses wheeled and went up the mountain, directly away from where she clung in mid air.

Larcha's ruse had worked. He had not died in vain.

3

FRALEY'S head reeled as she clung to the tree and listened to the receding hoof beats. She could feel the old tree sway under her; she had climbed so near to the top that her anchorage seemed very uncertain. She had a feeling that she was high above the world, held somehow in the hollow of God's hand, and she laid her white face against the rough old trunk and closed her eyes. It seemed as if she scarcely dared to breathe yet, lest the men return, much less could she think of descending from her stronghold.

The searchers climbed higher and higher, till they were silhouetted for a moment against the distant bit of starry sky, and then disappeared down the other side of the mountain. They had gone to search for her among their own kind, thinking she had taken refuge with some one. Their voices which at first had been loud and clear, floating back in angry snatches, were suddenly shut off as they dropped from view. She drew a deep breath of relief.

But—they would come back! When they failed to find her there they would come this way again and search! It was not safe to go down now. There was no other spot for hiding that she knew of within miles, and she dared not venture into the unknown while they were yet hot on her trail. Besides, she knew that her progress must be slow indeed for she must go cautiously. Well had she learned that there were many other men hiding within these strange mountain fastnesses, who would be no safer companions than the ones from whom she would escape. Indeed, the way before her seemed as beset as the way behind.

How good it would have been if the shot that had stilled old Larcha's barking, had reached her own heart, and sent her out of a world that was only full of sorrow and terror.

As the immediate fear of the men died away, and strength began to return to the girl's tired limbs, and steadiness to her heart, she began to think about the dog. Had he died at once, or was he lying there in pain and wondering why she did not come to him? Her last defender, the only one in the world left who loved her, and he was stilled—probably forever! There had not been a whimper from him since that shot and the dull thud that followed. And she had thought that he would go with her on her long strange journey! Now she must go alone!

It seemed hours that she clung there to her frail support high in the old pine. The night shut down more darkly. The stars flicked little pricks in the strip of sky above the mountain more distinctly, and a thread of a moon came up and hung like a silver toy in the east, far off to the right. She shrank even from the bit of light it gave, lest her enemy might return. She dared not try to run away yet.

She tried to make a plan for her going, but somehow everything seemed all mixed up. She could not be sure which way the men would return. Also, there were cabins, deep hidden among the spurs of the foothills, where dangerous characters abode. These she must avoid, although she had not even a very definite idea where they were located. There were paths which her mother had always warned her against in a general way, and yet, they lay, some of them, between her and the great east which she must seek. Arriving each time from her round of problems she would just close her eyes and pray: "Oh God, you show me the way please! You go with me!"

It was hours later that she was startled into alertness again.

Voices had suddenly risen on the night air, detached, drunken voices, booming up along the horizon as if they had just emerged from another world.

She shifted her hands on the resinous tree, and found them stiff and painful with their long clinging. She changed her position, and shrank closer to the tree. The men were coming back!

Terror seized her once more with its iron grip. She peered fearfully up at the strip of sky. She could see a slow procession of four, silhouetted against the brightness, riding crazily, but they were not coming toward her. They were going along the ridge of the mountain toward the cabin, drooping and swaying on their horses. They had been somewhere with their kind and were debauched with drink. How well she knew their attitude! How familiar were the noisy curses that floated back to her!

"Well—l-l-let 'er—go!" stuttered Brand as he righted himself after a turn in the saddle to look back. "S-s-she—c-c-an't git fur before m-morning! We'll round 'er up with Shorty's hounds! Good sport. What say, boys?"

A chorus of drunken laughter followed, and the voices

drowned themselves back of the cow shed, then disappeared behind the slammed door of the cabin. How often she had wakened in the night and heard them! Only now she was alone, and in their power!

She waited while the night grew wide and still. No more sounds came from the cabin. Then she began to ease herself slowly down to the lower branches, listening at every move. Her hearing, trained in the open, was attuned to the noises of the night. She was not afraid of the creatures that lived in the forest, that hid, and stirred, and stole abroad in the dark for prey. She felt herself akin to them as she stood at last with her feet again upon the ground and listened. She could tread the forest aisles as silently as they. She could go like a shadow of the night. She could make herself a part of the black background, and shrink into it at the first approach of alarm.

Stealthily, for she was aware that the men might have left some one of their number in hiding to watch the surrounding country, she crept from the shelter of the great rock on which the old pine grew, and, turning, gave one glance back and up at it. If she succeeded in escaping she would probably never see it again. She could not conceive of herself ever coming willingly back to that place, so she looked her farewell with eyes that were blurred with grateful tears. That tree had been her true friend.

Adjusting the bag that seemed almost to have worn a groove in her slender shoulder she went softly, swiftly forward until she reached the higher ground where the horses had stood.

There lay the old dog right across her path. She stumbled and almost fell over him, his body still warm. Dear old Larcha! He had died for her! Or had he? Perhaps he was not dead after all? She must not stay for even such a defender, but might she not carry him with her, a little way at least? If she left him here he would be a prey for wild beasts. She could not bear to think of old Larcha, suffering perhaps, deserted. A little farther on was the river. She could see the gleam of it in the faint light of the little new moon. Perhaps down there she could minister to the old dog, and he might get up and go with her after all.

With sudden hope she stooped and picked him up and started toward the stream. But it was a heavy tug, and more than once her heart failed her, for she began to realize that he was dead. The inert way the body lay in her weary young arms told her so.

At last, near the water's edge, she laid him down and looked at him. There was no hope. She had known that even before she stooped, for the chill of his body had been growing upon her. She knew too that she could not carry him farther. She must save her own strength.

Sadly picking him up once more she waded out into the water and dropped him in.

"Dear Larcha!" she whispered softly as the water closed over the faithful head, "I'll never forget you!"

Then she turned and waded down the pebbly bed of the stream.

The water was cold and sent a chill over her as she tried not to envy old Larcha. How simple it would all have been if only she might have died too!

When the water grew too cold for her to stand it any longer she stepped out upon the bank and ran to get warm, but soon took to the stream again, knowing that if the threat of following her with the hounds should be made good, it would be harder for the dogs to trace her scent.

Later in the night, when the little silver boat of a moon hung low and seemed to ripple at her from the water like a tiny lamp, she found a fallen tree lying across the stream in a shallow place. Its top branches were touching the bank she was on, and its roots had been torn from the opposite bank and were standing high in the air like a wall. It might be dangerous, but she decided to cross on that tree.

Tucking her scant skirts about her she waded out as far as she dared, for the current was stronger here, and then clutched for the topmost branches.

The water was cold and black, but looking behind she seemed already very far from shore, so taking firm hold of the branches she pulled herself along, slipping and almost falling, until she could clamber into the tree top and so work her way along the trunk until she came to the rampart of roots towering above her in the dark, like an impassable wall. Had she been a fool to try to get across, she wondered?

She sat down on the tree trunk to get her breath and examine the precious woolen bag that she had taken the precaution to strap high on her shoulders before entering the stream. It was not very wet. Only the least little bit on the lower edge. Her precious Bible and the things her mother had put in it would be safe! That was something to be thankful for, at least.

She sat down to rest for a moment on the trunk of the tree before she would explore what was back of that wall of gnarled roots and mud and moss. The dim bank of the other side of the stream seemed not far away. Could she climb over the roots and get to the land or would the water be too deep for wading?

Across the stream lay the darkness from which she had come. There was no gleam of light anywhere. The cabin on the mountain where her drunken enemies slept was in darkness. She could not even locate it. She seemed to have been traveling for years and to have come miles and miles, but her knowledge of the wilderness and the vast open country told her that the cabin was probably not far away. In the daylight she would be able to see it easily. She had never been so far as this before. Her mother had always limited her going. But the old mountains were over there, the mountains she knew so well. Her journey would be a matter of years, perhaps, before she got to a place that would really seem safe. With a feeling of hopelessness she turned and faced the task before her. Some hiding place must be found before daylight, where she could rest in safety till another night gave her cover to go on.

She found the roots above her hard to climb. They had been worn smooth and slippery by many waters, before they were uprooted. But at last, after several failures, she found a place where she could work herself around, clinging carefully from root to root, till she had gained the black shadow behind them. The bag on her back hindered her, and took her strength, the roots were uncertain and gave way in the most unexpected manner, switching her face, and sometimes proving stubborn where they should have yielded. When she gained the spot where she could look across the blackness that separated her from the shore, the bank seemed steep and abrupt, and the water black as night. If it had not been for the little stars reflected in its darkness she could not have told whether it was water or mere black space. Gradually her eyes grew accustomed to the blackness that reigned behind those roots, and she saw that the other end almost touched the shore with one big root, heavier than the rest. A little star was twinkling right beneath it and plainly showed a big flat stone where one could step.

Softly, cautiously, she put an investigating foot down and tested the water under her. If she could only swing herself by these wiry old roots, over toward that stone, she could get up to the bank she was sure.

The first root she tried snapped, and left her with only a single hold, her foot went down several inches into soft spongy mud, but she clutched for another root and caught it, and was finally able to get a footing farther on. At last she stood on the stepping stone and caught at the bending branches of another tree that arched over the water.

It was a hard, dangerous climb, even then, for her feet were wet and the bank was slippery and steep. Moreover her pack had become painfully heavy, and its straps cut deep into her weary shoulders. When she scrambled at last to the top she had only strength left to draw her feet after her, and sink down where she lay to get her breath. Now that she was safe across the water it did not seem to matter. There might be dangers twice as great as those she had escaped but her tired eyelids dropped over her eyes, and she lay there panting and disheartened, wondering how she was to go on. Suddenly the memory that her mother was gone surged deep into her soul, and everything was for the moment forgotten in the overwhelming realization. Nothing mattered but to weep her young soul out.

It seemed the more bitter to her that she had not been able to attend her beloved to her final resting place. She longed inexpressibly to go back and make sure that all was safe and right, but that was impossible. There would be no escape if she did, for that would be the spot where the men would look for her first. She shuddered at the thought of being found there, at the possibility of the terrible things they would say. The harsh unfeeling words of Brand when he had discovered that her mother was dead had seemed to her more cruel than all the rest. Her soul writhed at the memory. Out of all proportion to her other injuries this seemed to loom as the one unforgivable thing.

Silent sobs racked her weary young frame as she lay there under the low spreading tree. She dared not cry aloud, but there was some relief in letting the tears come.

A little stir high up over her head made her suddenly start and sit up, looking around her in the darkness. Was someone watching her? Had perhaps the men traced her to this refuge too?

But though she listened she heard only a little scratching of tiny forest feet, some bird or chipmunk perhaps in the branches, and the soft sighing of winds stirring a twig against a limb. It was very dark here, for the foliage grew thick and heavy, and the night seemed to have settled closer. Peering hard she could discern nothing but tree trunks, and concluded she must be in the woods. This would be a good place to sleep, but she dared not sleep. The night would be all too short for putting distance between herself and her enemies, without stopping for sleep. She would stretch out for just a few minutes to relax her tired limbs, and then she must grope on. It would not do to be getting out in the open at daylight. She must get somewhere under cover by dawn lest the men be out after her early. They would want their breakfast, and would be impatient at not finding her back. No, she had no time to waste resting. So in a very short time she gathered herself up, re-slung her pack on her back, and started groping on through the woods.

The trees fringed the river bank thickly here, and she dared not stay near the edge where it was lighter, because the bank was steep, and she was in danger of slipping down into the water. She must penetrate the woods, and get to the other side if possible before daybreak.

Looking up occasionally where the trees were not quite so close together she could see the distant stars, but they seemed very far away. If she only had a match or a candle! Yet she would not have dared light it if she had, she reasoned, lest someone see her and hinder her going. No, the dark was a friend, for God was in the dark, and He would show her the way.

Resting her soul in this thought she groped on from tree to tree, sometimes stumbling over a root, often coming in sharp contact with brush that scratched her face, clung to her garments, and left thorns in her hands.

It seemed that she had already been hours in that forest when she suddenly came to a break in the darkness, a soft lightening of the blackness that seemed almost bright in contrast.

Cautiously she went forward, for now she sensed some soft sound ahead of her, something more than the night wind. Nearer and nearer she drew to the sound and streak of light, till suddenly she was on the edge of the woods, and the sound was as of a giant breathing. She stood quite still, steadying herself by a tree, her own breath withheld, and listened.

Yes, decidedly, that was breathing!

Had some human being camped just ahead of where she stood? Perhaps there was more than one person. Perhaps she had come on some of her enemies resting in their search till daylight.

With her hand on her heart she stood trying to still its wild thumping and to get strength to go on, forward or back, she could not tell which. At last she began to steal cautiously around the tree, and made her way slowly along the edge of the wood, keeping near to the clearing because it was easier going and not so pitchy black!

As a misty dawn began to break she saw that the open space was like a wide valley with dark mountains beyond again reaching up to the vault of dim stars. If she could only get across that valley perhaps she would be out of the region of danger. That would be wonderful! And yet, there might be people camped here who would see her as the lights grew stronger, and she might not be able to get to hiding before the morning really came. But there was danger anywhere, and she must take a risk. Also, she was burning with thirst and there ought to be water in a valley. Of course she was faint with hunger, too, but she must not think of stopping to eat. If she could only get far enough away so that word of her would not travel back, then she could take her own time. But now she must press on.

Ahead of her under the shadow of a tree that stood out a little way from the rest, she saw a dark outline, seemingly an out-cropping of rock. She would go and sit down upon it for a moment and rest. Her limbs were so tired they trembled under her. And now she noticed other dark shapes scattered over the open space. Yes of course they were rocks. She must get away from the idea that they were people camped here. What a foolish idea! People would not scatter around like this to camp.

Then she heard the soft breathing again. Could that be a man wrapped in his blanket, sleeping under the stars?

To her right came more breathing, and a movement, as if some one stirred in his sleep. Startled, she turned her eyes back toward the woods which were not far behind her, and imagined she saw something moving there, and heard more breathing. It certainly sounded like human beings.

In utter panic she turned, she knew not which way, and started to run, but she caught her foot in the long grass and fell headlong. Her hands went wildly out to save herself, and came in startling contact with warm, soft, living fur!

4

SHE was too frightened and stunned to think, and things began happening right away.

To begin with, the rock that was covered with fur gave a snort, and a quick investigating nose came cold and wet to her face. There came a leap and a bellow, rending of the earth close to her, a blinding shower of dirt and grass in her face, a sound of prancing and a great body hurled about.

Suddenly all around her other dark shapes came alive and reared and roared and bellowed, and she knew what she had done. This was a herd of wild cattle and she had trespassed into their territory. In a moment more, if it were daylight, she would be torn and trampled to a horrible death. They were preparing to stampede. She knew enough of cattle raising to understand their habits. She was as good as dead now if they could see her.

But the darkness hung like a curtain between them and her.

The creature she had fallen against had backed off, and was snuffing about uncertainly, with angry roars, sleep and mist in its eyes, making it very plain that once it got a sight of this unknown enemy in the dark, there would be a quick ending.

Fraley held her breath and lay quite still for an instant and the big steer, turned and backed off again, facing away from her. Could she make an escape? Would her limbs obey her? If she could only get to a tree! Now she must move, while its back was turned. Those other dark shapes were forming in a mass. She could hear an ominous bewildered roar. If they should stampede! If they should turn this way—!

With a quick catlike stealth she lifted her body an inch or two from the earth, and began to creep on hands and feet, inch by inch, away from the dark creature. Its own bellowing drowned the soft sound of her movement at first, and then as she grew bolder and moved faster something clinked in the bag that hung across her shoulders, as it swung down and hit the ground in her turning. Whatever it was, the creature about-faced and gave another roar. Trembling so that she seemed almost paralyzed, Fraley sprang to her feet and fled blindly, in the dark.

The race was on. The enemy sounded the battle cry, and a stamping of hoofs told her that she was pursued. A thousand giants, breathing hard, came behind her, a living angry fiery tornado. Was she going to the woods, or out into the open? There was so much dirt in her eyes she could not make out. Was she going to fall again? Would she never—reach—*anywhere?*

It was at this instant that her outstretched hand touched the trunk of a small sapling, and, straining her eyes ahead, she saw that the darkness of the woods was just before her. But how was she to find a tree to climb in the dark? Could she escape from those angry, flying creatures if they ventured in among the trees?

The roar behind her now was deafening, and they

were coming full toward her. Could they see her? Did they have eyes that could see in the dark like a cat?

An instant more and she swung herself under the low branches of another tree, and gained a footing inside the darkness! Sharply she turned to her right, and dashed in and out among the trees, slid behind a tall old oak, out of breath, her heart feeling as if it would burst with fright and exertion.

She peered around her tree, and saw that the cattle had paused, baffled at the barrier of trees for the moment. But she dared not trust to that. They were still making angry sounds, a mob cry. Perhaps they were consulting how they might find her and vent their anger for their rude awakening. She had heard awful tales about those who had got the ill will of a herd of cattle!

Putting out a groping hand her fingers touched the plumy branch of a pine! Her soul thrilled! Another pine! There would be branches she could climb!

It was not a great king of a tree like the one that had been her refuge before, but it was taller than the cattle that were after her. For now she could hear the crash of a branch, the crumpling of bushes under the heavy tread as first one creature and then another ventured blindly within the thicket. Without more hesitation she clung to the trunk, and drew herself up with new strength born of her necessity.

The tree swayed as she put her foot at last upon the lower branches, and the stir of swinging branches drew on the enemy. She clutched the resinous trunk tenaciously as her foot slipped, and almost fell back to earth again, but struggling desperately she at last got a footing, and crept up. The whole tree swayed with her weight, and trembled. But she was above those awful horns at last, unless the creatures tore the tree down. Could they do that? The one that had followed her was snorting and pawing just below. His horns were tangled in a branch, tossing the piney plumes.

Then a curious thing happened.

While she waited breathlessly, swaying in the tree top, a call sounded out below in the meadow, the cry of the angry leader of the beasts. In quick reply the whole herd turned and stampeded in the other direction, those struggling, tangled in the edge of the wood, crashing behind. The limbs cracked and snapped as they passed. Young saplings bent and were trampled under foot. Old dead branches that reached low enough for the flying horns were broken off like pipe stems, and the whole dark bellowing pack hurled themselves away toward the valley.

Fraley hung there in wonder and listened to their going. Then she closed her eyes and put her tired face against the gummy pine trunk and cried softly.

When the sound of the flying herd grew faint in the distance she opened her eyes and looked to the edge of the forest.

Little faint streaks of pink had taken the place of the starry strip above the mountains, though it was still very dark in the woods, but she could see that out in the open it was gray with dawning.

Softly, cautiously, listening at every move, she slid down at last to the ground. She was stiff and sore and moved painfully. Also she was faint with hunger, but this was no place to stop and eat. This must be the beginning of the cattle lands. She must get away from here before daylight. There would be men coming when morning broke and that would be worse perhaps than those awful cattle. She had heard all about this region. There were not only wild stretches of rich pasture land filled with cattle—many of them stolen cattle—but they were guarded by men, outlaws, such as those from whom she had fled. She must be on her guard every instant, or she would only be rushing into new dangers.

It was growing lighter now, even in the woods, and she was able to steer her course.

But now she began to be painfully aware of her burden, for the straps had become twisted and were cutting into her flesh. Also the old coat dragged heavily upon her and her hands and feet were torn and bleeding with the branches and bark. She had a stone bruise on one foot, and a deep cut where she had slipped on a sharp stone in the river. All these aches began now to cry out for relief. She began to wonder how many thousand miles she had yet to go. Could she ever make it? Here she had only been out one awful night and she felt ready to lie down and die. Oh, if she only could!

Bravely she drew a deep breath and struggled on, but there were tears running down her white cheeks, though perhaps she was not even aware that she was crying.

The dawn was creeping up fast now. Overhead there was a rosy glow.

Presently she heard a soft tinkle of water over stones, and came upon a little brook rippling along through the forest. Ah, here was refreshment!

She remembered the old tin cup, and unslung her bag to search for it.

She would have breakfast here beside this brook, and then perhaps she would be rested enough to go on.

But when she came to open the bag the tears started afresh, for it brought back so clearly her last talk with her dear mother.

Tenderly she unfastened the strings that held the bag shut, and looked within. The scanty folded bits of coarse clothing made from salt bags and the like, smote her with fresh sorrow. The little pockets along the sides of the bag, made with her mother's neat stitches, even though the thread was coarse with which they had been set! How dear every stitch would always be! And mother had made it for her!

It was light enough now to see everything, but she went through her investigation with great care so that nothing should slip out and be lost in the woods.

One pocket held needles, thread, a few buttons, the old scissors with one broken point, the other point stuck into a cork for safety, a pencil, some folded bits of cloth for patches, a pincushion with a few pins. Another held a broken comb, and a tiny broken mirror that had been one of the wonders of her childhood. That pocket was her little vanity case. Another held a small piece of soap and a wash rag neatly hemmed. There was a larger pocket that held some little bags, one filled with corn meal, perhaps a pint in all, another a small piece of salt pork wrapped in paper, and a piece of cheese. There was a handful of shelled corn in another. Then tucked in between the bags, and wrapped carefully in cloth were two little glass bottles with screw tops of metal. She knew her mother treasured them as relics of her own childhood that she had brought them with her into her far western home. One of them contained sugar and the other was half full of salt. This was her little pocket of supplies, and, save for the bits of corn bread she had brought, they were all that stood between her and starvation. And she knew that these had been saved at infinite risk and sacrifice to the dear mother who had packed the bag, for Brand, who brought home all supplies, kept a keen watch upon everything.

Fraley did not discover all these things at first. She was too weary and faint to look carefully, too overwrought with sorrow to identify everything. Also the light was not even yet strong enough to tell sugar from salt there in the woods. But she knew that her mother's tender hand had been on everything, and her love had put them all in. Later she discovered that another pocket contained a small piece of candle, and a few matches in a tiny box wrapped up in a bit of woolen cloth.

But it was the sight of the old Bible sewed into its neat cotton cover that broke her down, so that for a few minutes she sat there and sobbed softly to herself.

At last she roused herself. The tinkle of the water was so inviting. She took out the old tin cup and dipped herself a drink of water. Oh, how good it tasted. She drank deeply, and then leaned down to the brook and washed her face and hands, using the bit of soap, and setting up the broken mirror against a tree while she combed out her pretty hair and tried to make it tidy.

She felt a little better then, and ate a part of the corn bread she had brought. She must not eat it all, for it might be a long time before she could get more when this was gone, although there was the meal and the matches. When she got far enough away where it would be safe she might make a little corn cake and bake it on a hot stone over a fire of twigs. But not now. She must hoard every crumb of the corn bread.

She drank some more water, and then lay down and shut her eyes. It felt so good to stretch out flat and relax. She must not go to sleep, but she would rest a little while, five minutes, perhaps.

When she opened her eyes again she did not know where she was.

Two slender fingers of warm sunshine were touching her cheek, and shining on her golden hair, and a bird was singing over her head. She looked up to the trees, and down to the brook, and at the knapsack lying open beside her, and then she remembered.

As long as she lived she would never forget that moment when she awoke and realized that she had been asleep—perhaps a long time—and had been cared for and was safe. The words that came to her lips with a kind of sweet amazement were:

"I will both lay me down in peace and sleep, for thou Lord only makest me to dwell in safety." God had made good that promise to her in her terror and loneliness! There was almost triumph in her face as she looked over the things in her traveling bag, and found them all there.

Presently, realizing that the warm color of the two rays of sunshine that had penetrated the trees above showed that it was late in the day, perhaps even past midday, she gathered herself together to go on. She dashed more cold water from the brook in her face, and felt refreshed and able to travel. She drank again of the brook and was glad of the sweet water. She dipped her feet in for a last wash before she started, and then she began to strap up her bag. But in stuffing the things back again she found two hard objects which she had not noticed earlier in the morning in the dim light. They were wrapped carefully in the clean garments her mother had made and tied about with bits of string. Curious, she unknotted the string and found, first an empty bottle with a good tight cork. It seemed to be perfectly clean, and a bit of paper had been pasted around it which said "FOR WATER" printed with pencil.

Again quick tears came to her eyes at the thoughtfulness that had provided for all her little needs as well as it was possible. Now, she would be able to carry a little water with her for a time of need for it was not likely that brooks of clear water like this one would be frequent along the way.

She filled the bottle from the clear deep spot where the water bubbled up in a little pool, corked it firmly and set it upright in one of the pockets so there would be little danger of its upsetting. Then she investigated the other bundle, and almost cried out with pleasure when she found that it contained the old field glass which had been her father's and which, from her earliest memory, it had been the delight of her life to look through. She had not seen it since her father's death, and supposed, of course, some of the other men had appropriated it, as they had almost everything else that had belonged to him, in spite of all her mother could do. But it seemed she had been able to save this, hidden away perhaps under the old board beneath the bed which had been their only treasure chest.

Eagerly she unwrapped it and adjusted it, turning it toward the distance in each direction, delighted when she sighted a tiny bird in the branches, a squirrel sitting under a distant tree eating a nut it had just unearthed from last winter's store. Now she would be able to sight the distance, and see if an enemy was at hand! And her mother had known that. Oh, what a wonderful mother! It was almost as if her guiding hand were still there, to find all these things ready. A hungering came over her to unwrap the old Bible and see what had been written in it, but she knew that she must not take the time to do it now. Her first business was to get out of this region as fast as her two feet could carry her. Something over two thousand miles she had to go in all.

How far had she come already? As much as ten? She could not tell. No journey in her past compared with this one. But the thought of it was appalling, as the figures loomed before her, ten into two thousand—even supposing she had already made ten! She knew that ten was nothing to the men on horseback. She knew they thought little of a journey of a hundred and fifty miles. They could easily come after her and catch her although she had been doing her best for days, if they chose to think it worth while. The country was so wide and open, and her knowledge of it so very limited. Oh, it was a terrible chance she was taking to expect to get away from seven determined men with seven good horses and unlimited friends to whom they might appeal for help all along the way. Yet she must go on and do her best.

She buckled the old strap of the field glass across one shoulder, fastened up her bag carefully, and sprang to her feet. She must get on. The slant of the sunbeams was decidedly low, it might even be late afternoon. She must get some idea of where she was before night fell again. She must not risk another attack of wild cattle.

She decided to follow the brook a little way, and before long came out to the edge of the larger stream again, but, she judged, much farther down toward the East than she had been when she entered it, for she could see no trace of the fallen tree on which she had crossed. There was probably a curve in the stream that hid it, and the woods grew close, the trees leaning far over the water in some places.

The sun was already far down to the western horizon. She must have slept even longer than she had thought. She gave one quick searching glance about and finding no one near she held up her field glass and searched the valley.

There were some cattle grazing quietly across the stream. She could even see the mark of their branding on one or two near by, but she was safe here. They were too far away to notice her. She searched the valley behind her, the way she must have come last night, as far as she could see, but only cattle here and there dotted the peaceful scene. There were no horses nor riders. She turned her glass up toward the heights across the valley, and searched them step by step, back as far as her eye could reach. Was that her old pine that had given her refuge the night before? It stood out like a dark spike against the sky, with rock below, and other trees around, but it was so tiny, and so far away in the shimmer of the afternoon sunshine, that she could not even be sure it was the same tree. Behind it and above it, she could not see. If it were her tree the cabin would probably be out of sight from the point where she stood. But, if it were her tree, how far had she come? Could one see ten miles even with a glass? She did not know. She did know that a great mountain might be many miles away and still be visible, soft and purple against the sky, but one could not see detail on a great mountain, one could not tell one tree from another at a great distance.

She searched the way again, on the ridge along the mountain up which the men had ridden after they had shot Larcha, but there was no sign of horse or rider, and with a breath of relief she turned and hurried along the edge of the stream.

It was rough going here, and took more time than she ought to spare, because, for every rod she progressed, she must travel three or four sometimes in getting around trees and climbing steep banks, but it was very peaceful and lovely here and gave her comfort and a sense of safety.

As she hurried along she occasionally raised her glass and searched the horizon again in either direction, and at last saw, through an opening in the woods, that the forest was past, and she was approaching a place where the trees were thick only along the stream.

That would mean that there were broad pasture lands perhaps, and she must be wary. It would also mean that she would be out in open where her moving form could be seen unless she stuck close to the fringe of trees along the stream. She remembered how often her mother had spoken about being able to see her coming a long way off because the sun shone on her gold hair as if it were bright metal. She must do something about that before she went out into the sunshine. Would there be something in her bag she could tie over her head? Then she remembered an old gray rag in the pocket of the old coat she wore. It was the remnant of a silk handkerchief her father had owned in his better days, but long since worn beyond recognition as such. The edges were frayed and frowsy, and there was more than one hole in it, but it was large enough to tie around her head.

Gravely she took it out and adjusted it, spreading it over her whole head and covering the bright curls till not a thread of them showed, tying the ends in the back of her neck firmly. Then she buttoned the old coat to her throat, slung the bag around under her arm like a fishing basket, and marched on. If anyone sighted her perhaps they would think she was a boy out fishing. If she had only thought to hunt out her father's old hat, but she was not sure that it had not been taken by the other men. Nothing had been safe after he was gone.

She hurried along as fast as she could, for she began to feel again the weight of her bag, and her feet and limbs ached with the continuous going.

She had been used to running free in the open all her life, but a long continuous plodding journey she had not known. For sixteen years she had lived in the cabin, her only excitement the wandering to the limits her mother had set for her, her only pleasure climbing trees and looking off at a world she did not know, and might not explore. Well and strong she was indeed, and able to stand much hardships, for she had never known even comfort in her life, but this long strain of going over rough uncertain ground, her loss of sleep and lack of food, added to the sorrow she was bearing, were beginning to tell on even her splendid young constitution. She longed to drop down again and sleep, but she knew she

must not. This was her best time for going. She must get
to a good sleeping place before night.

So she plodded on, keeping as near as possible, when
she emerged from the woods, to the fringe of trees along
the river bank.

But finally the fringe of trees grew thin, and then
stopped entirely, and the river broadened into a sheet of
silver. And now the land on either side was flat for long
distances, with mountains far away on either hand, and
she could see far and wide, even without the glasses. The
sun was distinctly behind her and her own shadow went
flat and small and black before her, so she knew she was
travelling in the right direction.

She trudged along several miles in this wide open
space, growing more and more secure as she went on.
There seemed to be no cattle on either side as far as she
could see, just wide, lonely landscape, and she was glad.
But she was beginning to feel as if she could not drag her
feet very much farther, and kept looking ahead for a spot
where she could rest securely.

The landscape, however, offered no refuge at this
point, and the horizon stretched ahead bright and golden
in the low afternoon sun. It seemed to her as she looked
through her glass with a faint despair at her heart, that
she could see almost to New York, and there was
nothing between. Would she ever be able to make it?

At last she sank down in the grass and opened her bag.
She must have something to eat. There was a sudden
weakness upon her. So she took out her stores and ate
another portion of corn bread, and a few small bites of
the salt meat. To her starved appetite it tasted like the
most savory meal. Then she drank a cup of water, corked
the bottle carefully, tied up her kit and stood up.

The river was off at her left now, a rod or two away,
for the ground where she was seemed to be an easier path

for her feet than close by the river bank. The sun had turned the river into a broad band of gold, and the west was bright with its horizontal rays, blending sky and earth at the horizon into a golden haze as if an eternal city were just beyond that point. With her glass Fraley swept the land back of her and to either side and came at last to the view straight ahead, catching her breath at the beauty of the day that was departing, the exquisite tintings of the foliage, and sky and clouds, rejoicing that there was not even a sign of cattle anywhere about, save a few scattered ones miles away behind her.

Then, suddenly, as she looked, fear crept into her body like a great hand that gripped her as in a vise, for, out from the golden distance, along the ridge that led from as far as she could see, back along the line of the opposite mountain, and on toward the cabin she had left, there moved a little black dot!

At first she thought it must be a speck on the glass, and she carefully breathed upon it and polished it with her sleeve, but no, when she looked again the dot, growing rapidly larger, was moving on toward her. As she watched it, scarcely daring to breath, it gradually became three moving dots, one lighter than the rest, and still coming on over that ridge of the opposite mountain.

She tried to tell herself that she was nervous, excited, seeing things—that this was some sort of mirage. Her mother had told her of mirages on the desert—but this was not the desert.

Larger and larger the dots grew, nearer and nearer they came, racing along the ridge. They were so near now that through the glass she could distinctly see that they were horses, bearing riders. A conviction grew upon her that it was some of the men from the cabin out on a search party after her, and her knees grew so weak they shook. She dropped to the earth suddenly as if she had been shot as this fear grew to a certainty, and, keeping a sharp lookout, with lowered head, she crept on hands and knees toward a clump of bushes down by the river bank. Oh, if she had stayed over there instead of daring to take the more open ground! Perhaps they had already sighted her. Yet, unless they were carrying a field glass, they might not have seen her. Brand had a field glass she knew. But was it Brand or some of the others? Or was it only some passing cowboys who knew nothing at all about her?

When she reached the screen of the bushes she crept close, and thus in ambush trained her glass once more on the riders.

They were almost opposite her range now, and she could see them plainly, although they must be a long distance away. The air was clear and still, and she could hear them shout to one another, though she could not hear what they said, and once she thought she heard a curse flung into the golden evening. But as they came opposite she saw distinctly that two horses were dark, and one was white, and the white one was lame in his left hind foot.

Like little silhouettes they moved across the opposite ridge of mountain. Now she was sure, though she could not see the men's faces, that the one on the forward dark horse was Pete, the other dark one would be Shorty—they always went together; and the white horse was Pierce Boyden's, the man she hated and dreaded most of all except Brand Carter.

As she watched them through the screen of the bushes, they suddenly drew rein, and stood together, pointing off in her direction, as if consulting about their route. Then they turned their course and came down from the ridge of the mountain, winding like tiny puppets into the dark pathways of the mountain side. There was a patch of trees that hindered the sunlight and hid them now from view, and Fraley lay in her covert trembling. Oh, had they seen her through a glass, and were they coming to trap her here as she hid?

Perhaps Brand had called out Shorty's vicious hounds, and they were even now coming upon her from the other direction. Perhaps that pointing on the mountain ridge had been signalling to the others. They might all be upon her in a few minutes, and what could she do? There was positively no place to which she could flee in the wide open landscape, and there was no possibility that these sparse bushes would cover her if a search party came near. Oh, if there were only a hole in the ground!

Then it came to her that she might cover herself with grass. Perhaps they would not get here before the sun was much lower, and they might not notice, though the hounds would surely search her out if they were along. But it seemed the only thing she could do, so she fell to pulling the grass about and piling it into a great heap beside her.

She crouched as close to the bushes as she could get, burrowing her body into the loose soil, till the old coat was almost on a level with the surrounding ground, and the precious bag containing her treasures was beneath her. Then she set to work as well as she could to cover herself with the grass she had pulled, satisfied at last that she would not be noticeable unless some one came quite near. She put her face down on her arms, and lay still under her camouflage, and, before long there came a sound of voices, and of hoof beats ringing across the water.

Fraley in her flimsy refuge, cringed, and held her breath!

5

FRALEY'S worst fears were realized as the enemy drew near. It was indeed, as she had guessed, the three men, Pete and Shorty and Pierce, and, as she had thought, they had come that way in answer to a signal from Brand who had found the body of the dead dog lying in the clear water of the river.

The three men came riding down from the mountain, and halted a little way from the water just across from the clump of bushes that hid the trembling girl, and there they waited till Brand came riding up on the other side. He forded the river not two rods above the little grass mound which covered Fraley's old coat, and she held her breath and tried to keep from trembling, as she listened to the splash of his horse's feet when he stepped out into the water.

She could hear all they said. They were not drunk now, and their curses were so much the more cold blooded and deliberate, as each man told with a coarse laugh what he would do to the culprit when he found her. Fraley shut her eyes and wondered if hell were like this, and wondered again, as she had done many times of late, why God made men.

It appeared that there were other search parties out for her now. Shorty had been warned, and was to pass the word along. Not a man within the outlaw's territory but would rise to the occasion and keep a keen lookout along his border. She heard them name the places, and gathered much helpful information from their discussion, the only trouble with it being that there did not seem to be any direction she could turn in which she might find egress into the world beyond. They had shut up the gates of their world, and guarded all their defenses. How could she hope to escape?

She had no words with which to pray, but she lay there calling in her heart to God, and presently, seemingly without reason, the men all turned their horses and galloped away across the valley. Cautiously she peered through the thicket to watch them, marveling that they were gone, not daring to come out of her covert lest there be someone still in ambush lurking behind her.

She lay there until the damp ground chilled her to the bone, and a sick dizziness descended upon her. She wondered how long it took people to die of starvation. She was not near that yet, for there were still stores within her bag, but she felt a strange apathy about eating anything. If she could only lie there and sleep herself away out of this life!

But Fraley had been too well taught to let herself give up so easily, and soon the stillness all about her began to give her renewed assurance. Now was the time for her to find another hiding place The sun had gone lower in the west. It was almost down to the horizon.

Cautiously she peered out. It was all very still.

She rolled herself softly over and looked about. She took out the glass and searched in every direction. Far away to the northeast she could see those small specks climbing the mountain again. Dared she rise and get across the wide stretch of open space now? If they looked back with field glasses could they sight her?

She decided to keep low, and move slowly. No one could notice a flat thing on the ground. So she crawled until her muscles were too tired to go that way any longer, then she rose half way and ran a few steps, dropping to her knees and lying flat down again, till she made another survey, and so she slowly progressed across a space that seemed interminable. She kept going and going and never getting any nearer to anything.

And now the ground began to rise. She was sorry for that, for it would make her more visible from afar, but a careful survey of the horizon showed her three enemies just going over the ridge of the opposite mountain and the other riding far off to the northeast. She would be safe from them for a little while at least, and perhaps could get over beyond the hill somehow. Perhaps it was safer south than north, although she had an inner conviction that it was in that direction she would find the great herds of cattle. She rose and ran again, till she was ready to drop.

There was a tree on the little hill. Its foliage was scant, and would give little shelter from an enemy's eye, but it might give her an outlook beyond, and help her to know where to go, or where not to go which was much more important.

As she climbed the hill she began to hope again. If she could only get beyond the bounds where these men had no holdings—out beyond where they dared to go! She knew there were such bounds for her mother had often told her so, and warned her to keep close around the cabin where she belonged, for until she was beyond these bounds there was no safety. And now she began to understand why her mother had not dared to try to get away. It was hard enough for one to hide. Two could not have done it even so long. Neither could her frail little mother have endured the long journey on foot, and the exposure.

The sun had slipped its last gold-bound crimson edge behind the mountain as Fraley reached the tree, and she stood up with more assurance now. There was no brilliant sunlight to pick out her little figure as it stood upright upon the hill.

The tree was not quite at the top of the hill, but from its highest branch she felt she could see over, so she unstrapped her burden and laid it on the ground, while she took a tired hold of the tree, and began to go up, hand over hand, knees gripping the trunk hard, feet clinging like well-trained hands. Oh, she knew how to climb. It had been her one sport as she ranged her own mountain, keeping in sight of mother's signal, an old cloth she hung out on the line behind the cabin whenever she wanted Fraley to return.

So now, she went easily up into the branches, and clung there, searching with her glasses first the place whence she had come, then the opposite mountain, lying dark against a bright sky. It all lay peaceful and serene. She could now see bunches of cattle grazing here and there, or going down to patches of water to drink. Then she turned her eyes to the south.

The ground sloped down here to another valley which stretched out and narrowed farther on into a deep pass or cut between more mountains she did not remember having seen before. They were hidden from the cabin on her own mountain by the range that shut in this side of the valley she had just crossed.

There were no cattle in this pass, though she could see them farther back in the new valley, and as she studied every bit of ground within sight she could see, just below her, half hidden among a group of trees, a little log cabin. That startled her, for she feared it might belong to some of the gang of outlaws against which she had been warned. Her impulse was to slide down the tree at once and fly again, but a certain intuition warned her not to be in a hurry. So she clung quietly to her tree and studied the little log house in the waning light. Its single window on this side reflected the faint glow of the flame in the sunset sky, but there was no light of candle within, and the rude chimney gave forth no smoke, although this was the hour for preparing an evening meal if the occupant were at home. The place looked lonely and deserted, and she half decided that no one lived there till she noticed, a few rods beyond it, half way up the crest of the hillside, a cow tethered to a long rope. Then she decided that the householder was gone from home, and might return at any time now. For no one who valued his cow would remain away without milking it. It would certainly be wise to get beyond this house before the owner came back.

Having thus decided, she gave one sweep of the landscape with her glass to make sure all was right, then slid down the tree, took up her bag and hurried froward, keeping just below the crest of the hill where she could study the house, ready to fly back over on the other side if she saw signs of human approach.

When she had got past the back of the cabin and nearer to where the cow was tethered, the creature broke out bawling, and Fraley, accustomed to the ways of a cow, noticed that her bag was full. The poor thing needed milking, and no one was at home.

With sudden pity for the cow, she paused and looked around sharply. The landscape was very still, and deep shadows were beginning to gather in every hollow and crevice. It was twilight down there by the log cabin. If she only had a pail she could relieve the poor cow, and perhaps get some milk for herself. That would help greatly. Yes, down there on a bench by the door of the cabin was a pail turned upside down. Dared she steal down there and get it? Perhaps she was a fool to think of it, but she could not bear to see the poor cow suffering.

She hesitated and the cow started bawling again, as if she knew what the girl was thinking, and Fraley took a sudden resolve. This was something she must do.

Softly, cautiously, she stole down and secured the pail, swiftly flew back again up the hillside and behind the cow. With quick furtive glances about she knelt and began to milk, and soon the pail was foaming with the sweet warm liquid. The fragrance of it made the famished girl faint with her need of it. And when she had finished and the cow was comfortable again, she took out her tin cup and drank deeply. She had a right to that much surely, after having performed this service for the cow.

When she had drank all that she could she took out her little water bottle and carefully filled that full, setting the cork tight again. Then she carried the pail carefully down the hill and put it on the bench. There was nothing near with which to cover it, but at least she had done what she could. Then, having tiptoed away from the house, she fled up the hill and away, on feet that were suddenly frenzied at the thought of what she had done. Perhaps the owner of that cow was a friend of Brand's and would presently meet her and punish her for having drank his milk, and meddled with his cow.

Yet she was going now on the strength of that milk, with fleeter step than she had traveled all day long. New strength seemed to have come into her veins with that sweet warm draught.

There were woods beyond, and if she could gain them before she met any returning householder, perhaps she would be safe for another night. She had her eyes upon that narrow pass, out between the mountains. If she could gain that, and get beyond, perhaps she would be out in the world where safety lay.

It was growing dusky now, and the way was dim and indefinite. Rough stones cropped up and almost tripped her, little hollows appeared in unsuspected places and almost threw her. Yet her feet seemed to have been given wings for the moment; she fled over all difficulties, and, breathless at last, gained the shadow of the scattered woods.

The rose color and the flame, the golden and the green were fading now from the western sky, and the little pink clouds catching reflected glory in the east were scurrying away to the dark. There seemed to be no creature stirring, and the ground where she was travelling had grown rough and pebbly. The grass was scant, which gave her relief, for she knew there would be no cattle about, and she did not want to repeat the wild terror of the night before.

She kept along the edge of the woods again, with her face ever toward the mountain pass in the distance. She would go as long as she could see, then find a place to drop down and rest till the moon came up, and get on a little farther. So she kept on at an incredible pace—for one who had traveled as far and been through as many strenuous experiences as she had—until suddenly she came to a little nook that seemed made for rest, two trees with their roots locked together in a kind of natural couch.

The woods were behind her as she dropped down upon it, and the ground below her sloped away to a sort of gravelly bed, perhaps the bed of an old stream. Across a wide stretch of this she could see the looming darkness of the mountain beyond, that continued on to the pass which was almost invisible now that it was quite dark.

There were more of the friendly stars above than there had been the night before. She looked up and was glad they were there.

She gathered the old coat about her, drew closer the knot of the old handkerchief that covered her bright curls, placed her bag on the roots, curled her feet under her coat, lay down with her head pillowed on the old Bible, and soon fell asleep.

Back across two mountains and a valley her enemies drank and plotted to ensnare her, while behind her, and around her, were creatures of the dark, but none of them came near her, as she slept guarded by an angelic band or perhaps, even by the loved mother whose body was lying in a rude grave in the other valley. Who knows?

The moon rose, and grew bright. It sailed on high for hours, looked down on the little soul hid among the branches, and stole away on its course to the west. The stars twinkled dimly, and the night waned.

Up through the mountain pass on horses came two riders through the night. Their voices were low but distinct in the clear air. Their horses were weary, as though they had come a long way that day, and they rode slowly and talked deliberately. The horses' feet clinked on the rocky road as they went. The sound pierced the night and seemed to stir the little shadows as they came.

Something reached the young sleeper as they drew nearer, and she woke sharply in alarm, but did not stir. Her senses seemed to be startled into breathlessness. Were these her enemies come again to find her? And dared she try to escape again through those dark unknown woods? She felt too stupid with sleep to dare to climb a tree, and the travelers were too near now for her to move without giving them warning of her presence. No, she must just lie still, with her face hidden, and hope they would pass by without noticing her.

The voices came on, low, angry, troubled, disheartened. They did not sound like drunken voices; and with relief she noticed now that they were not any voices that she knew.

"It was that Pierce Boyden done it!" said the voice of one of the riders resentfully. "I seen him. But you can't do nothin' about it. He's too slick with his gun. You gotta let him get by with it."

"She was there, then? You're sure she was there?" the other voice questioned anxiously.

"Oh, yes, she was there. I seen her all right. I trailed her down—" Fraley's heart stood still with horror. These must be some of Brand's gang, and they had been trailing her! But what had Pierce Boyden to do with it? Had he some fiendish plan to trap her, and make her pay for her escape?

Then the older voice spoke again, gravely as if perplexed:

"But I thought that woman was dead. I thought they told you they saw her buried."

"Oh, you mean the old 'un," said the other man. "Yep, she's dead alrighty. No mistake! But the young 'un is at the old stand, an' she's ninety times as peppy as her ma! She's a looker, too, got bleached hair an' has the boys right on her string. She keeps 'em all a guessing, too."

"And you think Boyden did it for her sake?" questioned the elder.

"Positive! He's jealous as a cat. I stood right beside him an' I saw him look at her an' then I saw him draw a bead—!"

The riders suddenly rounded a curve behind the trees and their voices were drowned in a breeze that sprang up and tossed the branches about.

Fraley sat up and strained her ears, but could only catch detached words now and then that meant nothing, and there she sat for some time trying to make out what the men had meant. Draw a bead. Then they were not talking about her after all, perhaps. It must be some other girl. Who were these men? They did not sound as if they were friends of Pierce Boyden. The older voice sounded sad and different from the men hereabout. Perhaps it was the owner of the log cabin where she had milked the cow.

But she could take no chances. She must get away from here as soon as it was light enough to see a step before her. It would not do to go yet however. The men might be returning soon, or others of their party might straggle on behind. She must wait until she could see ahead of her or sne would run into more difficulties.

She let her head drop back again on her hard pillow and closed her eyes. She did not intend to go to sleep again, just to rest until she felt it was safe to go on; but the weariness of her young flesh asserted itself, and she was soon soundly sleeping again, so sound that she did not hear a stealthy foot on the trail ten feet from her couch, nor hear the sniff of an inquisitive nose, as the creature paused and tried to analyze the new scent. Then across the valley a dark shadow stole into deeper shadows, and all was still again.

Day was just dawning when she was awakened again, this time by a leaf softly fluttering down on her face. Looking up startled she saw two bright eyes above her, as a saucy chipmunk frisked away on a slender limb and chattered noisily.

She sat up and looked about her cautiously. The

woods were very dim behind her yet, and still, save for a stray bird note now and then as some old chorister gave his warning cry preparatory to the early matins. Gray and dim also was the valley stretching out to the grim mountain beyond. But down at the end of the valley toward which she was facing, the mountain pass was lit with the rising sun, just the first pale streaks in the sky, rosy and golden, framed by the sentinel mountains on either hand—a wondrous picture to gaze at. Fraley caught her breath at the beauty of it.

But this was no time to gaze at beautiful pictures. She must be on her way before the enemy was on her track. If she could make the mountain pass before anyone came by, she felt she would have some chance. But it was a long way off, and she could not tell but perhaps it might be an all day's walk. Distances were deceptive. She had learned that yesterday.

Reaching in her bag she took out the little bottle of milk and drank its contents. She might need it more later, but by then it might have soured, and she must not run the risk of losing it.

She started on her way in the mist before the dawning, walking toward the rising sun. She found herself stiff and sore from lying on her humpy bed, and from the exertions of the day before, but the milk had heartened her, and she stepped forth briskly, trying to keep a straight course to the mountain pass.

The going was easier than the day before, for the trail was clearly defined as if it were in frequent use, and she got on faster than she had hoped. Before the sun was up above the mountain she was fairly beneath the grim straight shadow of this great stone gateway into the next valley—into a new world for her, she hoped. Nearer and nearer she drew to its foot, and passed between the rocky walls, looking up, straight up to heaven with a new awe upon her. She had never been right at the foot of a great sheer mountain like this before, and it almost oppressed her with its grandeur. It somehow surprised her to note that there was foliage draped upon its rugged breast, trailing vines putting out new leaves of tender green, gray moss and lichens covering the bare rocks in other places, here and there a small windflower growing, unafraid, from a crack in the stone, and blossoming a childish pink or blue, blowing in the wind as happily as if it had opened its eyes in a safe sweet meadow instead of on this bare cliff. And up toward the summit one or two temerarious pines had set courageous fingers in a crevice, and were growing out above the pass like truants, daring others to swing high and wide and free.

As she entered the gloom of the pass itself she paused and took a brief survey of the country she was leaving behind her. It lay green and still in the early light, and the few cattle she could distinguish were, most of them, lying down as if they had not wakened yet. There was no sign of human kind, no horses even in sight, and with relief she turned and hurried forward, wishing to get beyond this place before anyone could meet her or come behind her.

The trail was rougher here, and stony. It hurt her feet sometimes so that she had to stop and rub them, but she had no time to think of discomfort. It seemed so long to the end of the pass. The mountains were as thick through as they were high. It was like a great tunnel without a top through which she was passing. If she were caught in here there would be no place to hide. Perhaps she should not have attempted it in this growing daylight! She dared not linger.

The sun was three hours' high when she reached the end, her breath coming in quick painful gasps, for she had almost run the last mile, so great had been her panic.

The sound of a stone rolling down the mountain, the dripping of water from the crevices of rock startled her like shouts in the open. She kept a furtive watch behind and before for other travelers, and when she found she had really reached the end of the gloomy pass without molestation she could hardly believe her senses.

It was bright morning now, out in the world to which she had come. The valley was filled with grass, and dotted here and there with trees. This latter fact gave her new hope, for at least a tree was a place of refuge from cattle, if not from men. Cattle and men were her two enemies. There were some cattle in this new valley, but they were off to the left, and seemed to be quietly grazing. Perhaps she could pass beyond them without attracting their attention. The way was wide and comparatively smooth, and though she was worn with the excitement of the past hours, still she could walk fairly fast, and made good progress. Every step onward meant one nearer to freedom for her, and though the bag on her shoulders dragged heavily sometimes, she went forward with good heart, determined to get across one more wide open stretch before she need fear meeting other travelers abroad.

In the wide distance there glittered water, like a sheet of silver, but it seemed as far away as fairyland or heaven. To it her eager footsteps were now directed. It was as if she were in a wide sort of cup, with mountains all around, and mountains in the distance just beyond the glittering water. She felt safe and protected. And yet it was through this same valley that the two men who passed her last night must have come. She must not be too trustful.

Thus reasoning, she kept a constant scanning of the distance in every direction, and arrived about high noon at a small foothill where there were groups of young trees, and a spring of water that trickled down into a tiny stream and disappeared in the valley again. She was thirsty now, for she had eaten some of the salt pork, and the last of her corn bread as she walked along, and for the last half hour had been parched for a drink. She dipped her cup in the spring and enjoyed the clear cold water, dashing some in her face, smoothing her hair back with her wet hands and tying the kerchief over her head again. But she could not stop for more than this tidying. She felt that she must utilize every moment of this bright peace and quiet to get on into safety. This long-continued absence of anything to make her afraid was almost too good to be true, and she must not rest secure.

She hurried up the hill, after cooling her hot feet in the water for a moment, and when she almost reached the top she flung herself full length upon the ground and began to creep up. She would not make herself a target for any eyes that might be searching the landscape. So she crept up till she could peer over, and then slid slowly back, her heart beating fast. The valley below her was full of cattle, and riding among them were three horsemen, seemingly rounding them up. Far away, at the upper end of the range, she could see two more horsemen riding toward the others. Her one quick glance was enough to tell her that Pierce Boyden was one of the men among the cattle, and that he was riding his white horse. The back of another looked like Pete but she could not be sure, and she waited no longer to identify the others, for a great panic had seized her. She rolled down that hill, and darted out into the golden day across the open like a frenzied creature. She ran and ran until she was breathless, and still she kept on, staggering through high grass, crushing through brush and brambles, wading a little stream that came in her way regardless of its depth, and the fact that it was wetting her brief skirt, and soaking up the edges of the old coat she wore. She seemed to have always been running, and still she ran on, panting for breath, her eyes blinded now, unable to see whither she was going, until suddenly she stumbled and fell across a tree trunk that had been hidden by tall grass. She lay there trying to get her breath and wishing she need never have to rise again, afraid to open her congested eyes lest the sun would blind her, too weary to even think.

6

IN a few minutes it began to dawn upon her senses that she was no longer out in the sunlight but was lying in the cool shade somewhere, and all about her everything was very still. Cautiously she opened her eyes and saw she was lying in the shade of a mountain that loomed above her, and off beyond it she could see the water flashing, a silver sheet in the sun.

She sat up and looked around, half dazed by her fall, her head feeling queer and dizzy. She got out her field glass and put it up to her bewildered eyes, but presently she identified the low green hill in the distance as the one she had crept up a while before. She had then come safely across the wide spaces, and was close to the water, incredible as it seemed. She had thought that water a whole day's journey away when she sighted it from the little hill.

Glad and thankful she rose and tried to walk. Her whole body was stiff and sore, and her feet were swollen and bruised with the stones, for she had not tried to save them in her flight. But she felt she must keep on around that mountain till she was out of sight of the valley she was leaving.

It was just as she reached the turn where a moment more would open up a new vista to her troubled gaze, that she turned back once more to look and saw the big drove of cattle pouring from a narrow pass between the little hill and the opposite mountain, and among them were five riders!

Horrified, she flattened herself against the rock that loomed above her, and peered through the branches of a tree that grew out from the side of the mountain, watching, fascinated, dumb with hopelessness. They were a long way off, but it would not take them long to catch up with her, and where could she flee? Unless the rocks and the mountains opened up and took her in, or fell on her to hide her she was lost; for the moving procession seemed to be coming straight her way.

She hugged the rock, her fingers reaching out along its surface, like a child who clings for protection, and a strange thing happened. Her hands found a wide crevice in the rock, a sort of fissure, and looking, she saw it was an opening where the rock had split away, making a fissure some seven or eight inches wide, with part of the split rock fallen out making a screen in front. It was wet inside as if a small stream or spring had worked a way behind the rock, and the opening was small. But could she slip inside? If she could she would be practically hidden.

Shifting her bundle, she flattened herself as much as she could and squeezed between the rocks. A sharp jagged edge bruised her shoulder, and her foot slipped on the mossy stones as she went through so that she struck her face, but she accomplished it, and slid behind the fallen pieces of mountain.

Safely hidden, she found that she could peep through

the crevice and watch the oncoming group. There was a great bunch of cattle, and the men were riding hard to keep them in check. They seemed to be coming directly toward her, and were probably going round this mountain straight to the lake, toward which, five minutes before, she herself had been happily hurrying, thinking to find safety. The men on horseback were so close now that she could see the ugly set of Pierce Boyden's jaw, the cruel blue eyes, the sensuous lips, as he dug his spurs deep into his horse's flanks and rounded up a tricky steer. And now she could see the long scar on his cheek that glowed an angry red. In a moment more he would be where he could see straight into her hiding place!

She shrank back and fell to trembling, not daring to look any longer, slipped down to her knees on the cold wet stones, with her face against the wet rock, her eyes closed, and prayed.

The cattle herd swept on, with trampling of hoofs, and shouting of the men, but she began to realize that they were not going on toward the water, but were rounding the mountain back of her. Perhaps the cattle had tried to stampede for the water, and that was why they came so far out of their straight course; but at any rate they were going on, and in a very short time they were out of sight and sound.

It was a long time before the girl dared creep from her hiding place, and then so fearfully, so tremblingly that she found it hard work to squeeze through the tiny opening. Fearfully she gazed about her, studying the farthest corner with her glass. Her enemies were gone again and she safe once more!

With her hand touching the great rock, she crept on around her mountain, knowing that her strength was spent. She must find a place in which to rest.

Perhaps a mile further on, around the other side of the

mountain, she came upon another great rock split away from the mountain, leaving a hollow place behind it like a cave. Here was shelter surely, and before her lay the great sheet of silver water, almost round, and clear as crystal.

The shore line seemed deserted. There was no sign of shack or habitation of any sort in sight. If there were humans living about, it must be beyond the thick foliage which clustered at the upper end, and that would be too far to see a small lone figure creeping in behind a rock. She needed food, but she was too tired to eat the salt meat, or the dry meal which was all that she had left, so she crept to the edge of the lake, filled her cup, drank plenty of water, then stole back to her cave, arranged her hard pillow and lay down. There might be processions of enemies going by, but she was out of sight; the mountain behind which she hid might be full of wild animals, but the thought did not occur to her. Utterly spent, she lay down and slept, and knew not when the second sun went down upon her pilgrimage, nor when the stars came out or the young moon like a silver boat was reflected in her lake, upside down. It might even have been that some night creatures crept about her feet and sniffed at their strange companion, but she slept on.

It was early morning when she woke again, startled and wondering where she was. A sparkling new day lay before her, with the lake in white ruffled wavelets, lapping softly on the pebbly shore.

She stole from her hiding place and looked around, but there was no one in sight. She would have liked to take a swim in the clear water, as she and her mother had often done on days when the men were away and the trail to the river free from intrusion, but she dared not, so near the enemies' territory. Those cattle were probably being driven somewhere to be sold, and it might be that while Pierce and Pete and the others were away, she would be more free to escape from this region entirely. She must not delay. So, adjusting her bag to her shoulders comfortably, she went down to the water's edge, filled her water bottle, tucking it safely into the bag, and then stooped for a refreshing dash of water in her face and on her arms. She took a long drink, too, lapping the water Gideon fashion, and felt better. Now she would hurry on at once.

But before she could rise, the sense of another presence near by brought a great fear. Turning her head she saw not five feet away from her, standing beside his black horse, her old enemy Pete. He leered at her with a wicked grin of triumph, knowing that he now had her in his power.

For an instant she was too frightened to think or move, and the strength seemed to be ebbing out through her feet leaving her helpless there before him, as he stood gloating over her. Oh, if the water would but rise and receive her out of his sight! She had a wild thought of flinging herself into it, though she knew Pete carried a wicked weapon, and would shoot with unerring aim, only to wound and capture her at last. Pete was a great swimmer too. She could not escape that way.

Then in her terror she seized upon the only weapon at hand, the pebbles and sand at her feet. With a quick motion, so deadly quick and subtle that Pete was taken off his guard, she flung the two handfuls of sand and tiny pebbles straight into those two evil eyes, and springing past him as he cringed with sudden maddening pain she flung herself toward the fiery black horse. Would he let her mount? He was known as an ugly brute, and had always seemed to her to possess a demon spirit like his owner. But he was her only hope now to get away.

Perhaps the horse too was taken unaware by the

daring of this slip of a girl, a little white, frightened, flying creature who hurled herself upon his back and dug her bare heels into his sides.

The bridle had been flung over the saddle, but she had no time to grasp it, for when the beast felt this new rider upon his back, he began to rear and plunge and she could only throw her arms about his neck and cling with a desperation born of her terrible plight.

Failing to dislodge her at the third plunge, the horse whirled with a peculiar motion all his own that would almost have flung off a leech, and started to run. The running was almost like a bolt of lightning, or a ball shot from a cannon, and had not Fraley been trained by her father to ride a wild western pony fearlessly when she was a little child, she would have stood no chance whatever in this race with death. But she had early learned to hold on, and now as the horse fairly flew through the world with a wild unbridled freedom that was breath taking and horrifying, she clung as she had never clung before, each second seeming a year of horror. The bag across her shoulders banged its weight against her, and each instant seemed about to be torn away from her by the motion—would she ever be able to find it again if it dropped off?—Her hair blew wildly over her eyes and whipped her face unmercifully. She expected momently to be flung to earth, and her heart was beating so wildly that it seemed to her it was about to burst. Was that a shot she heard? She could not be sure, but she felt rather than saw that they had skirted the lake and already left it behind.

Then just when it seemed that her strained muscles could not hold on another second the horse stopped stock-still so suddenly and unexpectedly that the aching muscles, set rigidly for the motion of swiftly shooting forward, suddenly lost their grip; and when the horse as suddenly rose upon his hind legs and shook himself with a spiral motion, Fraley went limp and slid to earth in a crumpled little heap, everything gone black around her.

When she came to herself and looked around the horse was gone, and a deadly inertia was upon her. She felt too languid even to raise her head or her hand, and somehow did not seem to care whether she was in danger or not! She wondered if perhaps she was dying.

Gradually her memory returned, and with it the sense of danger. She began to bestir herself slowly and at last rose to a sitting posture and took account of stock.

Her first anxiety came when she discovered that the bag was not about her shoulders. But on further examination she found that it was lying only a few feet away, one strap torn and some of the contents scattered about.

With trembling limbs she crept over to it and began gathering up her things, the slow tears rolling down her cheeks.

When she came to the field glass she remembered Pete. Perhaps he was already almost upon her. She put the glasses to her eyes, and searched the distance fearfully, but there was no sign of living creatures as far as the eye could reach, not even a glimmer of a lake. The horse must have brought her a long way, but he would probably return to his master. It would not take Pete long to give the warning to his mates, and they would surround her. For by this time Pete was probably recovered from the sand she had thrown in his eyes, and he would be angrier than ever. No torture would be too great for her punishment.

In new panic she looked around and discovered a forest not far away. Could she get to it? Fear winged her feet and gave her new strength, and she started in haste for the only shelter offered.

And then it took nearly an hour to get to the edge of

the woods. By this time she was faint with hunger and worn with anxiety, and could hardly drag one foot after the other. She sank down at last in the heart of the forest, too spent to do anything for a time but lie with closed eyes and just be thankful she was sheltered.

She was not hungry now. The anxiety and fatigue and the shock of the fall had taken her appetite away, but she was sick and dizzy for lack of food and knew she should eat something.

She dared not make a fire to bake her meal into cakes, and she dared not eat salt pork alone lest she be tormented with thirst. She had taken the precaution to wash and fill her water bottle when she first went down by the lake, but that would not last long, and there was no telling how far she might have to go before she found water again.

But she must eat or she could not go on, so she took out the little bag of meal and forced herself to chew some of the dry meal slowly, washing it down with sparing sips of water, till at last she felt a little better.

And now her uncharted course led her through the forest, one of the tall primeval kind, with dim sweet light filtering from far above, and distant birds flying from branch to branch and singing strange sweet songs. Little squirrels raced and chattered from bough to bough, and the air was delicious with balsam breath. The paths were smooth here, soft and resinous with pine needles, and little pretty cones she longed to stop and pick up. It was a place she would have loved to linger in, and once she sat down at the foot of a great tree, looked up the length of its mighty trunk, and drew a deep breath of relief. It was like finding sanctuary from trouble to walk these forest aisles and she dreaded to leave it.

It was late in the afternoon when she finally stepped fearfully out from the woods, wondering if after all she had not better remain there for another night. The sun could not be more than two hours from setting now, and the world looked strange and different as she paused and tried to get her bearings. There were still some mountains in the distance, but they did not look quite like the mountains she knew. They were far away, and purple with a misty light upon them, and the land ahead of her looked flatter, and had been fenced in places, though there were still wide stretches of land without fences, with just a sort of hard flat trail over them. This must be what men in the world called a road.

Strange that just going through a forest, even a wide forest like the one she had traversed, should make things different. Here there seemed to be no friendly hidings, few trees together that could be climbed in time of need. She hardly knew how to adjust herself to this new outlook.

She stepped timidly down from the wooded bank, and started along the cleared smooth way. It was even easier going than in the forest, and she made good time. But what, she wondered, should she do if enemies on horseback came along that way and met her? Here were no convenient holes in which to burrow, no kindly mountain to offer shelter, only the open country wide and frightening and different. It seemed so far to anywhere, yet there was a way marked out, and on the beaten path she took her unknown course.

It might have been an hour she walked along, her feet growing sore with the dust between her toes, and longing for rest again, when a strange foreign noise began to grow upon her consciousness. It came from behind her, and she stopped in a nameless dread, as she saw an old horse jogging along the road at a steady pace, drawing a shackly vehicle of the type known as a buckboard. It was the rattle of the wobbling wheels, more than the thud

thud of the old horse's feet on the dirt road, that had made the queer noise, but the sight of the oncoming equipage frightened the little pilgrim more than anything that had come her way yet.

There was nothing to do but stand aside till the thing had passed, or take to the open and run, and she had sense enough to see that this course would lay her open to suspicion far more than to sit by the wayside and rest. So she sat down a little off the beaten track, and looked toward the sunset, as if she had come out for that purpose, even as she might have done at home by the old cabin in the mountains.

She could not yet see the driver of the equipage very clearly, but she knew that none of her immediate enemies drove such things as that, they all went horseback. Of course it might be some of their gang who had been sent to trace her, but if it was she would have to face it out somehow. She selected deliberately a spot of ground that was a bit higher than the road, and throwing her bag down, flung herself beside it, resting one elbow on the firm square of the old Bible, her hand slipped through the strap, if there came a need for sudden flight.

On came the buckboard, and presently she could see the driver quite plainly. It was a woman, dressed in an old dark cotton frock, with a man's felt hat on the back of her head. A few straggling gray locks of hair hung down around her ears, and her skin was darkly tanned like old tired leather. She sat slouched forward on the rickety seat, occasionally looking over her shoulder to a box of things that were lashed to the back of the rig. When she got opposite to Fraley she drew rein and stopped, gazing at her pleasantly, and not at all curiously.

"Howdy!" she said with a kindly leather smile, "want a lift?"

Fraley half rose, a frightened look in her eyes, ready for almost anything, but glad that it was a woman.

"Want a—*what?*" she asked doubtfully.

"Goin' my way?" explained the woman questioningly. "Want a lift? It's late fer walkin'. Hop in!"

"Oh!" said the girl, beginning to comprehend. "Thank you—I—How much will it be to ride a little way?"

"Not a cent!" responded the woman heartily. "We don't charge fer lifts out our way. I'm gettin' back to the ranch before dark ef I kin make it. Left the children alone with the dogs. Gettin' oneasy about 'em, so hop in quick! I ain't got time to waste!"

Fraley was coming down the bank swiftly now. The invitation sounded too good to be true, for her weary feet would hardly carry her down the slope, and the bag dragged heavily on her shoulder as if it were weighted with iron.

"You—are—very kind!" she said shyly, as she climbed up beside the woman. It was only after the old horse had started on his jog trot again that she bethought her this might possibly be a person sent by her enemies to lure her back to them. So she rested the heavy bag in her lap, and sat tongue-tied, choking over the thought.

"How fur be you going?" asked the woman turning kindly, uncurious eyes upon her.

"A good many miles," stated Fraley noncommittally. "I'm sure I'm much obliged for the ride," she added, as her mother had taught her was proper.

"Well, you mustn't let me carry you outta your way," said her hostess. "My ranch turns off to the right about fifteen miles beyond here."

"Oh, that's all right," said Fraley, relieved that it did not turn to the left. Somehow her instinct taught her that the Southern route was best, at least until she was farther east.

"Come fur?" asked the woman, still eyeing her admiringly.

"Yes, a good ways," said Fraley laconically.

"Well, where are you goin'? I don't wantta take you outta yer way."

"Why, down this road," said the girl, "I—you see, I'm just travelling."

"Ummm!" observed the woman in a tone that implied her answer was inadequate.

"I'm on my way to New York!" she added desperately, feeling that she must make some explanation. The woman reminded her a little of her mother.

"Umm! Yer young to be goin' that fur alone!" observed the woman affably. "What's yer ma think o' yer goin'? I hope ye ain't running away. Ef ye are I ken tell ya it don't pay! I done it, and look at me!"

"Oh," said Fraley, her tired eyes suddenly filling with tears, "my mother is dead! She told me to go. Yes, I'm running away, but not from anybody that has a right—"

"There, there, honey child, don't you cry! I hadta ast. You see I'm a mother, an' you is too little and sweet eyed to be trampin' around these here diggin's alone so near night. There's them that might do ya harm."

"But I have to go. I have—people—in the east."

"Well, thank goodness fur that!" said the woman warmly, "an' I'll take ye home with me to-night, and you can have a good supper and a nice sleep before you start on. You look all beat out. And in the morning my Car'line'll harness up an' give ya a lift over ta the railroad. It ain't so fur, an' she's used ta drivin' alone. She can take Billy along fer comp'ny on the way back."

"Oh, thank you," said Fraley again, still frightened at the way her affairs were being managed for her. She didn't want to go to a strange ranch. There would be men there, and there might be friends of Brand's or Pierce's. Then she would not be safe ever, for they would come and hunt her wherever she went if they once got track of her. They would claim she was theirs.

"My old man died three years back and left me with five children," went on her would-be hostess. "I thought we'd come to the end, but I stuck it out, and now Jimmie is fifteen, and he can do a man's work. I useta have a hired man, but he got drunk and I got tired of it, so now we just look after things ourselves."

"Oh," said Fraley suddenly relieved there were no men to face at the ranch.

"That's one reason I'm hurryin' home. Jimmie's plantin' t'day, an' he'll be tired, and Car'line's got a cut on her hand an' can't milk. I got two cows, and they'll be bawlin' fit ta kill. I don't let the young children milk; they're too fresh. Last time Billy tried he knocked a whole pail of milk over on himself."

"Oh, I can milk," said Fraley eagerly. "If you'll let me milk to pay for staying, I'd be glad to come to your house to-night."

"You got such little hands I wouldn't think you could bring the milk down," remarked the woman eyeing Fraley's little brown hands that lay relaxed in her lap.

"But I can," said the girl earnestly.

"All right. You can try. I've got an awful lot to do to red up. I'm expecting a man t'morra from over beyont the mountain. His name's Carter, Brand Carter. Mebbe you've heard of him. He's coming to look over some steers I've got for sale!"

7

FRALEY'S face grew white as milk, and her heart seemed almost to cease to beat. The sustaining power seemed to ebb away from her arms and shoulders, and her whole body slumped. With the relaxing of her position the bag on her lap began to slide, and in a second more would have gone out onto the road. But she rallied and caught it, and covered her confusion well with the effort.

"Say, you don't need ta hold that heavy bundle!" exclaimed the woman, alert at once to be kindly. "Here! Lemme put it back in my box. There's plenty a room there, and it can't get out! You're all beat out, an' you're white as a sheet!"

"Oh, thank you—but I'm all right!" urged Fraley, gripping her precious bag close once more. "I'd rather hold it. There are some very special things in it. They might fall out. It doesn't fasten very close together."

"But ain't it heavy? My land! I don't see how you ever managed carrying all that, hiking it! I think it's better to travel light. What you got in there? Can't you ship 'em on by freight?"

"Oh, no!" said Fraley aghast, "I wouldn't want to trust it that way! It's my Bible, that's the only heavy thing, and I couldn't be without it. Besides, I wouldn't be sure just where to send it till I got there."

"Why, ain't you got your folks' address?"

"Yes, I have the old address, but they might have moved," said Fraley evasively.

"Hmmm! Well, you could leave it to my house till you got fixed and let me know where to send it. Me, I wouldn't bother about just a Bible. You can buy 'em cheap anywhere."

"Oh, no!" said the girl horrified, "not like this one. This was my mother's Bible. She taught me to read out of it. It has things written down in the cover—things that she wrote for me! I promised her I'd never let it away from me!"

"Oh, well, that's diffrunt, of course, ef your maw wrote things down fer you to remember. I thought ef 'twas jest a common Bible why you cud git one most ennywheres. I don't see what use they is ennyhow! Except ta sit round on the parlor table like a nornament and hev ta dust all the time. Me, I didn't even bring mine with me when I cum out here. I hed too much else ta think about. I never missed it. I was too busy ta dust books. Besides, I never had no parlor table. Say, why don't you stay ta our house awhile? You cud be comp'ny fer my Car'line. Mebbe she wouldn't be so crazy to git out an' see the world ef she hed a girl her own age to talk to. She's got men comin' to see her, a'ready, an' she ain't much older'n you. There's one comes ridin' over the crest of the mountain every oncet an' a while. She's allus fussin' up when he comes. His name's Pierce somethin'. I didn't rightly git the last name, an' I won't ast Car'line, it would give her too much satisfaction. But I don't like his eye. It ain't nice. I donno why, but it ain't.

Say, whyn't you stay over a week er so an' be comp'ny fer Car'line? It might kinda make her more contented like."

"Oh, I couldn't!" said Fraley in a small disturbed voice. "I'm sorry, but I just couldn't. I really ought to go on to-night. You see I'm in a great hurry. I'll just ride as far as you go, and by that time I'll be rested and can go on. I really must get on to-night."

There was actual panic in her voice. Brand and Pierce! Then she was not out of their region after all! Perhaps she was getting into an even worse place. Perhaps Brand or Pierce would come to-night and find her in this woman's house!

"Naw, you can't go on ta-night!" said the woman eyeing her curiously, "I ain't lettin' no kid like you go gallivantin' out in the dark. There's wolves beyond the ranch in the forest. They come out sometimes. My Jimmy seen 'em. You ain't got no gun, hev ye? Well, you jest better wait till daylight. It'll be plumb dark now afore we git to my shack, an' time fer you ta rest. My Car'line, she'll git ya off at daybreak, ef that'll suit ya, but I ain't lettin' no child wander off ta get lost in the desert this time o' night. Ef you'd get inta the desert alone, an' lose yer way yer bones might bleach white afore anyone found 'em. You trust me."

Fraley's face could turn no whiter, but she said nothing more. Perhaps there would be a chance to steal away in the night.

The sky ahead was showing pearly tints with blue and green and fire pink like an opal. When she turned to looked behind her the sun was a burning ball just touching the rim of the horizon, and poised above a dark mountain. But she was relieved to see that so far there was no traveler in the long beaten strip of white road that rose and fell and rose again mile after mile as far as she could see, till the forest through which she had come intercepted.

The woman began to talk of her home, and the children, telling bits of family life, till Fraley grew interested. Her heart leaped at the thought of knowing another girl. Only once or twice had she seen girls of her own age, once when a party of tourists lost their way and stopped at the cabin to inquire. There had been two pretty girls in that company, dressed in lovely garments the like of which she had never seen before; and once she had seen some girls in the town when her father took her with him to buy her shoes. The ride had taken all day, and she had been very tired. He never took her again. He said it was too much trouble. It would be nice to know a girl—and to see some children. There had been no children near the cabin since her baby brother died of croup, and she was a tiny thing then herself.

It was quite dark when at last they came in sight of a speck of light in the distance. She could see nothing in the blackness but that light like a red berry, and she began to be afraid again.

"That's my place!" announced the woman cheerfully. "Now, we'll have some grub. I'm gettin' hongry. What about you? There! Hear the dogs howl! They know it's me jest as well zif they cud see me. We keep five dogs about the place an' there couldn't no stranger come within a half a mile 'thout we'd know it. You like dogs? Ever have one?"

"I had a dog—But—it is dead!" said Fraley in a low voice, and the woman could see the tears were not far away.

"Well, they will die, too. That's so! But they're right useful whilst they live. I reckon Car'line's got hot bread fer supper. You like hot bread? Car'line kin make it good. She knows how to housekeep real well, an' she c'n work the farm too, only I won't let her. I say that's man's work. Though goodness knows I've done enough of it myself, too. But that's diffrunt! Car'line ain't gonta!"

They were nearing the ranch house now, a long low building made of logs. The door was flung open wide, and a stream of light shot out into the night. A sudden shyness descended upon Fraley. She wondered what to say to these strange people. She had had no dealings with her own kind, and she remembered keenly the mirthful glances of the two daintily dressed girls in the lost party on the mountain. They had made fun of her bare feet, she knew as well as though she had heard the words they were whispering. What would this Caroline think of her?

Then the dogs broke about them with barks of joy, and leaped at the woman, as she halted the old horse in front of the door.

Fraley stood, in a moment more, inside the open door, holding her precious bag in her arms, looking like a frightened rabbit.

She did not know that she made a picture as she stood there in her bare feet, and the old coat and kerchief, with the light of a big log fire flickering on the golden curls that strayed from under the binding silk. The other children stood off, suddenly shy, and watched her, and she eyed them, and then stared at the great beautiful fire in bewilderment. She had never been in a room like this, nor seen a fire in an open fireplace.

Off at one side was a table set with dishes, neatly, and chairs drawn up. There was a foaming pitcher of milk and another of molasses, and there was a pile of corn cakes keeping warm on a tin on the hearth. There was a smell of appetizing meat cooking sending up exquisite steam from a kettle slung over the fireplace.

The baby of the house ran and jumped into her mother's arms, and the others stood around evidently happy that she had come home. It seemed like heaven to Fraley.

Car'line stood by the side of the fire and stared at the girl her mother had brought home. Said "Howdy" perfunctorily when her mother told her to, and went on looking at her curiously. The other children stood around and watched her.

There was a certain dignity about Fraley, even as she stood there in bare feet clasping her bundle, that made the others feel shy. But suddenly one of the dogs sprang through the door, went wagging from one member of the family to the other, wagged up to the stranger, sniffing about her skirts, and laying his muzzle against her hand. Fraley stooped down, and began to pat him, snuggling her arm around him. Here was someone she understood, and who understood her.

"Oh, he is a dear dog!" she said looking up, and he wagged his tail and whined in pleasure at her attention.

There was something in the tone of her voice, or the way she said it, that made the children stare again. This was a person of another kind. There was something fine in the quality of her speech that they recognized as beyond theirs, which Car'line, perhaps resented a little.

"He's fell fer you all right," said the mother as she removed the old felt hat she wore and hung it on a peg between the logs.

"I ken see he thinks you're jest right. Swing that kettle round, Car'line, you'll have that stew burned before we get a chance to get it et up. Whar's Jimmy?"

The boy appeared at the door, awkward in the presence of the stranger, but melted into a grin as he saw how the dog had made friends with her.

"She's a girl I picked up on the road," introduced his mother informally. "She's goin' to stay with us t'night. She's all right."

"I bet she is," vouched Jimmy. "Buck wouldn't take up with 'er ef she wasn't. Say, girl, you gotta dog t'home, ain't ya? He smells it on ya I guess."

"I did have," said Fraley sadly, drooping her head to hide the tears that stung her eyes, "He—got—shot,— two days—ago!"

"Aw shucks! Ain't that a dirty shame!" said Jimmy sympathetically.

Fraley liked Jimmy from that time, and the rest of the children gathered around her with clumsy affection, feeling that her love for dogs had made her kin to them.

They gathered around the table while Car'line took up the stew in big tin plates. Fraley had a nicked thick white one because she was company.

She took off her head kerchief and washed her hands at the tin basin on the bench as the rest did. Then she sat down as a guest at a table with strangers for the first time in her life.

And here, as before, they noticed a difference in her. She did not reach out and grab for things. She did not make a noise with her lips as she ate, nor swoop up gravy with her spoon; she did not fill her mouth too full, nor talk when she was chewing. She seemed to eat without doing so. She put things into her mouth with quiet little unobtrusive movements, as if eating were quite a secondary thing, yet she seemed to enjoy what they gave her and accepted the second helping when it was offered.

The children watched her fascinated, the candle light playing on her gold hair, and on her delicate features. She seemed like a creature from another world to them. Yet she was telling their mother that she had lived all her life in these parts, and the garments she wore were no better than their own.

It appeared that the cows had been milked by Car'line and Jim, so the guest had no opportunity to prove her abilities in that line, but she promised to be up bright and early next morning to do it before she left.

It was after the supper was cleared away and Fraley had helped with the washing up, that they gathered around the fire, and Fraley felt a sudden loneliness in the midst of this friendly family. She and her mother had been like this together, even though there had been but two of them, and now there was no one! If only this were thousands of miles away from the home cabin gladly would she have accepted the earnest invitation of her hostess to stay on indefinitely and visit. But the thought of the men who were expected on the morrow to buy steers filled her with terror.

"Say, why'n't you git out yer Bible an' read to us all?" asked the mother presently, reaching forward to stir up the fire with a long stick that lay on the hearth. "I'd like to see what it sounds like after all these years; an' it wouldn't do these children any harm to hear it oncet, too."

Fraley shrank from bringing out the dear relic, sewed so carefully into its cotton covers by the hand of the beloved; but she could not refuse when they had been so kind to her. She must do something to repay them for her supper and night's lodging. So she went to the corner where she had laid by her gray woolen bag and took out the Bible for the first time since her mother had committed it to her care. She was a little troubled as she did so because of the papers which her mother had told her were inside the book, but when she unwrapped the outer sheathing of cotton, she found that the cover was fitted tightly over the old worn boards of the original, and that the papers were securely placed within this outer jacket of cloth with a fold of the cloth turned inside over their edges. Then she need not explain everything to these strangers, and have them fingering over her precious papers and asking her all sorts of questions when she had scarcely seen the papers herself.

With quiet reserve she took the chair that her hostess had placed for her beside the table, where two candles pierced the gloom of the room outside the ring of firelight.

"Where shall I read?" she asked lifting her serious big eyes to look about the group.

"Any place!" said Car'line peering over her shoulder curiously, "Is it a story?"

"Yes, it's full of stories."

"Read what you like," said the mother.

So Fraley turned to a favorite chapter to repeat it.

The candle light flickered on the worn page, the edge almost in tatters, where the little Fraley had fingered it long ago when she learned it; and the sweet earnest face of the girl was bent over the book for a moment and then lifted, with her gaze across to the firelight, as she spoke the wonderful words.

The family watched her spellbound.

"Say, you ain't lookin' on that there book, how can you know what it says?" interrupted Jim finally, too puzzled to wait till she was done. "Are you all makin' that up?"

Fraley smiled.

"Oh, no. I know it all by heart. I forgot I was not looking on. I learned it when I was a very little girl."

"You learned that whole book?" asked Car'line incredulously.

"Oh, no, but a great many parts. I used to learn a chapter a week, and sometimes more. I know a lot of the gospels, and the epistles, and a great many psalms. You see this was the only book we had. I never went to school, so Mother made me learn out of here.

"Car'line went a whole two terms when we was back

in Oregon," boasted her mother, "but she can't read good like that."

"Oh, I can't be bothered!" said Car'line with a toss of her head, "I allus hev too much to do. And ennyhow, where's the good of readin'? I'd never hev ennythin' to read."

"I'm gonta send fer us one o' them Bibles, an' you better git practiced up, Car'line, fer I meanta hev it read now an' then."

"Gwan!" said Jim, "I wanta hear what it's like. Mebbe I'll read it."

So Fraley went on with her chapter, being many times interrupted in the course of her recitation.

The room was very still. Even the little ones listened with round wondering eyes, and the mother, nodding now and then as her memory brought back her vague former knowledge of the story that was being told, although it had never reached her soul before as a thing that had aught to do with her personally.

As the story of the death on the cross changed into the glory of resurrection, the faces round the fire grew vivid with excitement, and Fraley, led on by their interest told of Christ's appearance to the different disciples, and to the women.

As she paused, the great log that had been burning in the fireplace fell in two and sent up a shower of sparks, and the mother, more deeply stirred by the story than she cared to have her children see, rose and fixed the fire again, but Jimmy leaned forward eagerly:

"An' wot happened then? Gwan!"

So Fraley told of the ascension, taking the words from the first chapter of Acts.

"Oh Gosh! Then He's gone!" said the boy flinging himself back in dismay. "Wot was the use of risin' from the dead then? He might just as well be dead as up in the sky."

"Oh, no," said Fraley earnestly, "Because He's coming again. Listen!" and she began to recite again:

"'This same Jesus which is taken up from you into heaven, shall so come in like manner as ye have seen Him go into heaven.' And you know in that first chapter I read, He said, 'If I go away I'll come again.'"

"Well, did He?" The boy's brows were drawn in a frown of earnestness.

"Not yet. But He's coming sure, sometime. There are lots of places in the Bible where it tells about it. He might come to-night, or to-morrow. It says it will be when no one knows—not even the angels know. But it's going to be wonderful!"

"Gosh! Then you can't tell us the rest of it t'night!" he said in a disappointed tone. "I don't see why He had ta go away 'tall ef He was comin' back."

"Why," said Fraley puckering her brows in her effort to explain, "because He had something to do for us up there before He came back."

"What 'e hav ta do?"

"He had to take our sins up there and tell God He'd taken them all on Him when He died."

"Gosh! What for?"

"Because we were all sinners."

"Well, what did God care about that?"

"He cared because He loved everybody. He made them to be His children, and do right, and be His family, and everybody went and did what He told them not to do, and He felt bad. He had said everybody that sinned had to die, and He had to keep His word or He'd be a liar, so He sent His Son to die and make a way for everybody that wanted to come back and be forgiven."

The boy who had lived all his young life on the edge

of an outlaw's country opened his eyes in wonder at this, and silence filled the room for a long moment, while each listener thought over this new version of what life and sin and death meant.

Then suddenly the mother turned toward the stranger and saw that her face looked worn and her eyelids were drooping.

"Say," she said eagerly. "Whyn't you stay? You'all could stay awhile, ennyhow, and git good en rested, an' read this Book to us a spell!"

"Oh, I couldn't!" said Fraley starting up in alarm. "I ought not to have stopped over night—really!"

"Well, you all gotta go to bed now. It's way after bed time."

"Aw, maw!" protested Jim. "It's jes' this one night an' we wanna hear more."

"Yes, jes' this one night for you all, but this child's gotta go a journey in the early mawnin' and Car'line an' Billy gotta take her down to the railroad. Hustle down quick now, an' no more words."

Fraley slept with Car'line in a loft overhead that they reached by a ladder at the far end of the room, and presently the house was still, the fire banked, the door barred, and no chance to steal away as she had half contemplated doing. Jimmy was sleeping on the cot in the big room down stairs, just at the foot of the ladder. The little window up here was too small to crawl through even if she dared drop so far, and the mother with her brood slept at the other end of the loft. so Fraley, with her hand out on the bag that carried her old Bible, fell asleep. To-morrow, perhaps early in the morning, Brand was coming to buy steers, and maybe Pierce Boyden with him. But she was safe to-night.

8

THE household was astir early, for the roosters began to crow at daylight, and all the other creatures seemed to think it was time to wake up. Fraley made a hurried toilet and got down even before Car'line, who was prinking a bit for the ride to town.

She milked both cows in spite of their protests, for they somehow felt that she was above such work. But she insisted sweetly, and carried her point, and then they all sat down to breakfast, Jimmy in open admiration now for a girl who could both read books and milk cows.

"Gosh, ef you'd stay," he urged with his mouth full of corn cake, "we'd have a great time! Wouldn't we, Maw?"

"I reckun we would!" said the mother with a sigh of regret. "But p'raps she'll come back sometime when she gits done visitin' her kinfolks."

Fraley smiled. She was in a frenzy to be gone, but she could not hurry Car'line, who was enjoying her breakfast, and had just reached over and helped herself to another piece of fried meat.

"We don't have meat fer breakfast every day," vouchsafed Billy with his mouth full. "It's jes' cause o' you. I wisht you'd stay."

It was just as they were leaving that Fraley ventured her request in the mother's ear, as she said good-by.

"Please don't say anything about my being here to any of those men that come from around the mountain," she whispered. "There's someone I'm afraid of that might follow me, and I don't want anyone to find out where I'm gone."

"All right, child, I won't," promised the woman with a kindly pat. "You're a good girl, an' ef anybody worries you, you jus' come right back to us. We'll see that no harm don't come to ya. I'll see that Jimmy don't say nothin' too. Don't ya worry! Good luck to ya, an' don't cher fergit the Bible!"

"No, I won't," promised Fraley, "I've put the address safe in the Bible, so I can't lose it."

Then she went out and climbed up into the buckboard beside Car'line, her precious bag across her lap, and they started, Billy riding on behind atop of the wooden box that held the groceries yesterday, his legs hanging down and swinging.

Away they drove over the winding brown ribbon of a road, over humps and hollows, till suddenly and surprisingly the log cabin was lost to view, and the country stretched wide before them, taking on a new aspect with the mountains far away and very dim.

Fraley kept glancing behind her every little while to see if there was anyone coming. She made the excuse of talking to Billy, but the morning was new and no one else in the wide world seemed abroad at this hour.

They were coming into country where the land was often fenced in little detached portions, and small bunches of cattle were kept meekly within bounds. Car'line discoursed wisely of the different ranches that could be seen as they went along, talked of the people who owned them, and of cattle raising, as if it were a kind of sport. But mostly her talk was of the young men about, and of their interest in herself. She found Fraley not very responsive on such topics, but a good listener, and she grew more confidential and related how a man named Pierce Boyden came to see her sometimes, and how he had kissed her the last time he came.

"Oh, Car'line!" exclaimed Fraley startled out of her reticence, "I wouldn't let him!"

"Why not?" asked Car'line sharply.

"Because—" said Fraley earnestly, and then stopped, realizing what it might mean if she let this girl know she knew the man and hated him. "Because—why—men are—Why, Car'line, do you know anything about this man? He may be—a *bad* man, Car'line! Does your mother know he kissed you?"

"Well, I guess not!" said Car'line proudly. "He wouldn't do it before her! He's a gentleman, he is! He has great big black eyes, and black hair all sort of curly, and when he smiles he looks just like a king! You oughtta see him! He's the best looker I ever saw!"

"But he might be—a—cattle thief or—something! He might kiss—other girls!" Then mindful of the midnight conversation she had heard concerning Pierce, and feeling she ought to give a warning she added:

"I know a man—like that—hair and eyes and all—and he—he—kissed a girl down in a town beyond where we lived. She wasn't a nice girl. Men talked about her—at night—that is they said awful things about him—too! I wish you wouldn't do it, Car'line. Your mother has been good to me, an' I wish you wouldn't do it. You tell her what I said about that man, and you ask her if she thinks you ought to, won't you?" she pleaded earnestly.

"Like fun I will!" snapped Car'line angrily, "an' don't

you go to writing no highflown letters to her about it neither ur I'll tell her you did it because you are jealous of me, see?"

"Oh, Car'line!" said Fraley in distress. "You wouldn't!"

"Sure I would!" said Car'line gaily. "Just you try me!"

"But it wouldn't be true!" said Fraley quietly, as if that robbed the threat of its sting.

"I'm not so sure it ain't," said Car'line impishly, eyeing her companion with a furtive look, "I'll bet you know him!"

But Fraley's answer after a long wait surprised her.

"Yes, I know him."

"You do?" The other girl was startled. "Mebbe he's kissed you, too."

"Never!" said Fraley and her face was grim with indignation. "I would rather be—*dead* than have him touch me!"

Car'line laughed.

"Gosh!" she said. "Well, you would. You're one of them saints! I didn't know they had 'em round her s'near ta Rogues Valley. Well, I ain't. I'm jes' flesh an' blood an' b'lieve me, I know a handsome man when I see him."

From then on Car'line had the conversation all to herself and she rattled on proudly about the devotion of the different young men she had met till Fraley turned her thoughts away in self-defense.

The country round would have been interesting to her if she had not been in a frenzy of fear. Now she had given herself away to this girl who had no sense of loyalty to a confidence, and here she was almost as badly off as if she had just started from her home mountain. If Pierce found out she had been here he would get the word to Brand at once, and Brand would call the gang and ride after her. There was no use in trying to doubt that. Brand thought she was his property. The last few sentences she had heard him and his drunken companions speak on the terrible night of her escape left no doubt whatever what her fate would be if she were caught. She could not even claim the protection of this good woman with whom she had passed the night. Brand and his crew were stronger than a mere woman. He would ride and take her, that would be all of it, and after that she were better dead!

What could she do about it? Would any appeal reach this girl as it seemed to have her mother?

The town, as they called it, turned out to be five houses widely scattered, a general store, and a station. Car'line drew up at the station with a flourish of her broken whip, and a smile and a gay word for the two men who stood on the platform which was returned in none too courteous a manner.

"Well, here you be," said Car'line. "You got a hour an some minutes to wait I reckon, but I'll hev to be gettin' back. Pierce Boyden said he might be comin' down today an' I don't wantta miss him."

But here Billy rose:

"Aw, Car'line! Maw said you wasta wait till her train come. I wanna wait an' see the train come in. I ain't seen it only twicet in my life. I wanna wait!"

"You shet up!" said the elder sister in an ugly tone. "You shet up er I'll tell maw you're a cry baby!"

But Fraley was already getting out of the conveyance. Car'line's decision had brought intense relief to her. She did not mean to wait around any station and give Pierce or Brand a chance to waylay her, and if Car'line went now it would make her way much easier.

"No, don't wait," she said eagerly, "I don't need

anyone. It was kind of you to bring me, and I hope I'll be able sometime to repay you."

She wanted to ask Car'line please to say nothing about her being there, but when she looked again at the girl's angry eyes and arrogant chin she decided to leave things as they were. Perhaps Car'line would keep still on her own account, but if she did not she certainly would not do so for the asking. She was evidently angry at what Fraley had told her of the young man. Well, let it go at that. There were difficulties everywhere and this was just one more.

"Good-by, Billy," said Fraley wistfully, "and thank your mother for the pleasant time. When I come back I'll bring you something nice. Good-by, Car'line, and thank you for the ride."

Car'line lingered a minute to flirt with the two men on the platform, obviously showing off to the younger girl, and then, with a careless wave of her hand toward Fraley she drove away and was soon a mere speck in the distance.

Fraley, giving a quick furtive glance around, moved away from the vicinity of the two men. She looked up and down the shining track that gleamed sharply in the morning sun, and ran away in a bright ribbon as far as her eyes could see in either direction. She marveled that this was a thing to bind the distance. Her mother had talked about the railroad. She had come west—on the railroad—years ago. Fraley knew about the sleeping cars and diners, and the common cars. She of course could only afford a common car when she came to taking the railroad, but she was not ready yet. She would trust nothing but her two feet for the present. This getting mixed up with other people only seemed to make more and more trouble. But how was she going to get away with those two men watching her?

She studied the surroundings and read the sign over the store door. A store! She would buy something more to eat, some cheese, or crackers or something that would be easily carried. It would be interesting to go into a store, and she would have an excuse to get away from the station without attracting their attention.

So she hurried across the space between, and up the wooden steps of the store.

She had taken the precaution to tie one of her precious gold pieces from her belt, into the corner of her crude handkerchief, and knot it round her wrist under her sleeve, for she had expected to have to pay something if she had to take the train, so now with confidence she entered the store and looked around.

It was as interesting to her wilderness eyes as a great city emporium would have been to a villager, and she longed to stay and examine the wares, of which there were a great variety, all the way from plow and shoes to crackers and cheese and dress goods. The bright tin pans were fascinating, also a nest of yellow bowls, and there was a piece of cotton cloth covered with little pink flowers. But she had no time for such things now. She looked about and saw some dried prunes. Sometimes her father had brought home prunes with the groceries. Those were things that could be eaten raw, also there were apples. She bought two apples, after carefully asking the price, a quarter of a pound of prunes, ten cents' worth of cheese, for hers was all gone, three eggs, and a box of stale crackers that had been in the store indefinitely. The eggs she meant to use in mixing up her corn meal when she found a safe place to make a fire by the wayside. They would be hard to carry, but would make the corn meal go a great way.

She put the things in her coat pocket, placing the eggs carefully on the opposite side from the one on which she carried her bag, and while she waited for the store-keeper to make change she asked a few questions. The store-keeper told her about the trains, gave her an old time-table, and was quite voluble in explaining the difference between local and express trains. He informed her that the next train east would be there in exactly one hour and fifteen minutes "if she wa'n't late, which she usually was." He invited her to be seated and offered her a Kansas City newspaper a week old to read. He said his wife came from "back east in Kansas," but she thanked him and declined. She said she would go out in the sunshine awhile and walk around, and so she slipped away.

The two men were just getting into a cart driven by a third man when she emerged from the door, and she waited by the door to examine a pair of shoes that hung just outside, tied together by its strings. She admired the smooth stiff surface, and decided that some day she would buy a pair, but she must not spare the money now. She did not even ask the price, but the shoes kept her back in the shadow till the men had driven away, and then she ventured forth.

She walked back to the station, glanced around, and seeing nobody watching her, and nothing in sight either way, she began slowly to walk the rail that was next to the platform, balancing herself with her arms out, as if to amuse herself. When she had walked a few steps she turned and walked back, and the store-keeper nodded across to her and called:

"When ye git tired come over an' set" and she called back a smiling "Thank you," and kept on walking the rail.

The man went in presently, and she turned and walked the other way. This time she did not walk back, but kept on down the track toward the east. The man had said there was no train till the eastern local came by an hour from now. She need not be afraid, so she walked on and on till the little gray station and the little gray store were mere specks in the bright distance. And if the store-keeper came to look out at her again and missed her he did not trouble himself long about a stray stranger. She was going to take the train and she would likely look after herself.

But Fraley, when she came to a road that turned at right angles to the railroad, sprang from the track and started out across country, glad to get her feet off the hot steel, and on to the cool ground again.

The road she took led across a hill, and when she had climbed the gentle slope she looked around, took her bearings again, and after studying the long bright ribbon of tracks, decided to keep them in view as much as possible, for at least they were a clue to the world she sought and eventually they would lead her on the right way.

She sat there resting, sheltered by a group of trees. Feeling in her pocket she found that the eggs were still unbroken, and decided to eat one of the apples, for it seemed a long time since breakfast and she might not find such a good place to rest in again for several hours. The country here was broad and flat, and much of the forest had been removed.

As she enjoyed her apple, she suddenly heard a rumbling in the distance, and starting to her feet, she looked wildly around her in every direction, until finally she discovered a dark speck back on the railroad track coming along like a wild steer, or a whole herd of wild steers. In amazement she dropped down in the grass again and watched it, breathless, her eyes shining with wonder. This must be the train she was supposed to have taken!

How did people stay in their seats on a thing that went as fast as that?

Her mother had told her about the railroad trains, but she had never imagined it would be like that.

She watched it as it came on, and in another moment it was before her. Like a flash it passed, and was gone, a darting, disappearing speck in the distance! How strange! How wonderful!

She sat there visualizing the sight again, the great black puffing monster ahead. That would be the engine. Cars and cars hitched together, with little windows in most of them, windows close together, and the outline of heads of people inside at each window. At the last car there had been a black man wearing a white kind of cap that looked like paper, and a white coat and apron. He would be the cook for the dining car, or one of the waiters. Her mother had described it all. But somehow she had never thought it would be like this, rushing so fast! She was glad she had not taken that train, it would have frightened her. She resolved to wait as long as possible before she took to the railroad.

When Fraley started on again she had a sense of being comparatively safe for the time at least. If Car'line had told her plans to either of her enemies, at least they had not been able to find her at the train, even if they could have reached there in time. And perhaps if they thought she had taken the train, they would stop their search for her in that region. She did not realize that she had already gone beyond the bounds that outlaws had set for themselves, and that they would come no further out in the open seeking her. If they carried on their search they would have to conduct it through others, and it might be that those others would be in the most unexpected places, even far from where she started.

She did remember later that the store-keeper might

have seen her walking the track, and perhaps told someone, and so her old uneasiness returned to keep her on
the alert.

With very little rest she kept on her pilgrim way
during most of the day, but at sunset, well spent, she
discovered a little nook where two small hills came
together, leaving a tiny point of land jutting between
them at their base. There were trees above, leaning over
and quite sheltering the retreat, and a small brook, that
had been wandering around all the afternoon in the
general direction that the railroad took, ambled not far
away. It was an ideal spot to make a fire, hardly visible
from any direction. Fraley gathered sticks, and finding
three large stones, put the flat one across the other two,
making a very good fireplace. She soon had a brisk little
fire of twigs and sticks, and the top stone heating nicely.

She examined her eggs in the right-hand pocket and
found only one cracked, and that she broke into her tin
cup. She had no spoon or fork, but she stirred it with her
finger, and began mixing in the corn meal, with a pinch
of salt, and a little water from her fresh filled water bottle.
As soon as the stone was hot enough to sizzle at a drop
of water she dropped her little hoe cake on the stone and
it began to bake, sending forth such a savory odor that
she was almost afraid it would attract some wild thing of
the forest, or perhaps some wilder humans, but the cake
went on baking, and the soft blue smoke from the tiny
fire rose straight up between the sheltering pines on the
banks above, and nothing came to molest or make her
afraid.

She was just eating the last crumb of the hoe cake
when there came that low terrifying rumble that beto-
kened a train. Three times that afternoon, since the first
train in the morning, had the silence of the open been

broken by that sound, and now that she was becoming more accustomed to it, it seemed even friendly.

So she sat quite still by her little fire, and watched a freight train slamming by, down beyond the mist of the meadowland. The smoke from the engine sent up a fiery glow in the twilight, and the end of the long, long train carried a little red berry-like light, that waved and winked and twinkled jauntily, as the train flung on into the prairie vastness.

When the train was entirely out of sight, Fraley put out every vestige of fire, even trampling the dirt into the spot where it had been, and pushed the stones under the bank where no curious passer would notice them. She then ascended the bank to find a night's lodging. She would not be afraid if she could find the right kind of a tree. True a tree was not always as restful as the ground, but it was safer, and could be ascended in a hurry.

She found one to her purpose just up the bank, a big pine—for she always took a pine if there was one about, she loved its sweet odor and its plumy tassels—and swinging up into it a few branches high settled herself and her bag quite comfortably for a rest. Even supposing she should turn in her sleep, there would be little danger of falling far, for the branches were wide and low and closely interlaced. She could almost rest back upon their springy resinous arms. She was high enough from the ground so that no animal would be likely to disturb her, and near enough to good climbing branches to easily get herself out of harm's way in case anything came to trouble her.

A drawing-room train from California swept along the railroad track near enough to be interesting, and Fraley, lying among her branches, watched. She could see bright windows and people sitting cosily together, doing something at little tables. Some of them seemed to be eating. She watched in wonder till the train swept out of sight, and then she thought of the pleasant home where she had spent the last night. Hungrily she wished for such a home. If only Mother were back, and they two could have a home of their own, where joy and safety and love abode!

She remembered each little incident of the evening before; the faces with the flickering firelight on them, the wonder in their eyes when she read the Word of God. She had not realized before that some people did not know the Bible—except perhaps such men as Brand who had deliberately chosen to go away from God. And sometimes even he spoke in his anger words that showed he must have heard some of the Bible.

From the branches she could see the stars coming out one by one, and the moon beginning to climb the heavens, and she repeated softly to herself: "When I consider Thy heavens, the work of Thy fingers, the moon and the stars which Thou hast ordained, what is man that Thou art mindful of him—"

On through the psalm her mind went, as if she were talking to the invisible One. But she was not quite finished before her eyelids drooped and she was asleep, rocked in the arms of the great pine.

The Atlantic and Pacific Express woke her in the early dawning, rattling through the land in two sections, its sleepers still dark-windowed where the travelers lay asleep. Rubbing the sleep from her eyes to watch its trail against the dawning, she found thanksgiving in her heart that the night was past and she was still safe.

Slipping down from her piney bough, a little stiff from her cramped position, she pattered softly down to the stream, to a spot where she had noticed low growing trees, and a sheltered pool. Here shut in by the foliage and the dark she could safely bathe.

Ten minutes later she returned to her shelter of the night before, assembled her fireplace and some wood, and baked another little cake out of the last of her meal. She might not find another opportunity to do this conveniently, and the meal would be wasted.

She had put on fresh undergarments, and washed out the brief ones she had been wearing since she left the cabin, and now she hung the wet things around the fire to dry while the cake was baking. With her bit of comb, and the broken mirror she combed her hair out and spread it to dry over her shoulders, and then she ate her cake, saving a small piece to eat on her way. There was one more egg in her pocket, still unbroken, and that she could eat raw for lunch if there were no chance to cook it.

By the time she had put out her fire and broken camp, the flimsy garments hanging on the low limb over the fire were dry. She wrapped them up, stuffed them into the bag and started on into a new day, almost sorry to leave the pleasant retreat that had housed her so comfortably.

The morning proved long and uneventful. The way was rough in some places, unless she wanted to climb the hills and get farther away from the railroad, but she felt that it was the only guide she had to her unknown port, so she trudged on, through boggy land, or rough stubble grass, and about noon she came in sight of a small village.

9

IT was only a small straggling village, a settlement it would have been called in the east, but it looked like a swarming hive of population to the girl whose eyes were trained by mountain loneliness. She stood uncertain afar and studied it through her glass.

The railroad wandered before her, cutting a clean steel gash across the country shining in the midday sun. She studied the buildings in detail, and finally came to the one closest to the tracks. That would likely be a station. Then her heart stood still. There were two riders just arriving, and one rode a white horse!

That was enough for Fraley. She put down her glass and dashed into the bushes, making a wide detour around that village, and resolving to keep as far as possible from human habitation for the next several days. Would she never be free from her enemies?

The detour carried her far out of her course, and for three hours she lost track of her railroad entirely, and began to think she would never find it again, but it rediscovered itself to her toward evening near a brown lake set about with reeds and reflecting dark pines in its depths.

She had steadily avoided human habitation so far, but as night drew on again she felt a strange dread of the loneliness. The lake looked large and dark, and the world seemed interminable. A dislike of passing that sheet of dark water possessed her, and she was aching in every muscle with fatigue. She was hungry too. She had eaten the raw egg early in the day, the apple at noon with the last bit of corn cake, and later in the afternoon had eaten some of the dried prunes with a few of the stale crackers and a little cheese. Her store of eatables was growing very low, and how could she go on unless she ate. Even though she had dipped deep into her supply she was not satisfied, but felt empty and faint as she dragged on her weary way.

As it neared the lake the railroad plunged into a dark forest and was lost again, and Fraley, half running, found herself sobbing as she tried to keep on higher ground because it was wet down near the tracks, but at last in desperation went splashing across the marshy land straight over to where the railroad grade rose up high and dry.

She had been watching the trains ever since she had left the station where Car'line had conducted her. She knew that there would be no train either way now for some time, for the usual afternoon expresses had passed. Should she venture to walk the track a little way? She could keep a sharp lookout, and roll down the grade quickly if she heard a train coming. There was a double track, and she had noticed two freights passing yesterday. She could walk toward the one that would be coming west.

She stood, hesitating, at the foot of the steep grade, and then started upward. It was difficult climbing, especially with that heavy bag to carry, but she struggled up, and at last reached the top of the grade and stood, palpitating, on a tie. She looked back and saw nothing but track and landscape as far as her eye could reach. She looked forward and saw the dark lake at the foot of gloomy mountains on one hand, and marsh land on the other, the track plunging into the depths of the forest just beyond the lake. But there was light beyond. She could see that the wooded place was not of great extent. Should she try it?

The memory of those two riders she had seen at that village gave her impulse and she decided to press on.

It was hard, nervous work walking the ties, and her feet were sore from the climb through the cinders, her head dizzy with watching her steps and both distances at the same time. It seemed the longest walk she had ever taken, but at last she got beyond the woods and came out into a wide stretch of country that was brilliant with sunshine.

"Oh," she said aloud, "oh, I'm so glad!" and found there were tears running down her face. It had been a terrible strain, walking that track through the dark wood, with water on either side down below the grading, and the dread of a special train, perhaps, rushing at her unawares.

She slid down the grade as soon as she got beyond the marshy land, and was glad, indeed, to get on firm, dry ground once more.

The place about here looked more inviting than where she had been all day. There was a house a long way off and, apparently, roads going here and there. There was even a stretch of land that seemed to have been made ready for planting. A plow stood in a furrow as if it had just been left for a while. Also there were pleasant, friendly trees along the way, and a smooth road presently presented itself to be walked on. She was almost too tired to keep on much longer, but she must until she found a safe place to sleep.

She was watching the way to choose smooth spots for her feet were very sore, when suddenly she looked up and saw a rider coming toward her on a black horse, and her heart stood still with fear.

There was not time to study him through her glass and see if he was one of her enemies. It might be that he had not yet noticed her. She turned and fled like a streak of light but, to her horror, as she ran she heard the man calling. She did not stay to hear whether he was calling her or someone else. She fled for her life back on the road, back to the last tree she had passed. She flung herself upon its trunk as she had often done before, and shinned up into the thick branches, where she was completely hidden from view. The branches were so luxurious that she could not even look out herself without parting them, and she did not dare do that. Silently she waited, seated on a high bough, frightened eyes staring down, ears strained to listen to the horse's hoof beats on the hard earth.

Yes, he was coming on. Had he seen her? Was it Brand, or Pete? Was she caught at last? It was of no use to cry out, for that house was too far away, even if there might be friendly people in it. Her only chance was to keep silent and hope he had not seen her. Perhaps he lived in that house and had been calling to someone on the porch. Perhaps he had not seen her at all, or if he had he might have missed where she went and would ride straight by.

But no, the horse had stopped. There was a sound of someone springing to the ground, and then she heard steps. He was coming toward the tree.

"Oh, I say, you up there? What are you? A bird or a

girl? What do you seem to think you are doing up there anyway?"

The voice was crisp and hearty, and the eyes that looked up were full of merry twinkles. Fraley leaned forward and stared down and answered in a frightened little voice:

"I'm—just resting—a little!"

"Oh, I see!" said the young man jovially. "Well, would you mind if I interrupted you a minute to inquire the way? I'm a stranger around here, and I guess I've made a wrong turn. I want to get to the log schoolhouse, wherever that is. Can you tell me? You see I'm lost."

Fraley looked down at his nice, lean, tanned face, noticed the wave in his brown hair, and the merry twinkle in his eyes, and lost some of her fear.

"But—you see—I'm lost too!" she said gravely.

"The dickens! You are?" said the young man, and bent over, laughing, "Say now, that's a great joke, isn't it? Well, perhaps I can help you then. Where were you going?"

"I—don't—quite know," she vouchsafed in a small voice. "I'm travelling."

"Oh, I see!" said the young man sobering down and giving her a quick, surprised glance.

"Well," he said at last, "I see you're a lady, and, I should judge, a lady in distress, and I hope I'm a gentleman. You needn't be afraid of me, if that's what's the matter. I'm perfectly respectable. Suppose you come down and let's talk this thing over. Where were you really heading for?"

Fraley sat very still for a minute, and then answered slowly, "Why—I—suppose New York, in the end. But it seems to be a long ways off."

"You bet your life it is!" said the young man bitterly. "I'd like right well to be there myself if I hadn't been chump enough to promise to stay out here and hold down another fellow's job while he goes to the hospital. But I'm here, and I guess I'll have to stick it out. How about it, will you come down and help me decide which way we ought to go, or do I have to come up there?"

Fraley looked wildly about and at once uncurled her feet from under her dress, where they had been tucked out of sight.

"Let me help you," said the young man, reaching up a friendly hand.

"Thank you," said Fraley solemnly, "I can get down alone," and she proceeded to swing herself off the high bough and drop with a graceful little spring to the ground as if she had really been the bird he had suggested.

"Well, that was some jump!" declared the young man, surveying her as she stood silently before him, watching him with wise, half-frightened eyes.

The kerchief had caught in the branches, and was hanging on her back, and her golden hair was flowing in waves about her shoulders. Even in the old overcoat she was lovely; barefoot and tired and ragged, she made a picture there in the wilderness.

"Now, what are we going to do about it?" asked the young man after he had surveyed her. "What good jokes do you know?"

"Jokes?" she said looking puzzled. "I'm not sure what you mean. But there's a railroad over there, just behind those bushes, down there. It goes east that way, because that's where the sun rises."

"The dickens it does? I take it you've watched it rise too. Well that's something, only the sun isn't rising now."

"No, it's almost sunset time," said the girl gravely, "were you going east or west?"

"Well, now, that's what I don't know. You see, I started from a ranch where this friend of mine is supposed to board, and I'm due at that log schoolhouse at seven o'clock. I've got to get there or bust because I told this fellow I would. He's counting on me! It isn't my kind of a job, but I'll have to do the best I can with it, and I've got to get there. By the way, how can I serve you? You said you were going to New York. Do you want to get to a station? I should suppose there would be one somewhere along a railroad eventually, although you can't, most always, sometimes, tell in a new country like this. I could perchance take you to a station if we could find one lying around loose."

"No, thank you. I thought I would walk a little farther first," said Fraley shyly, "it costs a lot of money, I guess, to ride on the cars, and I haven't very much."

"Oh!" said the young man, "so it's money is it? That's my bugbear too. Not for myself you understand. I happen to have been born with plenty and I can help you out in that way if you'll let me."

"Oh, no," said Fraley shrinking away, "I'll be all right. But I'm sorry I can't help you. I've been travelling all day and I haven't seen any log schoolhouse—that is nothing that looked like that—"

"I see," said the young man. "Well, what about some supper? I'm getting perfectly hollah! Suppose we just sit down here under this tree and have a bite and talk it over. Perhaps that will help."

"I'm sorry," said Fraley again, "but I have nothing but some crackers and a few prunes. You are welcome to half of those if you like. They are not very nice."

"Oh, but I've got a real lunch," said the young man. "The lady at the ranch put it up for me. There's enough for a regiment, and I do hate like the dickens to eat alone. Won't you share it with me? Then we can decide what's best to be done."

Fraley looked troubled. It was not quite her idea of etiquette nor safety, this picking up a strange young man in the wilderness and going out to dinner with him under a casual tree, but he waited for no acquiescence. He stepped over to his horse and began to unstrap a box from the back of the saddle.

"Gaze on that!" said the young man opening the box and disclosing neat packages wrapped in wax paper, and glimpses of golden oranges.

"Oh," said Fraley looking with amazement at the arrangement, "that is wonderful!"

"Now, let's sit down here and eat. I'm simply ravenous. We had lunch at eleven o'clock, and I expected to reach this place an hour ago and have time to get all primed up for the evening. Here, let me fix that knapsack of yours so you'll be comfortable!" He sprang forward and lifted the bag from her tired shoulders and placed it down by the tree trunk.

"Now, tree-lady, drop down there and rest against that. There's nothing breakable in it I'm sure, the way you lighted down from that tree."

She obeyed him because she did not know just what else to do, and because she was too tired to stand up longer.

He dropped down on the grass in front of her and opened the box again, handing her out one of the little wax paper parcels.

"How's that? Open it and see what it turns out to be. If I can judge by the lunch we had it'll be something pretty delectable. They think because I'm taking the job of their preacher that I must be fed on nectar and ambrosia."

"Is this nectar and ambrosia?" asked Fraley seriously looking down at the package she held, still unopened.

The young man laughed.

"Something like that," he said. "Try it."

"Oh, but I mustn't," said Fraley handing it back to him. "You will need every crumb you can get if you're really lost. It's such a long way to anywhere out here. I know for I've tried it."

"The dickens you have!" said the young man. "Well, now, that's too bad because I never eat alone, and if you won't I won't, you see, and we'll just starve together!"

Fraley looked at him in astonishment and then she laughed, a rich sweet childish gurgle of fun.

"I'll eat some," she agreed, and opened her little package.

She found delicate slices of fine white bread with slices of chicken breast laid in between. And when she put it in her mouth she thought it was the best thing she had ever tasted.

There were other little packages with other sandwiches, some with fragrant slices of pink ham between them. There were hard boiled eggs rolled in paper. There were olives and pickles, and chocolate cake, and cookies, and white grapes and oranges, a feast for a king! There was coffee amazingly hot in a thermos bottle! And in the wilderness!

Fraley ate silently at first, until the faint sick feeling was gone, and then she looked up with a smile:

"This is just like Elijah under the juniper tree, isn't it?"

The young man stared at her.

"Beg pardon, who did you say?"

"Elijah! Don't you know? The first time he was in the wilderness the ravens fed him, and then the time he was so discouraged under the juniper tree an angel came and baked him a little cake—"

"Am I to understand that I am an angel or a raven?" asked the young man. "Consider, I beg you, for it will make a great difference to me whether you think I'm a raven or an angel."

Fraley looked up and laughed.

"But I mean it seriously," said the young man helping himself to his third ham sandwich, "It may make a great difference to me all my life whether you consider me a raven or an angel. And who is this person Elijah that you seem so intimate with?"

Her face grew sober again.

"Oh, don't you *know* Elijah?"

"Sorry but I never had the pleasure of meeting him," said this strange merry gentleman as he handed her a bunch of luscious grapes. "I'm a graduate of one of the best colleges of the land, too, and I suppose I ought to have heard of him at least, but I simply can't recall his identity."

Fraley looked troubled.

"It's a long story," she said, "I'd have to begin at the beginning to tell it all, but you can read it."

"I detest waiting for a thing when I want to know it at once. Just give me some clue, I may know the gentleman after all."

"Why, he was a prophet, you know," began Fraley looking at him hopefully.

"A weather prophet?" asked the young man catching the word lightly.

"Yes," said Fraley with a clearing of her expression. "That's the one. I was sure you knew him. He told Ahab you know, that there wasn't going to be any dew nor rain and it made him so angry that he told the prophet to get out of the country, and he went where there was a brook and the ravens brought him bread and flesh in the morning, and bread and flesh in the evening and he drank of the brook."

"Oh, I see," said the young man, "but that's the raven, where does the angel come in? I don't seem to recall the rest of the story. Where did the ravens get the sandwiches do you think?"

"Why, they weren't sandwiches," said the girl earnestly. "I don't think people fixed them like this then, it doesn't say anything about it, but God sent the ravens you know. He told Elijah He was going to do it, and He sent the angel to him too you know."

"No, I don't know," said the young man. "Where do you get all this? I don't recall ever having heard it. Tell me the rest. It sounds interesting. We have ten minutes before we have to start. I'm sure that will give us plenty of time to hunt out that schoolhouse, for it ought to be within a mile of us somewhere. I know just where I got off the track."

Fraley looked at the sun.

"It's getting late," she said uneasily. "I ought to start right away myself. I've got to get somewhere for the night."

"That's all right," said the young man easily. "I'll take you wherever you want to go. That horse is good for two riders as well as one. You can come on with me till I get this job done I'm in for, and then I'll carry you wherever you say. Why not come on back to the ranch with me till morning? My landlady will be delighted to take you in, I'm sure. I'll just tell her I picked you up on the road, and you need a night's lodging."

Fraley's eyes were filled with alarm.

"Oh, I couldn't really!" she said, getting to her feet. "I must be getting along fast. It is time I was gone now. The sun is going down, see, and I must find—I must get— somewhere—before it is quite dark."

"Where is it you have to get?" asked the young man springing up also.

"I—why—I—have to find the place. I don't know just where—and so I must hurry."

"Do you mean you are going to some house where friends live?" he asked eying her keenly.

The alarm was growing in her eyes and, when she did not answer immediately, he went on.

"Because there isn't any house anywhere near here except that one up there, I can tell you that, I've been riding around quite a bit, and I've got a pretty good idea of the lay of the land. Where is it you think you are going? You know it isn't safe for a nice little ladybird like you to be cutting around lonely places all alone like this. You don't *live* around here, do you? You don't *live* up in that old empty house up there, do you? Because I happen to know it's perfectly empty, for I applied my eye to one of the windows a few minutes ago, meaning to ask the shortest way to my schoolhouse. There isn't a stick of furniture in the place."

"No, I don't live there—" she said, "but I can find a place—I always do—!"

"Do you mean to say you've been hiking it like this for long?"

"Oh, not very long," evaded Fraley, intensely worried now and anxious only to get away.

He looked at her steadily, and there was something strong and clean in his eyes that allayed her fears. Then he spoke.

"Well, I may as well tell you the truth, I'd been watching you for half an hour from that upper road up there. Several times I saw you drop down as if you were all in, and you dragged along as if you couldn't go much farther. Being somewhat lost myself a little farther didn't matter, so I thought I'd come down and offer you a lift.

But when I saw you run and disappear into a tree I just didn't know what to make of it, and so I thought I'd come and see anyway. Now, Ladybird, you needn't tell me any more than you want me to know, but I certainly don't intend to leave you in this God-forsaken spot alone at this time of night, unless you tell me you have a protector lurking somewhere in the neighborhood that will see that no harm comes to you. The people I'm staying with told me there were some tough characters not far from here, and it isn't safe for a girl to be here alone."

"I know," said Fraley gently, "but this isn't a God-forsaken place, it isn't really. God has taken care of me in a wonderful way—if you knew."

"Well, that may be so," said the young man, "but I guess He's sent me to do the job this time, and I intend to do it. You can take me for a raven or an angel whichever you like, but I'm going to stick by till I see you in a safe place. You look too much like a stray angel yourself to be lying around loose on the desert. Now, shall we go?"

"But—where are you going?" asked Fraley wide eyed again, and troubled.

"Why, we are going to find that schoolhouse. I'm going straight back to the crossroads and take the other road. If it isn't this one then it has to be the other one. I was more than half sure it was when I took this one, but I wanted to see where this led. I've never been out to this part of the country before. Come, lady, let's mount. You ride in the saddle and I'll sit behind. The horse looks long enough to hold half a dozen."

"Oh, I can easily walk beside you," said the girl shyly.

"Walk, nothing! What do you think I am, Ladybird, a sheik of the desert? No, you get on. We'll manage fine. I went to a military school once for a year and the horses was the best thing I did there. Now, are we all set? Well, how about continuing that serial story? I want to hear about those angelic sandwiches. What was it, bread and meat in the morning?"

"Oh, the angel baked a little cake. It was another time you know, under the juniper tree, after the big testing on Mount Carmel!"

"The testing? What was that?"

Fraley began to tell the story, and as she told it the young man marvelled at her simple, pure language. How was it that a girl in these wilds, dressed as she was, could yet speak English as if she had been well educated? She must have been away to school somewhere. And yet, there was a lack of sophistication that made that seem impossible.

But there was something about that simply-told story that was gripping. He stopped his wondering about the speaker and listened to the tale.

Where did she get the language in which she spoke? For Fraley as usual was using the words of the Book, the matchless words that cannot be improved. Occasionally she condensed in a few words of her own, but for the most part she clung pretty closely to the text.

The sunset lay upon the world as she reached the ending of her story.

"I say, where did you get that tale?" asked the young man as the sweet earnest voice ceased speaking. "It's rare, and I never heard it before."

"Why," said Fraley, "it's just in the Bible. How could you miss it?"

"Well," said the young man studying her curiously, "you see I've been rather busy with a lot of other things, and well—I stopped before I got to that, I guess. But I can see now my education has been badly neglected. That's a great tale. And you say it's in the Bible? Do you know about what page? Perhaps you could help me find it. It might be just the thing I need to-night."

"To-night?" said Fraley, puzzled. "Why, yes, of course I can find it. It's in the first book of Kings, about the middle somewhere. But you don't find things in the Bible by pages. You find them by books and chapters, you know."

"Oh yes, of course, that was what I meant of course. I wonder if they will have a Bible at the schoolhouse. One would think they ought to, but you can't always tell. You see I haven't brought one with me. I came away in a hurry."

"Why, I have my Bible with me," said Fraley, half reluctant to have a stranger handle it. "You can read out of mine."

"The dickens, you have?" said the young man, astonishment in his voice. "Well, now that's rare. You see I have to hold a service to-night in that schoolhouse and I was just figuring what to do about it. It isn't really my job, but as I told you I couldn't refuse to help a fellow out when he was in such straits, and he swore he wouldn't go to the hospital unless I'd promise faithfully to get someone here in time for this service to-night, and failing in finding any of the people he suggested I had to come myself."

"Are you a minister?" There was a ring of interest in the girl's voice that almost amounted to awe as she asked the question. "Then you *are* an angel! God's ministers are called angels several times in the Bible."

The young man gave her a startled look, and then suddenly, he discovered that he was passing the cross-roads, and drew the rein sharply to the left, starting down a better worn trail than the one they had been traveling.

"This is the way, I'm positive," said he, taking a card out of his pocket and consulting a diagram traced on it with pencil. "Yes, this is where I should have turned before. But in that case I shouldn't have seen you and that would have been bad, wouldn't it? I couldn't have been even a raven then. The schoolhouse ought to be about two miles from here, and then we'll have plenty of time to look up that story in your Bible. Now, what was that question you asked?"

10

"YOU are a minister!" declared Fraley joyously. "To think that I should have found you out here in the wilderness. You see I never saw one before and so I did not know you. I thought a minister would look older."

"They do come young, sometimes," affirmed the young man, eyeing her curiously. "But where have you lived, angel lady, that you never saw one before. I fear you're kidding me."

"What is kidding?" she turned her large serious eyes on him, and he found it rather difficult to explain.

"I mean you are joking with me, birdlady. You surely could not have lived your years to this time without having seen many a preacher?"

"No, I haven't really," she said earnestly. "I lived on a mountain and we never saw anybody except men who came now and then. They—were not the kind—of men, ministers would come to see!"

"You don't say!" said the young man thoughtfully, and watched the pure outline of the girl's profile as she sat before him, her head slightly turned towards him, the warm tints of the setting sun bringing out the delicacy of the features, the soft modeling of the sun-browned flesh.

"I am so glad I know you are a minister. Now I do not need to be afraid of you any more. My mother has told me what wonderful men ministers are!"

Ah! There had been that kind of a mother! That explained some things.

"But you see, I'm not!" said the young man after a thoughtful pause. "I'm all kinds of sorry to disappoint you, but you see I'm only a raven after all."

"Why—but—you said you were going to hold a service?" she questioned with a look as if she had leaned upon something that looked strong and found it failed her.

"That's what I'm undertaking to do. I don't know how well I'll make out, but I'm making the best kind of a stab at it that I know how. You see it was this way. This fellow that was coming out here is a minister all right I guess. I don't really know much about him. He was a poor gink that had studied himself pretty near into the grave and hadn't any strength left. He got up from a sick bed to go to his train so he would get here in plenty of time to get settled and begin on this service to-night. He's a stranger to me. I only saw him about half an hour before I had to leave. You see he was taken awfully sick in the street, and was almost knocked down. In fact he fell as he was crossing the street toward the station, and we picked him up unconscious. I happened to be driving my car that way and was the first one to pick him up, and of course I landed him at the hospital and thought that would be the end of it, but on the way there the poor boob came to, and insisted that I take him to the train instead of the hospital, and he wouldn't take no for an answer till I promised I'd see somebody took his place out here. Of course there was nothing to do but promise, but when I got him to the hospital and the doctor got on the job he found there had to be an operation, and the poor guy was so upset that I just stuck around a few minutes. He seemed to cling to me like a drowning passenger to a lifeboat, and boy! I couldn't shake him. He said he had three friends, any one of which could take this job and I promised to see that one of them went by the next train, and stuck on the job till he got there. So he went happy to the operating room and I went to hunt my man and get him shipped out here."

Fraley's vivid little face was turned to listen and he paused to wonder again at the delicacy and refinement of it. It was like finding a rare exotic in a wilderness.

"Well?" she said breathlessly.

"Well, would you believe it, I couldn't get one of these guys to come. The first one had got married and gone on his wedding trip, the second one was off in Maine being headmaster of a boys' camp, an all summer job; and the third had gone down to Jersey to take charge of a church. There I was, and by the time I got the last man chased to his hiding place it was just about time to leave. There wasn't a soul I knew would come out here even for a week till I got time to hunt somebody else. I called up several men I knew that do this sort of thing but they were all busy for the summer. I tried to sleep over it but I couldn't get asleep so I got up and took the midnight train. I couldn't get away from that guy's face when he made me promise to come, and here I am. I had to keep my promise, didn't I?"

"Of course," said Fraley. "But—how are you going to do it? Doesn't a man—have to know how? And doesn't he have to be set apart, or—or—blest or something the way they did with the Levites before they could minister before the Lord? You—might make some—mistake!"

"Blest if I know. I'm doing my best, aren't I? Angels could do no more," the glib tongue replied.

The girl looked serious and troubled.

"I—should think you'd—be—afraid. You know God sent down fire from heaven on Nadab and Abihu for doing something like that."

"The dickens He did? What did they do?"

"They offered strange fire. I don't know just what that means, but it was something they hadn't been told to do. Something they were not supposed to do."

"How did you know all that?" he asked wonderingly.

"Why, it's all in the Bible," she said simply as if that settled it.

"Say," said he wonderingly. "You know a lot, don't you? I wish I knew some of those things. I never realized there were things like that in a Bible!"

"Why it's easy. You could begin now. You learn a few verses every day," she said, as if that were the most natural thing in the world.

"You don't say!" he responded studying her earnest young face and wondering how a soul like this had come to be on the bad old earth.

But now, with a little turn of the road around the side of a hill, they came suddenly upon the log schoolhouse.

It was still light and the young man alighted and turned to help the girl, but found she had sprung to the ground before he could get to her.

She sat down on the step and began to open her bag at once while he tethered his horse, and when he came back to her she handed out the Bible in its cotton binding.

He took it curiously and marked the worn condition of its pages. Truly this old book had seen hard usage. He gazed at it reverently. The Book of God. Some inkling of what the Book had been meant to be to the human heart was revealed to him as he looked at the worn pages and then at the face of the lovely girl who had been fed upon it.

"Well, now, where is that man Elijah?" he asked gravely. "I've been thinking, don't you think it would be all right if I just read that story to the folks? That ought to be something anybody could do, to read a story."

She pointed out the place where it began and ended, and he sat down on the step of the schoolhouse and began to read in the dying light. And when the light failed he took out a pocket flash he was carrying and turned it on the page.

Fraley dropped down in the grass and leaned against a tree watching him as he read, and wondering what her mother would think if she knew she was here alone with a strange young man.

The young man was still reading when the first member of the congregation arrived. He swung himself from his saddle, a long lank man with a discouraged droop to his shoulders, and a kindly look in his eyes. And behind him on two mules rode his bright-eyed wife and her two boys.

The man said "Howdy" and unlocked the schoolhouse door. Presently light streamed forth from the door, from a swinging kerosene lamp and from four candles in different parts of the dim interior of the building.

The young missionary with his finger between the leaves of the old Bible rose and went inside, and Fraley stole into a shadowed corner, slipping into a seat and looking about her in wonder.

So this was a schoolhouse! All these desks for the scholars, two to a desk. And that smooth dark surface running around the front and sides of the room must be a blackboard. She had heard her mother describe it all.

People began to drop into the schoolhouse now by ones and twos. The tall thin first comer rang an old cracked bell, and the echo of its reverberations seemed to come back in relays from the mountains round about. Fraley sat in her corner and listened with awe. No visitor in a great cathedral could have felt more thrill than she as she listened for the first time to the call to worship as it rang out in that primitive countryside.

Most of the people who came looked old and tired, although there were a few with little children. Perhaps it was the shadows of the weird candlelight, and the high smokey kerosene beacon overhead that made them all look so scared and sad.

Three women came in together, and a little, little boy. Two more and a man. A little girl and her father. Then some more men, three of them. You could hear the thud of their horses' feet as they arrived, or the rattling of old sun-warped wheels on the hard earth. They seemed to steal almost furtively in, and slide into their seats. Finally the place was half full. Fraley counted them as they came, until thirty-nine had arrived. She had never seen so many people together in her life. But as each man came, she shrank back farther into the shadow, and scanned him anxiously. She was always looking for Brand, or Pete, or Pierce. Yet none of them would be likely to come to a prayer meeting unless they came for some evil purpose. And, as each new man entered, she quickly glanced from him to the young man sitting by the table in front. He was her friend, he would protect her, she felt sure, in case anyone should come after her.

So, at last, she settled back into comparative comfort to enjoy what was going on. It was all wonderful to her.

There was a thing up near the table that looked like a brown box, and presently a woman that looked younger than the rest came up and opened its lid and sat down before it. There seemed to be a lot of little white and black stripes inside, and Fraley wondered what it could be. There was a pile of books on the top of one of the front desks and the old man who rang the bell took them and distributed them. Fraley accepted hers wonderingly, and puzzled over the queer lines with dots on them that went between the reading.

The young missionary was whispering now with the woman who sat before the box, and looking through one of the books, and presently he announced that they would sing number ninety-three. Everybody opened the books and fluttered the leaves through and Fraley opened hers and found there were numbers on each page. She had no trouble in finding the right one. Then a strange sound broke the stillness. The woman at the box was moving her fingers up and down the black and white stripes and making the sounds, and it was a tune— a tune Fraley's mother used to sing to her sometimes, when they were very happy together, all alone:

> "Rock of Ages, cleft for me,
> Let me hide myself in Thee."

Why, that was like the place in the rock she had hidden behind! She had not thought of it then, for her mother had not sung the song for a long time.

And this must be a hymn book she was holding. The box was some kind of musical instrument, perhaps a piano, or an organ. Her mother used to play the piano. She had told her about that, and Fraley had always had a longing to play one sometime.

She joined her flute-like voice to the tide of dragging song that was sweeping round the little log schoolhouse, and lo, the hymn rose and soared as if a million songbirds had suddenly joined the company. Tired old voices, rose to the key, and felt thrilled with the music, because this sweet, new voice had broken into their worship. The young man at the desk heard, and looked up in pleased surprise, presently adding a fine baritone, and the little schoolhouse rang with the old, old song. Flickering candles, smoking lamp, breath of the pines drifting in, weird shadows in dusty corners, sad, tired, sinsick souls, one sorrowful lonely child of God, and one astonished flabbergasted man of the world, trying to do something he did not in the least understand!

When they had sung three songs the young man stood up. He looked around on the people, and the light from the candle that stood on the table before him flickered over his face and made him look like a nice, shy, little boy standing there facing into the shadowy schoolroom.

"Friends," he said looking about on them with his engaging smile, "I'm not the minister you expected here to-night. He's very sick in the hospital, back east, having an operation for appendicitis. I'm just the man that picked him up on the street and carried him to the hospital, and I promised him I'd see that somebody came out here to take his place. He wouldn't go under the operation till I'd promised. He said he had given his word that he would be here without fail. I tried to get somebody else to come that knew how, but I couldn't, so here I am. But it's a new job for me, and you'll have to excuse me if I don't do it very well. Perhaps you'll all help me."

Then he opened Fraley's cotton-covered Bible and began to read at the beginning of the story of Elijah.

The room was very still as he finished with the touch of the angel's hand on Elijah's shoulder, bidding him rise and eat and go forward.

The young man closed the Bible and looked at his

strange audience half bewildered for a moment, then he said, as if it came right out of his heart:

"My friends, I guess there is something in this story that will do us all good, to-night. I know it has made me think a lot. Suppose we each one think about it. Now I wonder if anybody else has anything to say?"

Back in the corner by the door the tall thin man arose and began to pray, and then another and another of the old men who looked like gnarled sticks but had kindly eyes, followed him, and a very old man leaning on a stick testified that he had served the Lord seventy years and found joy in doing it, and then a little tired looking woman asked for a hymn, and so the meeting unrolled itself till the young leader sat in amazement and watched.

The climax came when one man prayed "for our young brother who has brought us the word of God to-night" and Fraley thought she saw her missionary man brush away a tear as he rose when that prayer was over.

"Well, friends, I guess God heard all those prayers," he said. "I sure feel I've got something out of it."

They lingered after the closing hymn to shake hands with the new leader, and with the little stranger back by the door, and their kindly welcome seemed lovely to the girl.

She looked back wistfully at the long, low, shadowy room as she stepped out. It would always be a sweet memory to her, the hour spent there in the candleglow.

Out in the starlight the sky seemed to stoop lower, as if God were very near.

The tall man padlocked the schoolhouse door, and one by one the worshippers mounted their horses, or climbed into their shackly conveyances, and disappeared into the darkness, and Fraley was left standing on the steps while the young man went for the horse.

When they were mounted again and on their way he said gravely.

"Well, you had the right dope, little girl. I guess that service got by, didn't it?"

"It was wonderful!" said Fraley, starry eyed.

"Oh, I don't think that," he answered seriously, "but I can see there is a lot more in it than I ever thought there was. Jove! Think of that old man, poor and lame and almost blind, saying he's happy! But now, little sister," he said, bringing his attention back to Fraley, "we've got to make some plans for you."

"Oh," said Fraley, suddenly brought back to earth, "you mustn't take any more trouble with me. I've been thinking about that. If you'll let me down at your ranch house and just tell me the way the road goes I'll keep right on to-night. I feel real rested now and I mustn't waste any more time."

"Look here, little tree-lady!" said the young man, pulling the horse up short and leaning around where he could look at her. "I thought we settled that thing long ago. You are not going to be left to wander the darkness alone! Understand that? I was made a man so I could protect woman and I'm going to do it! And from all they told me at the ranch to-day I know this region around here is no fit place for you, even in the daytime, let alone night. So that's that! Do you understand?"

"But—" said Fraley, a worried pucker between her brows.

"No buts, please. I've got a plan. Listen to me. First, tell me a thing or two. Why are you traveling alone like this? You know you haven't explained yourself at all. Beyond the fact that you're a sort of a lady-tramp, bound ultimately for New York, I know nothing at all about you. Don't you think I have a right to an explanation? Can't you trust me?"

II

"WHAT do you want to know?" asked Fraley almost sadly, suddenly reminded of her sorrowful past.

"Where did you come from, where are your people, and where are you going?" asked the young man. "You may trust me absolutely. If there is something you want kept secret I'll be as mum as an oyster, if you know what that is."

"I've never had one," said Fraley smiling, "but my mother had."

"Well, an oyster never tells anything," said the young man solemnly, and Fraley suddenly laughed.

"I'm not afraid of you," she said, "but it's not a happy story. I lived in a cabin on a mountain, and I've hardly ever been away from there. A little while ago my father was killed, and the men that were with my father raising cattle were not good men. My mother was sick, and before she died she told me to get away as quick as I could. She had a brother in New York, and I am going to find him."

"But why did you start out to walk? Do you know how far it is to New York?"

"I know it seems very far," she said with a sigh, "but if I keep on I'll get there some day I guess."

"You poor little ladybird," said the young man with his voice full of tenderness. "But tell me, why did you not take the train? If you didn't have money, surely some of your friends would have loaned you some—"

"We hadn't any friends," said Fraley gravely.

"No friends? Well—but—why, surely your father's friends—the men you spoke of—even if you didn't like them they aren't inhuman are they?"

"I think perhaps they are," said the girl seriously. "They wouldn't have let me go if they had known. They wanted me to stay and cook for them. They—" the girl's voice shook and her slender shoulders quivered at the memory, "they came home drunk—and I heard them talking— They were *terrible!* I was afraid, and I got out of the window and ran away. I meant to get gone before they came back, but I couldn't bear to leave my mother lying there all alone, dead. She told me to go without waiting, but they came—sooner than I thought—"

"You poor kiddie!" said the young man, his own voice full of feeling. He felt a great longing to comfort her somehow, yet he laid no finger upon her. She was a little, white soul—like an angel.

"You poor, brave little kid! Didn't they find out you had gone?"

"Yes, pretty soon they broke down the door and got in and found me gone. I could hear them break it as I ran. They came after me, and they shot Larcha—!"

"Who is Larcha?"

"My dear dog. He was going with me, and he rushed at them to keep them from finding me. He threw them off the trail—"

"But where were you?"

"Up in my big pine tree—"

"Up a tree! Oh, so that wasn't the first time you shinned up a tree when you were frightened. Do you always go up a tree when you see a man coming?"

"There was nowhere else to go."

"You poor dear little kid!"

Little by little he drew from her the whole tale of her journey thus far.

"I don't wonder you were afraid of me!" he said when she had finished the tale. "You are a wonderful brave little kid. And now, it seems to me you have done this bravery act to a finish and it's high time someone took care of you. How would you like to stay at the ranch house where I board for a little while till you can write to these friends of yours to come after you?"

"Oh, no!" said Fraley. "I must get away. You don't know what those men are. They would find out. They may know even now about where I am, and they would find a way to get a hold of me."

"Let them come on," said the young man gaily, "I'd just like to wring their necks for them."

"Oh, no!" said Fraley with fright in her voice. "No, you must never go near them. Never! They would kill you as soon as they would kill a dog. They don't care for anything. They would get behind you in the dark, and nobody would ever know where you were. My father—"

"You think they killed your father?" he asked looking at her keenly.

"I'm not sure," she said, "I think my mother thought so! Oh, promise me you won't ever have anything to do with them. Please, please let me get down now and go away somewhere in the dark! They must not ever know that you were kind to me, or your life won't be safe."

"Now look here, Ladybird, calm yourself. If you are so determined to go away I'll see you safe to somewhere in the morning, and I'll make good and sure that it is safe too, but to-night you ride with me to the ranch, and sleep in a real bed. You needn't worry about me. I can kid the eyeteeth out of any man that ever walked the earth or shot a gun if I try. In fact I've shot guns too, over in France, and I know how. I'm not afraid, and I won't run any risks. You needn't worry about that."

"You promise that?"

"I sure do. And now listen, I've been thinking. I have a whole perfectly good return trip ticket to New York. I bought it thinking I was going right back. I meant to telegraph and get somebody else to take this job out here before another service came due. But after to-night I've a notion to stick it out, at least till somebody else turns up that can do it better than I. So there's my ticket going to waste. It's only good for five days, and if you begin to use it to-morrow morning it will take you on the train to New York. How about it? Will that help any?"

"Oh, that would be wonderful!" said Fraley hesitating. "But would you let me pay you for it sometime when I have earned some money?"

"Why if that's necessary to your peace of mind, sister, perhaps I would, but it isn't in the least necessary. You see the ticket is no good to me if I stay here awhile, and you might as well use it."

By the time he had reached the ranch house he had convinced her that the ticket really needed to be used, and she was doing him service to ride on it, and she drew a long breath of relief.

"All right, Ladybird, that's settled. And now, I want you to do something for me. When you get to New York, just as soon as it is at all convenient for you, I want you to go to a bookstore and buy me a Bible. I'll give you some money to pay for it, and I want a very nice Bible, with a soft leather cover, the kind a minister ought to have. Will you remember? You see I haven't any friends back home just now that I care to have pick me out a Bible, they wouldn't understand. It needs somebody who loves it to pick it out, I imagine. Can you do that?"

"Oh, I shall be glad to do it," said Fraley, her eyes shining at the prospect. "That will be two Bibles I shall have to buy."

"Two Bibles? How is that?"

And then she told him of the woman who had befriended her on the drive and kept her overnight, and of the evening when she had read her Bible to them. The young man listened.

"So you too have been called to be a minister by the wayside," he said thoughtfully. "Well, I want you to let me pay for that Bible too. I would like a share in that if you'll let me. I'll give you the money in the morning, and I want you to use whatever is left over for something that you want for yourself, something to remember me by. Will you?"

Fraley solemnly promised, and soon after that they came within sight of the ranch house, its windows glowing red with friendly light.

Fraley shrank back as the door was opened. Somehow she dreaded this new contact.

The room was more formal than the one at the other log house, and the hostess a different kind of woman entirely. She was gracious and lovely, an entirely new type to the girl. Her hair was waved, and she wore dainty pretty garments. She had a lovely smile, and was graciousness itself when the young man introduced her as a young sister who had been at meeting and was on her way to the railroad station.

"I have promised to see her safely to her train," he said, quite as if that were one of the duties of a missionary preacher, "and I told her I thought you would be good enough to put her up for the night so that she might catch the morning train, as she has come a long distance, Mrs. Hartwick."

The lady swept Fraley a lovely smile, just taking her for granted as one of the natives, and that was all.

"Oh, surely, Mr. Seagrave. We've plenty of room, and are quite used to having people stop on their way. We always keep open house. I'm glad you brought her. Molly," motioning to a colored woman, "show this girl to the end bedroom. See if she would like something to eat before she retires. Good night, my dear. I hope you will rest well."

Another smile and Fraley found herself dismissed.

She could not understand why she felt so humiliated as she walked across the lovely room full of easy chairs, deep soft rugs, wonderful pictures and bright lamps. The lady had been pleasant. She had said nice things. But she had shoved her out. She had made her feel like a stranger and an interloper.

She followed the colored woman out through a little hall, but as she went through the door she looked back and caught one look from the young man who had brought her, and something in his eyes gave her comfort, it was a light and interest, and a dazzling smile, and she knew she was not alone.

The lady was watching her with amused eyes. It was good that Fraley could not hear what she said as the door closed behind her.

"It is well that girl is not staying around here, she is much too good looking to be riding around with our young minister!" she said, and laughed a little warning laugh that had a snarl at the end of it.

Seagrave turned inquiring eyes on his hostess.

"Good looking?" he said, "and what has that to do

with it?" The lady laughed, but the young man began to talk of something else and did not return to the topic. It was the next morning that the hostess got in her final sting for Fraley.

They were sitting at the breakfast table, which was abundantly laden with good things, but the girl was too overawed to eat more than a bite or two. She felt uncomfortable and only longed to get away. The woman and her husband were kind, and passed her everything, but otherwise ignored her, and again she felt that she was where she was not wanted, and her sensitive nature was crushed by the burden of it.

"Mr. Seagrave," said the hostess, "We've made other plans for you this morning. We're going to take you off on a riding party to another ranch about fifty miles away, and we're starting right after breakfast. We've arranged to send this little charge of yours down to her train with Molly and Jim, and they will reach there in plenty of time to put her in the car and see to everything for her."

A quick fright came into Fraley's eyes, and suddenly she spoke, surprising them all at her gentle accent and refined tone:

"Thank you," she said politely, "You need not trouble to do that. I am quite used to walking, and would much rather go by myself. I don't want to be a burden on anybody. You have been very kind to take me in overnight, and I thank you, but that is all I shall need, and if you will excuse me I would like to start at once."

She rose from the table with a grace and ease made possible by her eagerness for flight, and they all looked up amazed at her poise. The lady was almost embarrassed.

"Oh, no, my dear. You misunderstood me. It is no trouble whatever to send you down to the train. We always arrange to do that for our guests. You see the man usually drives over every day or two anyway on errands, and it will be no trouble whatever. We were glad to have you with us."

But the young man interrupted her, rising with his watch in his hand.

"I beg your pardon, Mrs. Hartwick. I'm sorry to spoil your plans but I've given my word to personally see this little sister on the train and I must do it. Another time I'll be glad to ride with you if I may. And now, I wonder if you can spare another horse for my friend to ride. Or, perhaps we can manage as we did last night."

"Oh, you can have the horses of course," laughed the lady to hide her chagrin, "but it seems to me you might be a little easier on your conscience. Jim and Molly would do it just as well as you."

"That may be so, but I'm going," said the young man pleasantly.

"Well, then, John, we'd better go too, and go on from the station. It will only make the ride a little farther," said the lady determinedly.

Fraley's heart sank. She felt like darting out the door and flying anywhere to get away, but Seagrave caught her eye with reassurance.

"Sorry," he said, "I'll have to spoil your plans again. I've got a lot of business to attend to down at the station. I've got to send telegrams and wait for answers, and I simply couldn't make it to-day. I'll have to hang around and wait for Long Distance connection with the hospital too. I want to ask how our friend Dudley is getting on, and if he is in shape at all, I need to find out several things before I can go on here."

"Oh, you could wait to write," pleaded the lady.

But Seagrave was firm.

"I've got to get things straightened out," he declared, and then, in the nicest and easiest way possible he made his apologies and got Fraley out of that house and onto a horse, and together they started away in the sunshine, leaving the lady looking most discontented.

"I don't think she liked you to go," said Fraley, solemnly, after they had ridden in silence about a mile.

"That doesn't spoil the sunshine a particle for me," said Seagrave, smiling. "If I were thinking of staying out here indefinitely I might even change my boarding-house, but I guess, as it is, we shall manage to rub along and be good friends. I really didn't come out here for the purpose of amusing that woman, even if she does know how to put up a good lunch. Say, little sister, just hand me over that bag and let me carry it. It looks like a heavy load for you."

"Oh, no," said Fraley, "I like it. My mother made it for me."

"In that case I suppose it isn't heavy, but you needn't be selfish about it," and he reached over and lifted the strap from her shoulder, putting it over his own.

"You are very kind," she said, "I feel sorry to take you all this way just for me. I really can do very well alone."

"Well, I've expressed my views on that subject several times before so we won't need to say any more," he said jovially. "But listen now, there are a lot of things I need to know, and some things I must tell you before we get interrupted again. No telling but those persistent people may tag us after all, and give us no chance to talk. In the first place, you haven't told me your name."

"It's Fraley MacPherson."

"Fraley MacPherson," he repeated, taking out a pencil and writing it down. "That's an extraordinary name. I like it."

"And now, where are you going? Have you got the address with you?"

"My mother said she had put it inside the cover of the

Bible. I have not looked at it yet. There hasn't been any time, and I didn't need to know till I got somewhere near, but it is in New York somewhere."

"Well, we'll stop when we get over that hill out yonder, and let you look it up. I've got to know where you are going. I want to find you when I come back."

"Oh," smiled Fraley, "that will be nice. Then I won't be so lonesome."

"Well, now, do you know what to do when you get to New York?"

"Why, just get off the train, don't I?"

"Well, yes, but you know New York is a large place, and you want to be careful. You just go up into the station, you'll see how everybody else does, and when you get upstairs where the waiting room is you go and ask for the Traveler's Aid woman. She'll be around there somewhere. You can ask any of the red-capped porters, or officials and they will show you where she is. Then you tell her where you are going and she will tell you just how to take a taxi and get there."

"What is a taxi?" asked Fraley wonderingly.

"Why it's a public conveyance that you can hire to take you anywhere in the city. But you better get the woman agent to show you where to get it or you'll be lost in two seconds."

Fraley looked frightened.

"Oh, you'll get on all right," he reassured her, "but you better just let the agent manage things for you. It's her business to help travelers that don't know the city, and show them where to stay all night when they haven't any friends. You are sure you'll be all right when you get to your family?"

"Oh, yes," said Fraley, "my mother said her brother was very nice. He was always very fond of her."

The young man looked down at the sweet eyes lifted

to his, and felt grave misgivings at sending this young innocent out alone into the world. She read the thought in his eyes.

"You needn't worry about me, really," she laughed. "I'm perfectly all safe, and you know God is in New York too. The Bible says He is."

"I believe it," he said seriously; "I didn't know it before. Say, are there any more stories as good as Elijah in that Bible of yours?"

"Oh, many, many!" she said eagerly. "There's the blind man."

"Well, you hurry and send that Bible back to me. I've got to get up something to read on Sunday, you know."

"Oh, yes, take the blind man. I love that story! It's the ninth chapter of John."

"Very well, that's the one I shall read next Sunday!"

They had come to the other side of the hill now, and under a group of trees they stopped while Fraley took out her Bible and found the address she wanted.

"What's this MacPherson one?" he asked looking over her shoulder.

"That's my father's people," she said with reserve. "I might look them up too—I'll see when I get there."

"I know some MacPhersons," he said thoughtfully, marking the initials, "but they're not likely the same people. This address is away downtown in old New York."

That meant nothing at all to Fraley. She carefully put back the bits of paper on which her mother had written the addresses, and put away the Bible in her bag. The young man noticed with wonder the tenderness with which she handled it, almost as if the bag and its contents were holy things.

"It seems as if I oughtn't to let you go this journey all

alone," said Seagrave looking troubled; "you seem so little and unprotected."

She smiled up into his face.

"You are the first person except my mother that I ever felt was all right," she said innocently.

He smiled down at her with a worshipful look in his eyes.

"You are the first girl I ever met that seemed just as God meant her to be," he said gravely, and then knew that if he sat there looking down into her eyes any longer he might be tempted to say more.

"Now," he said looking at his watch, "we'll have to be getting on. I can't have you missing that train. But I want to give you this envelope first. I've written out a lot of directions for you there about the train and what you are to do, about new York and how to get about easily. You probably won't need them when you find your friends, but I wanted to provide against your being in a muddle. It's a big town, you know, and you can't trust everybody. Remember that! Trust God all you want to but don't trust men—nor many women either."

She took the envelope and looked at it interestedly.

"And here, in this purse I've put the money for the Bible, and the ticket, and a little extra change. You'll need it for tipping the porter."

"Tipping? What's that? And what's the porter?"

"Why, the man who looks after you on the train. You'd better get reservations right away. I'll try to get near a porter or the Pullman conductor myself and arrange that for you, but in case I don't, you ask for the Pullman conductor and get a reservation yourself. You'll have no trouble. I've written down what you'll likely have to pay for it. But you can give the porter a little something for waiting on you, and then you'll need to go into the diner for your meals."

"Oh!" said Fraley round-eyed. She wasn't sure she would dare. She wasn't sure that she was going this journey on the cars. If any chance at all presented itself for her to get away so that he wouldn't know it, she might slip off into the desert or somewhere and pursue her weary way, even yet. Now that she was getting near to the station she began to be more and more frightened at the idea of traveling on the cars with a lot of strangers.

They had lingered longer than they realized, and at the last had to hurry their horses to reach the station in time.

She found herself trembling as the great iron monster drew nearer to them, and Seagrave, kind and thoughtful for her, slipped his hand within her arm.

"You mustn't forget me, little ladybird," he said wistfully. "I'm coming to hunt you up when I get back. You know you are my friend. You'll remember that, won't you?"

"Oh, I won't forget you ever," said Fraley earnestly, "and I'm so glad I have one friend. I'm very grateful to you for what you have done for me, and I'll keep remembering your beautiful meeting."

"It wasn't mine, little sister, it was yours," he said, and then as the train drew to a halt he suddenly stooped and kissed her gravely, reverently, on her forehead.

"Good-by, little sister. You've done a lot for me, I think. Here, get on here, in this car. Yes, that's right, go in that door. The porter will look after you. Here, Porter!"

She stood an instant trembling, looking after him as he spoke to the colored man with the white coat, and then the train began to move, the porter swung on, and

Seagrave walked alongside, tipping his hat to her, and waving his hand. She watched him through sudden blinding tears, and tried to smile, watched him till the train whirled out of his sight, and then she turned to go inside.

12

IT seemed a strange unfriendly place that she had entered, somewhat like the entrance to a cave, solid walls, and a passage only wide enough for one to walk. The motion of the train, too, frightened her. She could climb trees, and walk out on a slender limb, she could wade rivers, she could brave the dangers of the night and the menace of wild cattle, but the motion of that train simply paralyzed her. It seemed that the earth beneath her was rocking and about to fall.

She put out both hands and steadied herself, and so, after a minute, began slowly to go onward again, inching along, and sliding her hands on the wall.

The porter with whom Seagrave had talked had vanished into the car behind her, and there seemed no one left in the wide world again. Why had she trusted herself to this strange way of traveling? Would she not see anybody at all all the way, and to where did this queer narrow room lead?

She came at length to the main part of the car, and saw high backed seats with green cushions, and people sitting in them, some facing each other. Some men were playing cards in one section, and their intent looks as they threw down their cards on the little table between them reminded her of Brand and Pierce when they were playing that way. She shrank back, and turned to her right to return to the door again. It was hot in this place, and she felt as if she could not breathe. But suddenly a little doorway hung with a dark green curtain presented itself. The curtain was shoved back, and there was a small room, with long green seats. By the window sat a lady who looked up curiously at her.

Fraley gave her a shy questioning smile, and the lady smiled back pleasantly enough. She was a curiously dressed lady, with trim, close-fitting, very short tresses, and a little tight dark hat. She was slim as a girl, though you could see by her face that she wasn't young. She wore a necklace made of beads that looked like drops of dew when the sun rises, and she had more colored stones in rings on her hands.

"Is this a place where I could sit?" she asked, shyly stepping within the door.

"Why, I guess so," said the lady with a swift startled glance at the slender bare feet. "You have probably got in the wrong car, but you can stay there till the conductor comes and he will tell you where to go."

Fraley sat down thankfully on the edge of the long seat.

"I have a ticket," she said as if presenting her credentials, "and some money," she added earnestly. "I can pay for my seat."

"Well, I'm sure the conductor will fix you up all right," said the lady kindly, wondering at the pure speech and refined accent of this barefoot child, and fascinated by her loveliness.

Fraley's eyes wandered to the window, startled.

"How fast we go!" she exclaimed. "I've never been on a train before!"

"You haven't?" exclaimed the lady. "That's strange. Where are you going?"

"I'm going to New York," said the girl, still watching the landscape. "Why, see! It's only the near-by things that are going fast. The ones that are far off, the mountains hardly seem to move at all. There! There they go! The mountains are going now. They're just shadows of themselves. Oh, I didn't think we could get away from the mountains so fast!"

The lady smiled and watched her amusedly. Presently she spoke again.

"Haven't you some shoes and stockings in that bag?" she asked practically. "I think you'd better put them on if you have. You know it isn't the custom to ride in the train barefoot. The conductor might not like it."

Fraley's eyes came to the lady's face now with quick alarm, and a flood of lovely color went over her face.

"Oh!" she said, and glanced down at her small white feet.

"They—are—perfectly clean. I washed them just before I started and we rode all the way."

"Yes, I see that," said the lady trying to make her voice sound less amused and more kindly, "but it just isn't the custom, you know. You might feel awkward, and I'm sure the conductor would feel he ought to speak to you about it. That's why I mentioned it."

Fraley's eyes went to the lady's exquisite little feet clad in sheerest gun metal silk stockings, and patent leather slippers with sparkling buckles. Then she tucked her own feet back as far as they would go curling one around the other unobtrusively.

"I didn't know," she said sadly, "or I wouldn't have come this way. I'd better get off the next time the train stops. Perhaps the conductor won't get around before that to see me. I can walk of course, only it will take longer."

"Walk!" said the lady laughing. "Why you would be an old woman before you got there."

"Well," said Fraley, "I suppose it wouldn't matter then."

"How absurd!" said the startled lady laughing. "Why don't you put on your shoes and stockings?"

"But I haven't any," said the girl, and there were almost tears in her eyes. "I had a pair once, but the stockings wore out, and then the shoes got too little and hurt me. They were red shoes and they had little tassels at the top. It was a long time ago."

The lady stared. Where had this amazing child lived without shoes and grown into lovely womanhood? Did she belong to some strange sect who didn't believe in footgear, or what?

"But why haven't you had shoes and stockings?" asked the lady curiously.

The color waved over the sweet face again. She lifted shamed eyes.

"Because we hadn't money to buy them. And anyhow they weren't necessary, like things to eat."

"Oh," said the lady with a little gasp as if she were in pain. As if anybody could be so poor as that!

She stared at the girl a moment and then she suddenly arose and sharply shut the little door between the drawing-room and the outer car.

"We've got to do something about this before the conductor comes," she said kindly. "I've got plenty of stockings here in my bag, and you go into the little dressing room here and put on a pair. I think maybe I have a pair of shoes that will fit you, too, nice low-heeled sports ones; we'll see. It simply won't do for the conductor to see you that way. He'll never let you stay in his car looking like that."

The lady swung open another little door and switched on a mysterious flood of light, and lo, there was a tiny washroom with towels and a looking-glass and sweet scented soap. Fraley's mother had told her about such an arrangement but she never expected to see one.

"Now," said the lady in a business-like tone, "we've got to work fast. You go in there and take off that coat, and that thing off your head, and I'll bring you some stockings. Have you any garters? No, of course you wouldn't have."

The lady vanished and Fraley stared at herself in the mirror critically, dimly realizing for the first time what part clothes play in the scheme of living.

The lady reappeared bearing biscuit-colored silk stockings and a pair of low-cut tan golf shoes with rubber soles.

"I should think you might get these on," she said as she put the shoes on the floor. "Now, let's see how the stockings fit. Your foot must be about the size of mine."

Fraley was not expert at putting on stockings, and the lady had to take a hand, and turn the toe inside, helping to sheathe the wild little foot in silk for the first time in its life.

"My! Aren't they pretty!" said Fraley surveying them in wonder after her two feet were arranged in the stockings.

Then she bent to the task of getting on the shoes, and found, to the lady's satisfaction, that they went on easily. They were even a little large, which was well for a first shoeing.

Fraley stood up and looked down at her feet. She took a trial step, and looked up.

"You couldn't walk up a mountain in these," she said with a comical helpless little pucker in her brow.

"Well, I think I'd make a better showing in those than without them," laughed the lady. "However, I'm glad they fit."

"How much—are these?" Fraley asked shyly, hesitating between the words, and not quite sure whether this was the correct thing to say or not.

"How much?" asked the amazed lady. "Why nothing, child. You're welcome to them. They're just old ones. I seldom wear golf shoes a second year, the style changes so often."

"The what changes?"

"The style. The way they're cut—the fashion, you know."

"Oh," said Fraley, "that's like 'The fashion of this world passeth away,' isn't it? I never knew that meant shoes too."

"You odd child! What extremely unique remarks you make! Really I can't quite classify you. But listen, is that your best dress?"

"No," said the girl looking down at herself doubtfully. "Don't you think this is clean enough? I washed it out in the brook not long ago. But I've got another one. It was made out of one my mother had when she was married. I am going to be very careful of it because it's the last thing she made for me before she died and I want to keep it always, but if you say I ought to put it on now, I will. I want to look right. Mother would have wanted me to look all right."

"Let me see your other dress!" ordered the lady.

Fraley went down to the bottom of her bag, under the Bible and the tin cup and the little packages, and fished out the old black satin frock, which was made something after the pattern of a flour bag.

The lady shook it out and surveyed it critically.

"It's rather mussed," she said dubiously, searching around for a good excuse, because she could see the girl's pride in her best dress, "and I think perhaps on the whole you'd better put it way if you want it for a keepsake. Traveling is rather hard on clothes, you know. Just let me see if I haven't something you could wear. You're about my size and I have several dresses I am tired of. I would just give them to my maid when I got home anyway. If you don't mind we'll put one on you and freshen you up."

"You're very kind," said Fraley with quaint courtesy, "But I don't think my mother would think it was right for me to take so much. Besides, your maid will be disappointed."

"Your mother would want you to look right," said the lady firmly, "and since she is not here why you'll have to let me decide that in her place. As for my maid she is just rolling in things I've given her, and won't know whether she gets one more or not. Wait, I think I have a little blue frock that will be the very thing."

The lady opened her suitcase again and produced an armful of bright silky things.

"These things go with it," she stated briefly as she handed out some flimsy little silk underwear of pale pink trimmed with frills of fine lace and set with a rosebud here and there. The lady was having the best time she had had since her childhood's last doll, dressing up this lovely child just to please herself and see how she would look in the right clothes.

Fraley looked at the pink things puzzled.

"What are these?" she said.

"They're undergarments that go with that dress to make it set right."

"But I have some nice clean underthings on," said Fraley proudly. "My mother made them."

"Well, take them off and put them away in your bag with your dress, and put these on. The dress won't hang right without the things that were made for it," said the lady as if that settled the matter.

Fraley accepted them because that seemed the thing to do.

"This one goes on first," said the lady, pointing to a much befrilled article, "and then this, and this."

The lady went out and Fraley took off her own things and slowly put on the strange slippery ones, and looked down at herself in wonder.

"I suppose," she said as the lady came back with a shimmery dark blue dress over her arm, "I suppose the fashion of my underthings is passed away, isn't it? And mother didn't know because we've been out there on the mountain so long."

"I guess that's it," said the lady with a mental note of the child's discernment. "Now, slip this over your head, and put your arms in here—"

The dark blue dress settled down over the girl's slimness and gave her distinction at once as all such little creations of a great foreign designer usually do. Fraley stared down at herself in delight, fingering the bright buckle with which the dress was fastened.

"Now, we've got to do something with that hair," said the lady speculatively. "Suppose you sit down on that stool and let me try something. You want to look like other girls of your age before we go out to the diner, you know. Your mother would want that. She wouldn't want you to look queer."

"Did I look queer?" asked Fraley studying this new self in the mirror over the wash-bowl.

"Well, just a little different, you know," said the lady with a smile. "Now, do you mind if I arrange your hair?"

"Oh, no," said the girl with a sigh of pleasure, "I wouldn't know how, I'm sure. You're very kind." Then after a minute, she added, "My hair is clean. I washed it in the brook night before last."

"You washed it in the brook!" exclaimed the lady in horror. "How on earth did you manage that? Were you in swimming?"

"Yes—" said Fraley hesitating a little to make sure this was quite true, "at least, I couldn't swim much, it wasn't deep enough."

"Well, it's lovely," said the lady in admiration. "Now, let's try a new way."

Fraley watched in the glass while the older woman combed her soft gold hair, parting it from forehead to the nape of the neck, and gathering each mass of golden curls into a softly coiled wheel over her ears.

"There!" she said standing off to survey the finished effect. "I think that's a good style for you. Now, wait till I get the hat that goes with that dress."

She came back with a little blue hat of soft straw with a bright pin gleaming at one side. She had also brought a string of curiously carved beads, and a little wrist watch which she said Fraley would need.

The girl stood up and looked down at herself, and then looked in the glass and turned back to the lady.

"It's like being clothed with Christ's righteousness, isn't it?" she said turning luminous eyes to her benefactor. "I wouldn't know myself at all."

"Mercy, child, what uncanny things you do say!" said the startled lady. "I think you look very well myself. You'd get by anywhere now."

"Yes," said Fraley shining-faced, "I think it will be a

good deal like this when I get up to heaven and see myself all dressed in the white linen!"

The lady looked at her aghast and said quickly:

"I don't know in the least what you mean, but don't try to tell me now, for it's time for the conductor to be coming around. What have you done with your ticket? You said you had a ticket, didn't you?"

"Yes," said the girl, "it's here in this envelope," and she drew it forth from the bag where she had slipped it when she came in to put on her stockings.

"Oh, well, you'll have to have a hand bag," said the lady and went out again to her suitcase, returning with a small strap bag of dark blue leather trimmed in silver.

"This will do. Now, put your ticket in there, and your money. They don't carry things around uncovered that way. And, what about that gray bag you have your things in? You want to keep all those things, do you? You wouldn't want to throw them away?"

"Oh, no indeed!" said the girl, a frightened look coming into her eyes. "My mother made the bag for me. It's been so convenient."

"Well, I was just thinking. They're not using that pattern of bag quite so much this season. Suppose I let you have this one of mine. I can easily put what things I have left in it, into my suitcase. We sent so many things home by parcel post that there really wasn't enough left to fill all the bags, but I didn't just care to throw it away."

So the old gray woolen bag found sanctuary in the extremely correct patent-leather overnight bag that the lady emptied for the purpose. Fraley went out in her new attire and sat down opposite the little door which was now opened for the coming of the official, and wondered at herself.

Then she began to wonder what her mother would have said to all this lovely array, and what her enemies would think if they could see her now. She had a passing wish that Caroline might have seen these clothes, and the lady who kept looking at her feet when she tried to keep the young missionary from going to the station with her.

And then her breath came a little faster, and her cheek flushed softly pink, at thought of that same young man, and the words he had said and the farewell he had given her. She could feel the touch of his lips upon her brow even yet, and she told herself it was like a blessing.

The lady was watching her with satisfaction. Not in years had she been so interested in anything as in transforming this lovely creature from a wild thing to a maid of the world. And yet, she would perhaps never be just like other girls. There was a freshness and a freedom about her that she would not want to have spoiled. A little training and she would be a wonder! An idea had come to her, and she was turning it over. As she was musing and watching Fraley, the conductor arrived.

The lady leaned forward with her own ticket, and told Fraley to get out hers. The conductor eyed her sharply.

"This young lady is traveling with me," she said handing over the two tickets. "She got on at the last stop. Can you arrange to put her here with me?"

"Tell the Pullman conductor," growled the official who snipped a hole or two in Fraley's ticket and handed it back.

Fraley took the ticket and studied it in wonder, reading its inscription as if it were something really interesting.

Suddenly she looked up at the lady who was still watching her.

"You have been wonderful to me," she said with a smile. "I can never thank you enough."

The lady spoke almost crossly:

"I've done nothing but what I pleased. Don't bother to thank me. I haven't enjoyed anything so much in a long time. Come, let's go and get some luncheon!"

FRALEY was very much intrigued with the diner. It seemed to her like a playhouse with all those little tables. With the pleasure of a child she sat down in the chair opposite to the lady.

The menu card interested her, too, and she studied it with fascination, but she knew very few of the names that were on its list.

"Would you like me to order?" the lady asked, watching her perplexity.

"Please," said Fraley. "Get me something that doesn't cost much. Just some bread and milk perhaps if that is cheap, or don't they have a cow on a train?"

The lady laughed.

"No cow, but plenty of milk! Don't you want tea or coffee?"

"No," said the girl decidedly, "Mother thought it wasn't good for me."

When the order was brought the girl opened her eyes in astonishment.

"Won't this cost a lot?" she asked with a troubled look.

"You're not to bother about the cost," smiled the lady. "You are my guest on this trip. You'll have use enough for your money when you get to New York."

"But that isn't right!"

"Yes, it's right if I want to. Now, eat your soup."

With a healthy young appetite she did as she was bid, and surprised her patroness with the easy way in which she handled her spoon and knife and fork, and the beautiful way she ate. Where did she learn it all? There was a mystery about this.

Nothing that went on escaped the bright eyes. After the lady paid the bill she laid some money beside the plate.

"What is that for?" the girl asked.

"A tip for the waiter."

"I thought so," said Fraley with satisfaction. "A friend told me about that. I ought to tip the porter too, he said."

"You needn't bother; I've done that. Who is this friend? Have you know him a long time?"

"His name is Seagrave. He is a good man. He had a service last night in a schoolhouse. I was there. I've only know him yesterday and to-day, but he was very kind. He brought me to the station and told me some of the things I would need to know."

"Is he young or old?"

"Why—he's young—with nice eyes, and a smile."

"H'm!" said the lady, "some theological student out earning his next winter's tuition, I suppose. What did he tell you?"

"Oh, how to get off the train, and up into the Pennsylvania station," recited the careful student. "He told me to go to the Traveler's Aid to find out about taking a taxi, and where to look for my friends, and where to find a place to board in case they were not at home."

"So you have friends?"

It almost sounded as if the lady were not glad.

"Yes. My mother's brother lives in New York. And my father's people live there too," she added the last as an afterthought.

"It's time you told me your name. I am Mrs. Wentworth, but you may call me Violet if you like. A great many of my friends call me that."

"Oh, what a lovely name. It's like your eyes. I'd like to pick you some of the flowers. They grow all over my mountain where I came from."

The lady smiled. This was the kind of thing she liked.

"But my name is just Fraley MacPherson," said the girl. "My mother was Alison Fraley and I have her last name, because she didn't want to forget it."

"That's strange," said the lady; "I know an Alison Fraley. She lives on Riverside Drive very near my home. But of course it can't be a relative of yours. I know some MacPhersons too, but they are very rich people. Where are your people living?"

Fraley told the address as she remembered it from having read it to Seagrave that morning.

"Yes, that's way downtown. Strange it happens to be the same initials. The one I know is Robert Fraley, too. He is a multimillionaire."

"What is that?" asked Fraley mildly interested.

"A man who is very rich indeed, richer than almost anybody else except just a few others like himself."

"That wouldn't be right, would it?" asked the girl with a worried frown. "A man ought not to keep more than his share, ought he?"

"Tell that to the millionaires and see what they'd say," laughed the lady. "I think you're rare. Tell me, how did you get your education if you've lived away off on the mountain? Was there a school anywhere near you?"

"Oh, we had a Book," said Fraley and opened her eyes wide in a way she had when she was astonished. "My mother used to hear me say my lessons every morning. I always learned a chapter a week at least, and then we had numbers, different kinds of them, and other things."

"All out of the same book?" asked the lady more amused than ever.

"Yes."

"What was the book?"

"The Bible."

"The Bible! How could you possibly study numbers out of that?"

"Oh, easily. At first I just had the numbers of the chapters and the verses. I counted them, and added them, and subtracted them and divided them. And then I began to hunt out the numbers of things in the stories. There were seventy of the children of Israel that went down into Egypt, you know, counting Joseph and his family. And there were six hundred and three thousand, five hundred and fifty of them when they came back four hundred years later."

The woman of the world stared as if she thought the girl had gone crazy.

"There was an old rock up a little way from our back door," Fraley went on eagerly, her eyes shining with joy at the remembrance. "I used to do my sums on that with a piece of limestone that made nice white marks on it. When I got the answers mother would come out and look at them to see if they were right."

"What did you do when the rock was full?" asked the lady interested.

"Oh, I washed it off, or sometimes the rain would

wash it off for me. I used to play games with the stories in the Old Testament sometimes. I would gather pebbles of different sizes for the people. There was a smooth white stone I always called David and a big rough red one with mica in it that was Goliath, and I used to set the armies out on the cabin floor, and then bring Goliath down to challenge them and little David would come and say he would fight the giant. I had a stone for the king too."

"Your mother must have been a very original woman!" said the lady listening interestedly. "I would like to have known her. The perfect idea of educating a child out of one book and doing all that!"

"Oh, but the book was the Bible, you know," explained the young student. "I used to have English work too. I used to have to write the stories off in other words, so mother could see if I understood. That was fun, putting it in another way but telling the same story."

The lady's eyes narrowed.

"You speak singularly pure English," she said. "I wonder—" but she did not finish her sentence. She was studying the girl's eager face and wondering what it would be like to have a young thing like this around her all the time.

"And what are you going to do first when you get to New York?" the lady asked at length.

"Why, first—the very first thing I'm going to hunt up a store where they sell Bibles. I have to buy two and send them back to people who are waiting for them."

"Bibles?" said the lady startled again. "Why should people be waiting for Bibles? I should think you would find a place to stay, first of all, and then hunt up your people."

"No, I must get the Bibles first," said Fraley firmly. "I promised. You see they are really needed."

"Whom are they for?"

"One is for a woman I stayed overnight with. She hadn't ever read it, and I recited some for her, and she wanted some more so much that I told her I would be sure to send her one. She wouldn't let me pay for my supper and my night's lodging, and you see I must let her know right away that I have not forgotten."

"Sort of a bread and butter Bible, then!" laughed the lady.

"A what?" asked Fraley. Sometimes this lady almost acted as if she were making a joke out of things.

"I mean you are sending it out of courtesy," she explained, her eyes sobering pleasantly.

"Not altogether," said Fraley. "There's a little boy there. He wants to read it."

"And why should you care whether he reads it or not? It seems abnormal for a child like you to be talking about reading the Bible. You are young and ought to be interested in all the gay things that are going on. You'll just love everything when you get to New York. You need to dance and flirt and have a good time generally. You've been too solemn and not had the right kind of a childhood. You are morbid. But New York will soon take it out of you, I'm afraid."

"If I thought that," said Fraley earnestly, "I'd get right off this train and go back. I would rather live out my life on a mountain than forget my Bible. It's the dearest thing in life to me, and I promised my mother I would never let go of it."

The lady shrugged her shoulders, and spoke soothingly:

"Oh, well, child, don't take me too seriously. Tell me who the other Bible is for?"

"It's for my friend, Mr. Seagrave. He had to go out there to preach without any Bible because he was called to go in a hurry in place of someone who was sick, and he gave me some money and asked me to send him back a Bible as soon as I possibly could. He needs it for Sunday. I am going to mark some of the stories in it that he is to read in his service. They are stories we talked about and he asked me to mark them for him."

"It seems to me he got rather intimate in one day," remarked the lady.

"Oh, no," said Fraley. "He was just friendly. He was what my mother used to tell me a gentleman was like. I never saw one before."

"H'm! What did you say his name was?"

"Seagrave," said Fraley, and suddenly felt a reserve coming over her speech. Was there the least bit of a sneer for her friend in this lady's eyes, and on her red lips?

"There are Seagraves in New York of course," said the lady thoughtfully, but Fraley kept her own counsel, and let her eyes wander happily out on the brightness of the landscape.

"Are your mother's people poor?" asked the lady suddenly.

The girl brought her gaze back to the lady thoughtfully.

"Why, I'm not sure," she said, "perhaps they are. I never thought. But what difference would that make?"

"You'd not want to be dependent on them if they were," suggested the lady, "perhaps they wouldn't be able to support you."

"Oh, I wouldn't want anybody to support me," said the girl happily. "I can get some work to do. I must take care of myself of course."

"But what could you do?"

"I could milk," was the eager answer. "I've done that a great deal, and I do it nicely."

The lady laughed amusedly.

"We don't keep cows in New York. The city is too crowded. So you'll have to give up the idea of being a dairymaid."

"You don't keep cows?" she asked perplexed. "How do you get along without milk?"

"Oh, we have milk. It comes on milk trains, in cans and bottles, packed in ice."

"Real milk? Where does it come from?"

"Farms and dairies."

"Then perhaps I'd have to go out to a farm or dairy and get work," sighed the child disappointedly, "but I'd rather be near people who belonged to my mother."

"Oh, they wouldn't take a girl to do that work. It is all done by men, or machines, nowadays."

"Machines? How could a machine milk a cow?"

"I'm sure I don't know. I never saw one, but I've heard that all the milking in large dairies is done by some kind of an electric contrivance that is made a good deal like a human hand. But what else can you do?"

"I can wash," she said brightly, "and cook a little. I can learn to do almost anything, I guess."

Looking at her the woman thought perhaps it might be possible.

"How would you like to come and work for me?" she asked.

"Oh, could I? That would be beautiful!" said the child enthusiastically. "What would you let me do for you? I could learn to do fine cooking like what we had to eat to-day perhaps."

"But I already have a cook, and a waitress, and a maid and several other servants. I don't need another. How would you like to be my social secretary? A sort of companion, you know."

"That's not work," said Fraley disappointed; "that's

play. I couldn't earn money honestly for doing a thing like that."

"Oh, yes, you could," said the lady, "and it's not play by any means. You would have to keep track of my engagements, and see that I didn't forget any of them. You would look after sending my laces to be mended and my jewels to be repaired or cleaned, or restrung, you know—and you would have to learn to answer my notes and send out invitations—all those things. Can you write?"

"Oh, yes," said the girl eagerly.

"Write something for me. Write me a letter. Here, take this and see what you can do."

The lady opened a gold-mounted handbag and took out a small notebook and a gold fountain pen and handed them to her.

Fraley examined the pen, and handed it back.

"I'd better get my own pencil. I'm not used to that yet, but I'll practice with it later if you want me to."

She opened the newly acquired bag, dug out her own little stub of a pencil and went to work. In a few minutes she handed over the paper. It was written in a neat plain hand and the spelling was perfect.

> Dear Mrs. Wentworth:
>
> I am glad I met you, and I love you. I hope God will bless you for helping me.
>
> With affection,
> Fraley MacPherson.

Mrs. Wentworth looked up surprised.

"Who taught you the form of a letter?"

"My mother used to make me write one to her every morning for a while, till she thought I understood. Sometimes she let me sign the end like the epistles in the

Bible. 'The grace of our Lord Jesus Christ be with your spirit.' I like that, but I didn't know whether that would do for the kind of letters you want or not so I didn't put it in."

"It would not," said the lady a bit sharply. "You showed good sense. Well, then, shall we call it a bargain? I'll hire you at a salary of two hundred a month. That will give you enough to buy some clothes right away. You'll need a good many for you will go out with me a lot. Do you think you will like it?"

"I'm sure I'll like to be with you and do whatever you want done if I can do it right," said Fraley. "I think you are lovely."

"Well, you may not think so after you've been with me a while. And if you get tired of the job of course I shall not hold you. I don't want you to feel under any obligation. I'm having my fun out of this, and I don't feel you owe me anything. But there's one thing I would suggest. Don't drag the Bible in everywhere. People don't all care for it as much as you do, and you'll turn everybody against you. You wouldn't want to do that, would you?"

"Why no, of course not."

The lady gave her a queer look, almost as if she were going to laugh and then she turned away and looked out of the window a long time. After which she turned back and said earnestly, "Fraley, you're a dear little girl. Don't let anything I've said worry you. I'm really rather a cranky old thing."

"Don't say that, please, Mrs. Wentworth."

"I told you you might call me Violet."

"I know. But it doesn't seem quite respectful. Mother taught me to be respectful."

"Well, I don't want respect. That makes me feel old

and I'm getting old fast enough without it. I'd rather you'd call me Violet."

"I'll try—Mrs.—Violet," she smiled timidly.

"That's right," said the lady. "Now, can you play bridge?"

"Bridge?" said Fraley. "What is that?"

"It's a game of cards."

Fraley's face darkened.

"No, I cannot play cards."

"I will teach you then."

"No, Mrs.—I mean Violet, please. I would rather not learn. My mother hated cards. The men played them when they were drunk. She thought it was what made my father lose—everything. I wouldn't feel right playing them."

"That's absurd, of course. However, I shan't press the matter now. You'll learn soon enough when you get into another world that those are all things of the past. You are leaving them behind and there will be new standards which you will have to accept if you want to be a success in New York. I am going to teach you how to be a success, little Fraley."

Fraley smiled but she did not look wholly convinced. She examined the tips of the smart little shoes she was wearing which had already become irksome; she smoothed down the satin of her chic little frock, and let the afternoon sunshine twinkle on the tiny platinum watch she was wearing, but somehow she felt a great depression. The new life began to look complicated. She looked wistfully out of the window, and thought of the Raven, her new friend, and that reverent kiss he had laid upon her brow at parting. She wished she could go to her own dear mother and talk it all over and find out what was right.

She drew a deep sigh. It was very stuffy in the train and her eyelids were heavy with sleep!

"You're tired, child," said the lady sympathetically. "Take off your hat and shoes and lie down there. We can draw the curtain or close the door and no one will disturb you. I want to read awhile."

So Fraley took off the new hat and hung it respectfully on the long brass hook over her head, took off the fine shoes and stood them in a corner by her couch, and nestled down on the pillow that the porter brought. She was soon sound asleep. One silk clad arm was under her head, and the long dark lashes lay on the lovely rounded cheek. A little late beam of sunshine laid bright touches on the coil of soft hair over her ear, and brought out exquisite tintings in the warm flesh. What a picture she made as she lay there sleeping like a baby, the little girl pilgrim, all alone! Something deeper than she understood stirred in the woman who watched her, over the book she was not reading. What if she should make this girl something more than social secretary! She would make a great sensation in her world, if she were launched in the way that she knew well how to launch a girl. Perhaps she would do it. She would go slow. She would find out first what kind of people she belonged to, whether they were likely to turn up later and spoil all her plans. Perhaps it would be well to investigate them before the girl had opportunity, and if they were undesirable, keep her from going to them at all. It would not be hard to do so, she judged, for the child was most tractable.

So the afternoon waned, and the sun went down behind the long express train hurrying east, and the sky on either side was spread with lovely colors left over from the main display.

Fraley woke up in time to see it, and to wonder for a

moment where she was, in such a noisy rush. She laughed when the lady smiled at her.

"I thought I was hiding behind a great rock in the hot sun," she said, sitting up and rubbing her eyes. "I guess I must have gone to sleep. Why, it is getting night, isn't it?"

"It surely is," said the lady closing her book. "Go smooth your hair and let us go to dinner. I like to eat while the sky is in good form. It makes it seem like a banquet."

Fraley got up and made ready, and they wended their way once more to the diner.

"I don't really need to eat so often," said the girl. "It costs a lot and I'm not used to meals very often."

"That is silly," said the lady. "People have to eat, and besides it is all there is to do here."

"Oh, I think there is a great deal to do," said Fraley happily. "There is so much to see. Such wide pictures out of the window, it is almost like climbing a tree and looking high over the world."

"Can you climb a tree?" asked the lady studying her and realizing her loveliness again. How well she looked in that dark blue. It brought out all the tints of her perfect skin.

"Oh yes," laughed the girl, "I always could do that. Can't you?"

"Well, no," said the lady, "not that I ever remember. I'm afraid I wouldn't look like much up a tree. There are no trees to climb in New York, you know," she reminded.

"Perhaps you do not need them," said the girl gravely, thinking how often a tree had been her only refuge.

"Need them? Oh, for shade? Well, no, we have our cool houses you know, and in summer we always go away anyway."

"I mean to climb to get out of danger," explained Fraley.

"Danger? What kind of danger?"

"Oh, bad men, and wild animals, and angry cattle," she answered coolly.

"Mercy!" said the lady. "Have you ever encountered such things?"

"Oh, yes."

"And taken refuge in a tree?"

"Yes, I don't know where I would have gone if there hadn't been a tree. I think God planted them just where He saw I would need them."

The lady smiled superciliously.

"Do you think He bothers about us to that extent?"

"Oh, yes," said the girl, opening her eyes wide in her earnestness. "I know He does. He took care of me every step of the way here."

"Well, what kind of ice cream do you want? I suppose the vanilla with fudge sauce would be the best, unless you prefer fresh strawberries."

"Oh, yes, strawberries! I've picked them on the mountain. How my mother loved them!"

"How you loved your mother!" sighed the lady enviously. "I wish I might have been your mother, but I'm afraid you wouldn't have been half so lovely as you are."

"Oh," said Fraley thoughtfully, gazing out at the violet and gold of the dying sunset. "It makes a difference where we are born, doesn't it?"

"It certainly does, princess in disguise."

"If I couldn't have been the child of my own dear mother, I think the next best thing would have been to have been yours," she said at last prettily, with a shy smile.

14

THE wonder of the night was having the berths made up in the cosy little drawing-room, and lying on the long couch at the side, with the lady over in the other berth in the soft noisy dark. The wheels beat a monotonous rhythm underneath her, and the night came close as they hurried along safe and protected through the dark land. The engine needed no guide. It had a set track to go on and it made no mistakes.

And Fraley thought how just as plainly her own little track was perhaps marked out where God who was her engineer could see it, and guide her.

Then as she heard the steady breathing of her room-mate and privacy settled down around her, she began to go over her meeting with the young man in the wilderness, and all the way they had come in their friendship in those few short hours. That kiss he had given her at parting sat upon her brow like a holy thing. She had a friend, and something told her he would always be her friend. Would he like her better in these new clothes she had put on? Had he liked her less for her bare feet, and faded clothing? It did not seem that he had noticed them. Out there in the wilderness perhaps it sort of fitted in with everything, and she was glad that he liked her first in her own plain simple things that she had always worn. Afterward, if she ever met him again she would like to have him know that she knew how to look as the world expected her to look, but she would always remember that he had not despised her in her old garments, and bare feet.

Then she remembered with a thrill of anticipation, that she had a letter in her new pocketbook from him that she had not read. She would get it out and read it in the morning while the lady was in the little dressing-room getting dressed. She shrank from reading it before her; she would ask so many questions. Instinctively she felt that this new Violet woman would not understand her friendship with this man in the desert.

She went back in her thoughts to the dim smoky schoolhouse with its candle light and quavering prayers; the sweet songs they had sung; and the voice of the young man as he read the familiar words from the Book. How close she felt to him as she thought of it, for he had enjoyed her Book, and had wanted one for himself. He had a sympathy and understanding for it that she felt the lady did not have.

When she woke in the morning the lady was still asleep.

Softly Fraley tiptoed up and got her letter, stealing into the little dressing-room to read it.

In a little delicate embroidered gown and kimono of silk that the lady had provided for her, she stood by the light and read, breathless with the pleasure of having a real friend who would write to her like that.

My dear Ladybird: [he wrote]
I am sitting up to write this because I am afraid I may

not have a chance to say these things in the morning without someone by to bother, and I do not want you to go into the wilderness of New York without some knowledge of what you are up against.

There followed some minute directions about ways and means, and what was wise and unwise to do in a great city when a young girl was all alone. Warnings that young Seagrave's friends would have been surprised he knew how to give.

She read them all through carefully, and then there came another bit of himself at the end:

And now, I don't just know how to tell you, Ladybird, what you have done for me. I was pretty much of a good for nothing when you found me on the desert yesterday, or when I found you in a tree. I don't mean I've ever been very sinful, you know, just careless, and always living for a good time. But you've somehow given me a new viewpoint, and I want to thank you for it. I mean to stick to the job. I'll just tell some of the stories, and put the folks to studying the Book. When you send me my Bible I'll get to work on it myself, and perhaps now and then, you'll remember to put up a prayer for the poor raven who was sent to feed you when you were hungry. I shall always be glad I met you, Angel lady, and please don't forget when you get settled to give me your address, for it may be your people are not at home and you'll have to find a boarding place. Don't forget that on any account, for I want to write you about my services and how you helped me through them, if you'll let me.

Your new friend,
A Raven.

And down in the lower corner of the sheet was written

George Rivington Seagrave,

with two addresses, one in the west, the other in New York.

But Fraley could hear that the lady was stirring in her berth now, and she folded the precious letter and tucked it safely away. She dressed quickly and came out looking fresh as a new-blown rose.

"Did I do my hair all right?" she asked, starry-eyed from her letter.

"You certainly did," said the lady admiringly, lifting a haggard face with the make-up sadly in need of repair. "You look like a new-born babe, my child. How do you manage it? I don't know but what you've improved on my coiffure. You certainly got the knack quickly. Well, I'll be ready shortly. I suppose you are hungry."

"Don't hurry," said Fraley happily, "I'll sit here and look out of the window. Isn't the world wonderful! And I want to read my Bible a few minutes too, I always do every morning."

Marveling, the elder woman took her way to the dressing-room, almost envying this child her relish for simple sights, and wondering whether after all she would ever be able to give sophistication to this strange young creature who seemed to be almost from another world.

"You certainly look a picture!" she said a little while later coming out in all her delicate war paint. "Put up your old Book now and let's go get some breakfast. They always have waffles on these trains. Do you like waffles?"

"I never saw one," said Fraley with the air of a joyous explorer.

Breakfast was a success. The morning was sparkling,

and the scenery wonderful through which they were passing. The people who sat at the little tables in the dining car were a never-failing source of interest to the girl whose circle of acquaintance had been so exceedingly restricted.

At one or two places during the day when the train stopped for some minutes, they got out and walked around, and Fraley managed her new shoes very well, although she confided to her new friend that it was much, much easier to walk without them.

"We'll have some that really fit you when we get to New York," said the new mentor, and noted with satisfaction how the girl beside her attracted all eyes, and how she went through this open admiration without a particle of self-consciousness. In fact she did not even seem to be aware of it. Perhaps that was because public opinion had as yet no part in her life, and pride of self had not entered into her soul.

Violet Wentworth felt that she had found a treasure in this lovely unspoiled girl, and she meant to use her as a new attraction to adorn her charming home. There was nothing like a new girl, with character and distinction, to bring a throng. She was proud of her sons, and of her reputation as a hostess. She was beginning to think that perhaps she would drop the social secretary idea and introduce Fraley as a young friend who was visiting her for a year. She would see how it worked out. Of course she would have to keep up the form of secretaryship for the time, until the girl got some of that Puritanism rubbed off, for she could see she would not be easily persuaded to accept her living for nothing indefinitely, not even in friendship—and of course it would be hard to make the unsophisticated child understand the real reason why she wanted her. And if she did understand, half the value would be gone from her fine simplicity. As soon as she got to know her own loveliness, it would vanish in pride and selfishness. Violet Wentworth had seen this happen many a time before with the different protégés she impulsively picked up here and there, but she somehow had a warmer feeling for this pretty child, and wanted to keep her as she was.

Secretly studying the child all the time as she conversed with her, Violet Wentworth was deciding just what coaching she needed to make her most quickly ready to move among the people of her own circle. Late in the afternoon she handed over a magazine she had been reading.

"There is a good little story; read it, Fraley. You ought to read a great many magazine stories, and novels. They will be excellent for teaching you the ways of the world. I don't know any way you can get atmosphere as quickly as by reading society stories. Unless perhaps the movies, and the theatre. Of course they are a wonderful help. Little habits and customs that no one would think to tell you about, you would acquire by watching, without realizing you were learning something new. It would simply come to you the way a baby learns the habits of her household into which she had been born."

Fraley took up the magazine and went dutifully to reading the story set for her. But as she read her face grew grave; and graver still as it progressed, and the color came brightly in her cheeks.

Violet Wentworth, watching her could not quite understand her reaction. But she did not seem to be enjoying what she had considered a little romance quite amusing and out of the ordinary. The child's eyes were flashing, and her lips were parted as if she were about to protest at something. When she had finished she handed over the magazine.

"Are people in the world all like that?" she flashed at the astonished lady.

"What do you mean, like that?" asked the lady, "Didn't you like the story? I thought it exceedingly well written."

"Oh," said the girl, "you mean the way it is told. Yes, I suppose it is well told. But why did they want to write such a horrible thing? It isn't like the dreadful stories in the Bible. They were all told to warn people or to teach some great truth that the people needed to know. But this story teaches a thing that isn't so."

"What can you mean, you funny little girl!" exclaimed Violet Wentworth, taking up the magazine and glancing down its columns to refresh her memory of the story which had already gone from her mind.

"Why, it makes that secretary girl fall in love with a man who already has a wife, and marry him, and *be happy* with him! Mother said that was a sin! The Bible says so too!"

"Oh, my dear!" laughed the lady. "What a little old-fashioned thing you are, to be sure. You'll have to get over talking about sin! There is no such thing nowadays, and people don't look at it that way. It is quite the fashion now to divorce and marry again, and nobody thinks anything of it. Perhaps half of the people you will meet will have been divorced once or twice. You mustn't think of it in the horrified way. The world is changing all the time, you know, and we are getting away from the antiquated ideas, and see that we have to do what fits the times. It certainly is better to be divorced if you are unhappy, and to marry someone you will be happy with. It makes the world a better place to live in for everybody to be happy, you know."

Fraley pondered this sophistry for a while and then she said with a troubled look:

"But God doesn't feel that way about it. The Bible says divorce is wrong. And besides, everybody wasn't meant to be happy. God said his children would have to bear hard things sometimes."

Violet smiled wisely.

"My dear, the world has progressed, and we must keep up with the times. You know the Bible is a very old-fashioned book. Come, let's forget it, and watch the sunset. I think it is going to be better than last night. Look at the lovely orchid next to the green."

Fraley turned her eyes toward the window, but there was a disturbed look in her face that her companion did not like. She must deal wisely with this prejudiced child if she wished to conquer in the end. It would not do to antagonize her. Therefore she put out her hand and patted the young hand that lay in the blue satin lap.

"You mustn't think that I object to your beloved Bible, little Fraley," she said. "It's all right, and it's very lovely for you to be so devoted to it, and all that. It really makes you quite unique and charming, only of course you have been shut in a good deal from the world, and you have got a narrow viewpoint. There's no harm in it, at all. It's really attractive for a young girl in this age of the world to believe in something uplifting like that. Only you have got some things a little out of proportion. But that will right itself. When you get to going to dances and house parties, and week ends, and theatre parties and the like, and when you have read some of the current literature, and gone to the movies a little you will find all this falling into line, and taking its place as it ought to do. But you must remember you don't know the world, and it is the world you live in, not heaven, now, and you've got to be like the world or you won't have a good time, and the world won't like you."

Fraley's face was still troubled, and she did not answer.

Violet saw that the girl was in no state of mind to
accept her sophistries so she soothed her.

"I've been thinking," she said pleasantly, as if the other
subject were finished, "that we ought to plan just what
we will do when we get to New York. There are always
so many things to think about just before one gets off a
train. You said you wanted to send those two books
before you do anything else. Suppose we attend to that
the very first thing. You can have the addresses all
written out for sending them, and it won't take much
time to select what you want. We'll drive to the store
straight from the station and get that off your mind.
Then you can enjoy New York."

She had struck the right note at last. Fraley smiled and
new light came into her eyes. She sat watching the
changing colors of the sunset, and when the darkness
came down, and the lights were turned on in the car her
face was bright again.

15

THERE was one thing in which Violet Wentworth utterly failed to interest her new protégée. It was a matter that she had never found to fail before and she was utterly at a loss to understand. Fraley MacPherson had no interest at all in the subject that has been all-absorbing to the most of womankind since Eve wore her first fig leaf, the question of wherewithal shall we be clothed.

Pleased she was with her new garments, often touching the cloth of her little frock gently as if she admired it, careful lest the least dust should fall upon it, guarding her hat from crushing with an instinct of one who had always worn good garments; yet when she was asked what else she would like to have in her wardrobe she smiled dreamily and said:

"Why I think I have enough, now, thank you."

Violet Wentworth was nonplused.

"Wait till we get in the shops," she said easily, "you'll see. You'll be charmed with everything."

"But I wouldn't need anything else but this," said Fraley genuinely surprised. "I've been very careful with this. It won't be hurt a bit by the traveling. I can save it for best and wear my other own old ones for work. This will do for dressing up."

"Well, that, little Fraley, is another thing you will have to wait till you get to New York to understand. Life is very different where I live. We don't go to bed at dark, and we have different clothes for all the places we go. Evening clothes, and sports clothes, and afternoon clothes, and street things, and party things. Oh, there is no end to the clothes one can use."

"Isn't it a lot of trouble?"

"Why, no. It's very interesting. Don't you like pretty things?"

"Oh, yes. I have always loved pretty things. The mountains in a mist, the sun rising across the valley, little green eggs in a robin's nest, the lichens on a great rock, an old tree against the sky when the sun has fallen the night before—and—my mother's face! My mother was lovely!"

"She must have been," said Violet Wentworth almost wistfully, watching the vivid little face before her.

The child was such a contrast to the feverish, artificial life she led, that it made her more than ever dissatisfied with everything; yet here was she at that very moment planning how she might force Fraley into the very same mould with all her little earth. Life was a strange contradiction, and a glimmer of the truth flashed at her now and then through the face and words of this unspoiled child.

The days on the train seemed like weeks to the girl. She began to grow weary of the confinement, but now they were coming to settlements, nearer and nearer together, and these were sources of great interest, seeing so many houses together, the paved streets, the many automobiles parked about the stations, the people coming and going in crowds, till it seemed to her that all the people of the earth must have congregated at one city.

Once there was a real procession passing the station just at the time the train stopped there, in fact they had come down with brass bands and all their nobility to see off some distinguished guest who was boarding the very train on which she was riding, and Fraley exclaimed at the throng.

"Oh, see, that must be something like the way the children of Israel looked when they started out of Egypt. There are women and children too, only of course there are no cattle nor sheep!"

The lady smiled indulgently, and Fraley quick to catch the lack of sympathy in her face, flushed softly and closed her lips. She was learning fast not to speak of her Book where it could not be appreciated. Would it always be like that in the new life to which she was going?

But each new town was a new pleasure. She longed to get out of the warm train and walk all over the streets till she knew the place as she would know a friend. What pleasure it would be to travel everywhere and get to know the world as she knew each individual mountain back where she had come from!

Chicago amazed her with its miles of buildings huddled close, and at her first sight of the lake she seemed almost frightened.

"Look!" she cried in an awestruck whisper. "Is that a—a—cloud—or—what?"

And when she learned it was called a lake, "But it is so big!" she said. "And it melts into the sky in such a strange way. I thought it must be an ocean."

The lady assured her that the ocean was much larger, and she sat with her face pressed against the window, watching till it was out of sight.

After they left Chicago the world was a continual

revelation to the girl from the mountains. So many, many houses, and people in them all. So many towns and cities, and always more on ahead! The wide stretching fields all plowed and harrowed and ready for the sowing, the miles of fences, the great barns and store houses. The groups of cattle and sheep grazing, the comfortable-looking homes, white with green blinds nestled among tall elms, or the great old stone farmhouses that had been there for years and looked to the young stranger as if carved out of her own mountain. She asked more questions than her benefactor could possibly answer, and the woman wondered that a girl could care so much for so many things that seemed to her utterly uninteresting. Why, some of those questions had never occurred to her, though she had traveled through this region all her life. She could not tell why certain types of fences seemed to be used to fence in cattle, and why some fields had only stone walls. She did not even know whether there was a reason or it was only a happening. She had never noticed that it was so. And it bored her to be asked.

But it continued to interest her to watch this girl, this new type of humanity, as she sat and planned how soon she could turn her into her own kind. Another pretty face on a useless creature of the world. That was what she wanted to make out of this lovely child of God.

And now, at last, New York!

Fraley was so excited she could hardly keep her seat. She wanted to stand up and press her face against the window, and watch each new station. She watched the porter curiously as he went from seat to seat brushing off the dust from passengers, polishing shoes and collecting baggage.

She almost protested when he came and took the handsome bag that now contained all the possessions she had brought from home.

"Perhaps I ought to take my Bible out," she whispered to the lady. "I mustn't lose that you know."

"He won't lose it," laughed the lady. "See, he has all my luggage, too. When we get out there we shall find our bags waiting for us. You will see."

She was much disappointed that they entered the station through an underground passage. She had thought New York would burst upon her like a vision of the heavenly city, shining and great in the noonday sun, and here they were rushed through darkness, with a ringing in her ears, and a strange bursting feeling in her head, and presently arrived in a great walled-in space lined with something that resembled stone, framed above with great stairs and galleries.

She stepped out carefully to the platform that was on a level close to the floor of the car, and stood looking up.

"Go on, Fraley, don't stop to look around now," whispered the lady. "You are holding up other people."

Fraley started with quick color in her cheeks and followed Mrs. Wentworth.

They got into a small cage a few steps from where they had stepped out, and the door shut and the whole little bunch of people with them began to rise into the air. It was a very terrible sensation not at all like being in the top of a tree, and Fraley's face expressed distress, but a glance at her companion showed that amused look that she had learned to dread, and she dropped her frightened gaze and tried to act as if she had been accustomed to ascend mountains in an elevator.

Violet Wentworth knew just what to do. They walked across a great open plain, with many people going in different directions, yet all having plenty of room. A great voice coming forth from above their heads somewhere announced a train to Washington, and another back to the Pacific Coast. She felt that she was standing in the center of the ways of the world. Here she was in New York! Yet she felt more of a pilgrim than ever. It was all so strange and cold and far away.

They walked across the wide space and through an archway and a great yellow chariot drew up before them as if by magic. It had no horse, and it looked magnificent to the unaccustomed eyes of the girl from the wilderness. The lady gave an order, and they both got inside. Then the red-capped man put some of their bags in with them and piled the rest in the front with the driver, and they rode away.

"Can this—be—a—a—taxi?" Fraley asked in awe. "It looks like—" But here she remembered and closed her lips.

"Yes, it's a taxi," said her mentor. "What do you think it looks like?"

"I was just thinking it looked something like what I thought a chariot might be."

"Oh!" said the lady, amused again. "I never saw one, but this is a mighty shabby old taxi. We'll have our own car by this evening, I hope. I telegraphed on to have it put in shape for immediate use, but as I wasn't sure then which train I would take I couldn't let them know when to meet me."

"Have you a family?" asked Fraley eagerly, half shrinking from the thought of sharing her new friend with others. "Have you any little children? Was that what made you so kind to me, because you are a mother yourself?"

"On, no," said the lady laughing. "Nothing like that, thank goodness. I've nobody to bother about but myself."

"But you have a husband?" said the girl fearfully. Men were such an uncertain quantity in this world.

"No!" said the lady quite crossly, "I haven't!"

"Oh, did he die?" she asked with sympathy in her voice. A dead man could do her no harm.

The lady was silent a moment staring out of the window, and then she answered sharply:

"No, he didn't! I might as well tell you for if I don't someone else will. I divorced him last fall. I've nobody but myself."

"Oh!" said Fraley in a little stricken voice and sat back silently thinking over the things she had said about people who were divorced; thinking of all the kind things the lady had done; of the pretty clothes she was wearing at her expense; trying to think of something that would be both suitable and true to say. But no words came to her lips. She could only sit back quietly and slide her small hand into the slim elegantly gloved one with a warm human pressure.

But the embarrassing silence was soon broken by their arrival at a book store, and Fraley's delight was great. Books! Books! Books! More than she had ever dreamed were in the world! Beautiful red and blue and gold and brown books. Books on shelves and on long tables that went down the room on either side.

Fraley's eyes sparkled with joy as she made her careful selections: a beautiful, expensive limp covered Scofield Bible with India paper and clear type for Seagrave, because the salesman recommended it as being most popular with ministers on account of its wonderful notes; and a large-print red-covered one with colored pictures for Jimmy.

They left careful directions for the mailing of the books, and Fraley proudly paid for them, and turned away with a shining in her eyes that was wholly unexplainable to the woman of the world.

"Now," said the lady, "are you ready to come home

with me, or do you think you've got to racket around first and locate your family?"

"Oh, no," said the girl seriously, "I'll look them up another time. I want to get started first and feel that I have a place to call home somewhere. I don't want to have them think they've got to do anything for me. They might not like it, you know."

"I see," said Violet Wentworth, with a shrewd look in her eyes and a satisfied set of her lips. Then there would not be any immediate interference of a family in her plans, until she had tried some things out and knew what she wanted to do. She got into the taxi and gave her order, feeling that everything was working out nicely.

Riverside Drive meant nothing at all to the little girl from the mountains, but when she saw the river, wide and shining in the afternoon sun, with the many strange boats plying back and forth upon its surface or clustered along its banks, she exclaimed with joy.

"Oh, this is going to be a wonderful place!" she said. "I'm going to love it. Now I can look off and see far away. It is almost as good as my mountains, this wonderful river. I felt so—shut in—before I saw this!"

She went up the steps of the Wentworth mansion with more wonder upon her, but turned before she entered the door and looked again upon the river, and at the palisades across.

"I shall come out here often and just enjoy this," she said as she turned to follow her friend into the house.

But inside the great hall she stopped and looked about her bewildered. The ceilings were so high, and the rooms so large, that she had a sense of desiring to reach out and hold on to something, lest she would fall.

There were thick rugs under her feet, and beautiful vistas opening out from wide doorways, with great mirrors in which she saw her small self reflected in several different views, and thought it someone else. There was one room in the distance where the walls were lined with books behind glass doors, and off in the other direction she could see a table set with dishes, and candles burning over a crystal bowl of flowers.

There were people there, also, a man who opened the door, and somehow reminded her of the porter on the Pullman. In the background was a woman, wearing a black dress and a white apron and cap or curious little white bonnet on her head; a young man, a boy almost, with brass buttons on his short jacket, lighting a fire in a room opposite the door. It was all bewildering.

She presently sensed without being told that these people were servants. She watched them and wondered how she should greet them, but found they did not expect anything but her shy smile.

The boy carried the bags up a beautiful staircase, and Fraley mounted it with interest. She had never seen a stair so high, and cushioned with velvet so that no sound came from a footfall.

There seemed to be unlimited rooms on the second floor, and Fraley was given one that opened across the hall from her hostess, a great beautiful room with windows looking out on the river, and a steamer hurrying down the river made a wondrous sight. She walked straight over to the window and watched it till it was out of sight before she even took off her hat.

"It is going to be wonderful here," she said turning as Violet Wentworth entered the door and stood watching her. "I am afraid I shall not do enough work with all this to look at."

"Well, forget it now," said the lady pleasantly. "I want to show you your room. I'm putting you here right across from me so that I can have you close at hand when I need you."

She did not explain that this room she was giving the girl was one which she had usually kept for honored guests, and that she was putting the child here because she wanted her near her, because she was growing fond of her, and because she longed to give her the best she had and see what reaction it would bring.

Fraley turned and looked at the beautiful room, stately in proportion, decorated and furnished by one of the greatest decorators in New York City, and at a fabulous sum. The effect was charming. To Fraley it seemed too spacious for her small self, too formal and beautiful for common use, too wonderful for the girl who had slept in a little seven by nine bedroom off the corner of the cabin on the mountain. But her heart swelled with appreciation of it all.

When the door to the white tiled bathroom was open, disclosing its shining spotlessness, with all its perfect appointments for comfort, she stopped and dared not enter. It was so white it dazzled her. White floor, white walls, silver-trimmed fixtures, and a lovely rose silk curtain to the bath!

"You do not mean that this is all for me, alone?" she said turning to the lady, and there were tears upon her lashes. "Oh, if my mother could know I have all this, she would be so glad. Oh, if she could only have had it I would be willing to go back to the cabin and stay alone. She had it so hard!"

"Well, she is probably glad you are here," said the lady, stirred almost to tears herself by the wistfulness of the young voice, "so just be as happy as you can. Now, will you unpack your own things, or do you want the maid to do it for you?"

"Oh, I will do it," said Fraley. "I want to do everything, myself."

"You can put your things in these drawers, and here

is one you can lock if you have any special treasures that you don't want the maid to touch when she comes in to wait on you."

"Oh, please, I don't want to be waited on," said the girl pleadingly, "I wouldn't know how to act."

"As you please. You'll get acquainted with all the ways pretty soon and then you won't feel so. Jeanne is very good, and knows how to put the last touches on a costume delightfully. She can teach you a great many things you ought to know. I shall tell her you have always lived your life quietly, and she will understand and not bother you. She is quick-witted. You will like her."

Fraley unpacked her shining bag, and took out the old gray woolen bag her mother had made for her. She locked her door and with the bag in her arms went and knelt by the smooth white bed and laid her face on the bag, beginning to cry.

"Oh, mother, mother, mother," she sobbed softly, "if only you were back again, I'd rather be on the mountain with you. Oh, I would!"

But presently she dried her tears and looked around trying to grow accustomed to her surroundings, and realize that this room was to be her home spot now, this beautiful room! If she could have seen a vision of this to which she was coming while she lay behind that riven rock, for instance, or while she was fleeing from the wild steers, or from the men who were her enemies, how astonished she would have been. So this was what God had been leading her to, all this time.

Slowly she unpacked the bag, taking out the old Bible, and looked around for a suitable place to put it, where she could easily use it every day.

Beside her bed was a little night table, with a silken-shaded lamp, a Dresden shepherdess under a pink umbrella. She laid the old Bible with its cotton covers down upon this table under the shade of the pink umbrella.

She put her mother's bag with the crude little cotton garments in the safe drawer and locked it. She realized by this time how odd they were beside the things that other people wore. She was not too proud to wear them still, but she knew that the lady would not like her to appear odd, and neither would her mother wish it; and moreover she did not want the critical eye of strangers on the precious garments that her dear mother had made with her last dying strength. So she locked them away tenderly.

Then she made herself sweet and neat and went softly out into the hall.

As the door across the hall was shut, and there were no sounds except far away downstairs, she went back to her room and sat down by the window to watch the river.

It was like having a new picture in place of her mountains, that great still river down there with the busy boats, so many of them, and off at the left, very far away in an evening mist of gold a place that looked like a very forest of boats, ships with tall masts.

She watched the pearly mists that began to rise as the evening came on, watched the sunset tints, and thought how even now they were out there in her western sky, back at the home mountain, and back at the ranch house where the missionary friend would be at this time of night perhaps.

She wondered if he had forgotten her by this time? It seemed a long, long two days since she bade him good-by. Was he sticking by his job?

Then suddenly she became aware of someone stand-ing in the open door, and looking up there she saw the stiff young person in her black dress and white apron and bonnet.

"Dinner is served. Madam says will you come down to the dining room?"

Fraley arose, fear born of formality upon her and followed the maid.

16

IT was an awesome room to which she was led, with high paneled walls in cream color, and rich heavy draperies over the white curtains at the windows.

The dishes were fragile and glittering, some of them like frostwork. There was a great deal of silver, and rich damask napkins with great embroidered initials. It was not at all like the neighborly little tables in the dining car. Fraley suddenly felt very small and awkward. It seemed a long walk from the door over to the table where Mrs. Wentworth stood, like some stranger in a wonderful sleeveless low-cut gown of deep rich velvet in dark red tones. There were ropes of little pearls about her neck and hanging low on the front of her gown. Fraley felt as if she did not know her till she looked up and smiled, but even the smile was rather absent-minded.

She was reading a letter, and seemed annoyed at something.

The tall gentleman in strange black clothes was standing at the door, and the maid who had brought her word about dinner being ready was at the other end of the room.

"When did this come, Saxon?"

"This morning, ma'am," said the gentleman, bowing obsequiously.

"And did you tell them when I would arrive?"

"I told the messenger that you were expected to arrive this afternoon."

"And nothing has come since? No telephone message even?"

"Nothing ma'am, except a box of flowers. I had it put in the ice box, madam."

"Have them brought in," said the lady curtly, and swept to her seat at the head of the table. The man pulled her chair out for her, and pushed it in when she was seated and then came and did the same for Fraley. The girl wished he would not. It only made it harder, but she tried to do just what Mrs. Wentworth had done, and to act as though it were nothing new.

There was nothing to eat on the table but little long-stemmed glasses of delicious fruit, and the lady began to eat it at once, tasting daintily, not seeming to care much about it. But to the girl it tasted like a wonderful heavenly nectar.

The butler brought the flowers in, wonderful roses and strange weird fluted things that her hostess said were orchids, tinted a queer green with brown markings. The roses looked like a sunset. Fraley had never seen roses before, not roses like those. Her mother had cultivated a sickly little bush from a root she had got somewhere before Fraley was born, and it produced little tight, red, purply pink button roses without any fragrance. But these looked as if they must have fallen from heaven, and the fragrance was like all sweet winds and perfumes melted together and flung upon the air.

The lady called for a crystal bowl and directed the maid in arranging the flowers in water. She seemed far more interested in them than in the delicious soup that was presently put before them. Fraley wondered if the flowers came from the lady's husband, but she did not dare ask. Perhaps he was feeling bad about their divorce, and wanted to make it right again. She watched the lady's lovely head as it was bent over the flowers, her white fingers, flashing with precious stones, giving a touch to the flowers skillfully, making them lie in the water as if they grew there, and lift their lovely heads like little people. Fraley was very much in love with the lady. She hoped with all her heart that she would make it up with her husband. The lady seemed absorbed and was not talking, so Fraley kept still and watched her.

"Rather nice ones, aren't they? One of my admirers sent them," and she laughed.

Somehow Fraley felt disappointed, but she tried to answer with a shy smile.

"I'd—like to—send you—some as nice—some day!" she said wistfully.

"Well, you can," said the lady as the butler took her only half-finished soup. "But if I were you, I wouldn't bother. You'll have plenty of uses for your money, and I get a lot of flowers. Sometimes I'm perfectly fed up on them."

The girl had a feeling that she was only half thinking of her. Presently the telephone rang, and the butler brought a message. It meant nothing to the girl, something about someone coming to call at nine o'clock, but after that, the lady was more cheerful, and the dinner went briskly.

There was half a little bird for the next course, and the mountain girl, who had lived on corn bread and bacon nearly all her life, with eggs and milk when it could be spared, felt wicked and wasteful, with so much all for her own. There were delicious vegetables and queer little entrées and a salad even more unusual than the things she had on the train, and the meal finished off with a delicate frozen pudding.

Black coffee was served in tiny cups and when Fraley declined it, the lady said to the butler, "See that there is milk for Miss MacPherson in the morning. She prefers milk."

"Now," said the lady as they rose from the table, "I am expecting callers. I wonder what you would like to do? As soon as we do some shopping for you I shall want you to come in sometimes and meet my friends, but to-night you can amuse yourself as you like. There's the library. Perhaps you'll find some books you'll enjoy, unless you think it's wicked to read any book but the Bible. And there are folios of engravings, and some signed etchings, and water colors in the drawer of the big table. There's the radio, too, and the victrola. I'll show you how to turn them off and on, and you can do what you like. I suppose perhaps you're tired anyway, after the journey. I surely am, but I shall be busy this evening."

"Oh, I'm not tired," said Fraley happily. "I'll love just to look around. And of course I shall enjoy looking at the books. This is such a wonderful house! I should think you would be the happiest woman in the world. You have just everything you want, don't you? Everything there is."

A strange look passed over the woman's face.

"No, I'm afraid not, little girl," said the woman sadly; "there are several things I would have liked that never came my way."

"But you never were hungry, or cold—or afraid—!" mused the girl.

"Yes—I've often—been afraid!" said the woman more as if she were talking to herself than the girl.

"We don't need to be afraid," said Fraley softly, with

her eyes full of a far-off longing, as if she were reminding herself of deliverance in the past. "God will always take care of us—if we trust Him. He sent—you—to me!"

Violet Wentworth suddenly walked over to the girl, with a quite new and tender look in her face, and putting her arms about her, kissed her. Then she walked away quickly into the other room, as if to hide her emotion.

Fraley went into the library and browsed around among the books. They were all of course utterly unknown to her. She had not even heard their names. Things beyond what she had seen herself she knew of only through her mother's telling. A bit of newspaper wrapped around something from the distant store, once a year perhaps, had been as near to a newspaper as she had ever come; and that was only a scrap now and then, treasured and puzzled over, but seldom complete enough to demand any real interest. Save for the old Bible which her mother had probably carried away with her more as a matter of superstition and sentiment, than for any real love of it at the time, no other book had come her way.

That Bible had become a liberal education to the isolated child, for from its pages alone her mother had contrived to give the little Fraley a rare knowledge of English and composition, an intelligent if not extensive idea of mathematics, a curious fragment of oriental geography, a vague glimpse into geology, botany, zoölogy and astronomy to say nothing of a thorough knowledge of theology.

So Fraley stood before those walls of books delighted, reading their titles, and wondering over them. They were not all of them such as a mother of such a girl would have selected for her daughter's perusal, but Fraley did not know that, and went over their titles selecting such as invited her interest.

Violet Wentworth's taste in literature was extremely modern. All the lurid, liberal, daring novels of the day were set in flaring rows across her shelves without discretion. For convention's sake she had of course, other rows, on the higher shelves—all the classics—and it was to these, after a dip into about twenty titles on the lower shelves, that the girl found herself drawn.

"They are more like the Bible," she explained later to Violet when she pointed out that those books on the lower shelves were the newer ones and therefore more important for her to read, as everybody would be talking about them and she must be ready to take her part in the conversation.

"But I don't like the people in those books," objected Fraley. "Now this one," she went on, taking up a volume of George Eliot, "has real people in it. They are living in earnest. But those other books down on the lower shelves, why, the people in them *like* to be bad! They just seem to be trying to hunt out new ways to do wrong! They are like the people before the flood!"

"They are up-to-date," said Violet with a firm line to her lips, "and they are what you ought to read to be well informed on your times. They will do a lot for you. They will show you how to move in the circle of my acquaintances, and do your work right. I want you to read them."

Fraley looked appalled.

"I'll try," she said slowly, "but—it doesn't—seem quite—right. Some of them—just make me *sick!*"

Her mentor laughed.

"You'll get over that, my dear. It's the way of the world, and if you live in New York you've got to grow up. You can't be a wild bird all your life. It's a part of your education."

"Of course I'll try to do what you want me to do,"

said Fraley looking worried, "but it seems like being among a lot of wicked, dirty-minded people."

"Well, you've got to get used to the world, or how can you ever live in it?" asked the elder woman with a firm set to her lips.

Fraley was silent for a full minute with her eyes wide and serious, then she said slowly, almost as if she thought the other woman would not understand:

"The Bible says you must keep your garments unspotted from the world!"

Violet Wentworth went upstairs from that discussion feeling that she had just put over another slaughter of the innocents.

Fraley continued to browse among the books, delighting in the top shelves, and dutifully skimming a few of the books on the lower ones.

But on this first evening she did little more than browse.

A little later when she was on her way upstairs with several books she had selected to read, she caught a glimpse of the caller as he entered.

She did not like his face. For an instant she almost thought it was Pierce Boyden come for her, so like he seemed to the other. Even the swift, furtive glance he cast about seemed like the way Pierce had always entered the cabin. She shrank back into the shadows of the landing startled, and so became an unintentional witness to the intimate greeting he gave to Violet who came forward at once from the big room on the right of the hall without waiting for the butler to announce the visitor.

The sight was most disturbing, the girl could not quite tell why. It was none of her business of course what this lady of hers did, or what relation she bore to this unpleasant caller, but she did long to feel that she was beyond reproach in every way.

So she went up to her lovely room with an oppression upon her which she could not shake off.

The room was in a soft light from a rose-shaded lamp by the bedside, and the covers were turned back for her convenience. A rose-colored satin quilt lay like a bright cloud across the foot of the bed, and on a chair lay rosy garments for the night, and a delightful negligee of rose and white chiffon with frills and tiny rosebuds of ribbon. Think of having things like this to wear when she was all by herself in her room! Nobody else to share its beauty! A sense of reluctance was upon her that she should have luxury when her mother had gone without everything lovely most of her life, and was lying now in that hasty unmarked grave in the distant valley. If only her mother could have shared all this!

She turned her back on the beautiful room, and went to the window to gaze out on the dark river.

There were lights below on the drive, cars hurrying by, lights off to the left where she knew the crowded city lay, lights across in the little park between the drive and the river, lights everywhere along the shore, and out on the river, on the boats. There were even lights twinkling across on the opposite shore, and high above on the palisades, where dim outlines of tower and roof marked noble mansions among the trees.

And up in the wide sky there were lights, her dear stars, come to New York with her. She would not be able to locate them all perhaps, but she found the Little Dipper at once, and it made her feel at home. God's sky, how wide and dear it was!

She stood within the shadow of the draperies that shrouded the windows and tried to shake off the oppression that was upon her about her dear lady, and she found tears upon her cheeks. Oh, mother! If only you were here! Oh God, show me how to walk!

There was a slight stirring and she turned to see the white-capped maid standing in the doorway.

"I am Jeanne, madam's maid. Madam told me to ask if there was anything I could do for mademoiselle."

"Oh, no thank you, Jeanne," said Fraley turning and smiling at the maid. "I have put all my things away."

"I could draw your bath," said the woman, "any time when mademoiselle is ready, and perhaps mademoiselle would like me to brush her hair. Mademoiselle has pretty hair."

"You are very kind, Jeanne, but I've never been waited upon. I've always done everything for myself, and I wouldn't know how to be taken care of. Only my mother ever did anything for me."

"One's mother is always best," said the maid unbending from her formal tone. "Is mademoiselle's mother far away?"

"She is in heaven!"

"Oh, that's too bad, mademoiselle!" apologized the maid sympathetically. "I beg your pardon, mademoiselle, I didn't know. But you're going to stop here in this house, now, and there'll be plenty of gay times to help you to forget."

"Oh, I don't want to forget, Jeanne; I love to think about my dear mother, but sometimes I feel just as if I had to cry."

"You poor little dear!" said the maid, now thoroughly won over. "Now, you just get a nice book and sit here and read, or get into bed if you like. I'll fix the pillows for you. That's what madam generally does. She most generally reads herself to sleep."

"I shall not need to read myself to sleep to-night,"

laughed the girl. "I'm sleepy already. That bed looks wonderful!"

"Well, then, I'll just draw the water for your bath," said the maid. "I know madam would be better pleased if I helped you and I'll get you some of madam's nice bath salts. They have such a pleasant odor, mademoiselle will like it I know."

"Call me Fraley, won't you, please?" said the girl. "It sounds more friendly."

"Very well, Miss Fraley," said the maid in a pleased tone. "Now, you undress and I'll have the water ready for you at once," and the persistent maid marched into the bathroom and prepared the bath.

Jeanne put the lovely rosy folds of the kimono about her shoulders and then departed, but when Fraley came out from her bath she was there at the door again.

"I just thought I'd come back and fix your hair for the night," she said. "It'll be a pleasure for me to handle such hair as yours. I used to work in a beauty parlor before I took a place as lady's maid, and they gave me all the fine ladies to do their hair. But now since everybody's bobbed there is little of that to be done any more. I was always sorry madam bobbed her hair. Of course she looks more distinguished this way, but she had such lovely hair, Miss Fraley, it was such a pity to do away with it. And she's so chic herself she could have got away with hair on her very well. You never bobbed yours, did you, Miss Fraley?"

"Do you mean cut it? No, mother liked it to grow. And then, I was living out west on a mountain, where I never saw other girls. I had only mother to please. But I wouldn't like my hair cut. God gave it to me and I'd like to keep it."

"That's what I always say, Miss Fraley, I say keep as near to nature as you can. Of course a bit of paint and powder now and then for pale people, but you, now, you don't need any. Your skin is like a baby's. You've got an odd name, Miss Fraley, is it a family name?"

"Yes, my mother's name was Alison Fraley."

"Why, that's odd now. There's an Alison Fraley lives on the drive. Is she related to you?"

"Oh, no, I don't suppose so. Mrs. Wentworth spoke of her on the train, but I've never heard of her. It is odd, isn't it, my mother's name?"

"She might be some kin, you can't tell. You'll have to ask her when you get to know her. She comes here a lot. Her mother is one of Mrs. Wentworth's crowd, and they entertain a great deal. You'll probably see a good deal of her. But she's not like you, one could see that at a glance. Of course she's handsome in her way, and very stylish, goes to all the extremes, and like that. But she hasn't got a good skin like yours, and her ways are very proud like. She'd not be conversing with a maid, kind like you are, Miss Fraley. She thinks she's above everybody. She'd be more like to throw her shoe at me if I spoke of anything but my work."

"Oh!" said Fraley distressed, "I am afraid I shan't like her."

"Oh, she'll not be like that to you, not if you are Mrs. Wentworth's friend. She dotes on Mrs. Wentworth. She went to Europe with her three months last summer. She's tall and dark, and a bit too bold looking to my thinking, but she's very popular. I can see you're going to be quite popular, too, Miss Fraley. You've got a way with you that makes people like you. Now Miss Alison, she is popular more because people are afraid she'll turn them down than because they like her."

"I'm sorry she's that way," said Fraley looking troubled. "I don't like to think anybody that has my mother's name is disagreeable. My mother was so dear!"

"I'll bet she was, Miss Fraley, or you wouldn't be what you are. I'll tell you frankly, there's not many girls to-day is as unspoiled and friendly as you are and that's a fact. Now, Miss Fraley, if you'll just step into bed I'll fix the pillows for you, and the light, and then you can read as long as you like. Can I get your book for you?"

"Oh, this is my book," said Fraley gathering the old cotton-covered Bible from the little bedside stand. "It was my mother's and I love it."

"It's not many young ladies nowadays reads the Bible," commented the maid, hovering about and patting the pillows, "I've never read it myself, but I've heard it has some very good things in it."

"Oh, it has, Jeanne! Sit down and let me read to you."

Fraley turned the pages and began to recite one of her favorite chapters.

The maid stood at the foot of the bed and listened curiously.

"That's beautiful, Miss Fraley," she said enthusiastically when the chapter was finished, "I never knew it was like that. If I had an education I might read it too, but somehow, when you read it, it sounds nice. I'd like to hear it again sometime, Miss Fraley, if you ever have time."

"Oh, I'll read to you every night, Jeanne, if you can come up here!" said Fraley eagerly. "I'd love to."

"I certainly appreciate that, Miss Fraley. I'll never forget your offer, but I know the madam when she gets herself going, will have your evenings all full. You'll be going out with her a lot."

"Oh, I don't think so, not much," said the girl, lying back on her pillow. "You know I'm here to work for her, don't you? I'm not here just visiting."

"I know she's taken you up, Miss Fraley, and that means you're just like a guest in the house, or a member of the family, and I've seen enough of this house to know she'll keep you going. But I'll be glad to hear you read, Miss Fraley, whenever you have the time. And now, would you like a glass of milk or something before you sleep?"

"No indeed," laughed Fraley, "I've already had more to eat to-day than I needed. Good-night, Jeanne, and don't forget to come to-morrow night."

"Thank you, Miss Fraley, for being so good to me. It's been a long time since I've seen a young lady I've been so drawn to as you, and I'll do anything I can for you, bless your little heart."

The maid withdrew and closed the door, and Fraley lay back on her pillows and watched the lights across from her windows and soon fell asleep.

17

THE maid brought a tray to Fraley's room next morning, and found her fully dressed sitting by the window
absorbed in watching the boats on the river and the
automobiles in the street.

"Here's your breakfast, Miss Fraley," explained Jeanne
setting down a dainty tray on the little stand, and drawing up a chair. "You could have had it earlier if I had
known you were up, but I was afraid to disturb you."

"Oh, you don't need to bring me anything, Jeanne.
Couldn't I go down? I've been waiting for Mrs. Wentworth to open her door. I did go downstairs once, but
there was nobody about and I concluded she had sat up
late and had overslept."

"She always sits up late in New York, Miss Fraley, but
she never rises before ten anyway. She takes her breakfast
in bed, and she doesn't have it till she rings for it. I
haven't heard a sound from her yet this morning, but I
thought I'd venture to see if you were awake, as you
went to bed pretty early last night."

"Oh," said Fraley, somewhat dismayed at a state of
things like this. On the mountain she had usually arisen

at dawn or a little after, and gone to bed with the birds.
"Well, then after this I'll come down and get my breakfast. That'll be less trouble for you, won't it? And I don't
need a thing but a glass of milk and a little bread or
something. Don't let anybody bother getting a breakfast
for me."

"It's no bother, Miss Fraley. The breakfast is always
cooked anyway, for the servants, and it's less trouble for
me to bring a tray up than for you to have the table set
in the dining room just for you."

So Fraley ate her delicious breakfast hungrily, and
presently Jeanne returned with a message.

"Madam says you're to go shopping with her this
morning and she'll be ready in half an hour."

Fraley had put on the little cotton frock of her
mother's make when she first got up, but when she stood
before the pier glass and surveyed herself, she realized
that it looked queer, here in this grand new home. She
did not understand it because it had always seemed nice
and appropriate enough, a whole, clean frock without
any ugly patches; but now, since she had travelled in a
Pullman, and watched the people in the diner, and more
than all since she had been with this lovely lady, she did
not like her own looks in this mountainmade frock of
faded cotton. So she had changed into the borrowed one
again. Now she was glad she had done so for her dear
Violet would not have liked her to go shopping in her
old dress, of course.

So she put on hat and coat and gloves and sat down
by the window to count her money. How much did
dresses cost? She seemed to have a lot of money left from
those Bibles, but one could never tell in this new world
to which she had come. There might be only enough
for a pair of shoes. The dear lady had said she must have
shoes.

But before her problem was solved there came the summons to start, and Fraley went down to find her lady arrayed in a smart street suit, with her face so startlingly fresh and lovely that she almost exclaimed over it.

But she seemed a distant lady, this variable new friend this morning. She was all business-like, giving orders for the day before she left, and somehow the girl did not like to speak intimately.

The car was at the door, a wonderful shining limousine, glittering and luxurious, with deep soft upholstery.

"Isn't this wonderful!" she said before she could stop herself as she sat down on the deep cushions and looked out of the clear glass at her side. "Why, it's like a little house!" The lady smiled:

"Do you like the car? It's a new one. It seems comfortable, doesn't it? Now, let's begin to talk about what you need. We want to get your wardrobe all in order before people find out that I'm home and begin to come, and I have so many engagements that I can't attend to anything else."

"I was thinking about it this morning," said Fraley, "I put on one of my old dresses and it looked kind of queer after I'd worn yours, so I guess perhaps I'd better buy a new dress to save this one if you think I've got money enough. The Bibles didn't cost as much as I expected, and I haven't spent any of the money my mother gave me, except for crackers and prunes and apples and cheese. How much do everyday dresses cost?"

"Oh, you needn't bother about that, child, I'll attend to all that. You'll need a lot of things besides an everyday dress if you're going to stay with me, and I'll just have them charged and then we'll take it out of your first month's salary. How is that?"

"Why, that is very kind—but—suppose something

happened to me and I couldn't do the work right, or I got sick and died. Then I wouldn't have paid for them."

"Well, I'd still have the dresses and things, wouldn't I?" smiled the lady. "And anyhow that's my affair. I say you've got to have the things if you stay with me, so I'll take the chance of your doing what I want you to do in payment."

"All right," said Fraley with a pleased sigh, "only I want to be honest. You see I don't know anything about what clothes cost, so I can't judge, but it seems to me my work won't be worth very much at first, anyway, though I mean to try very hard."

"You don't know how much of an asset you are, little Fraley," smiled Violet Wentworth, looking into the clear eyes, and noticing the sweet sincerity and purity that was an open vision to all who looked that way.

Fraley wondered what an asset was but she did not ask. She kept her eyes busy out of the window, for now they had come to the shopping district and the traffic was jammed.

"Why, it's just the way God takes us through hard things, isn't it?" she exclaimed suddenly, and then caught herself and flushed. She had not meant to think out loud that way any more, since she knew the lady was amused by it.

"I mean," she explained when she saw the look of question in her companion's eyes, "I mean the car, and the man who drives it. We don't have to worry about getting across that street, or be afraid we'll be run over, because the car carries us straight through, and the man who drives it is doing all the worrying."

"You certainly ought to have been a theologian," said the lady crossly. "Your mind is always running on things like that. But you mustn't call Burton 'the man who drives,' you must say, 'Chauffeur.' You'll have to remember that because it will mark you as utterly green if you don't. Burton! Stop here! Yes, the shoes! There's a place where you can park around on the side street. It's too crowded here for you to wait. We'll come around to the usual place."

The quiet elegance of the shoe shop overawed the child of the wilderness. She followed where she was led, and sat down as she was bidden. Violet Wentworth did all the rest.

"Shoes!" she ordered curtly, "for this young lady! She's not been used to high heels. Yes, sports shoes and street shoes, and don't make the heels too high even on the evening slippers! Make it an easy grade from the low flat school-shoe type, you know. Her foot has never been cramped."

Fraley sat and wondered and said very little.

Shoes and shoes they tried on her, now and again asking her if they were comfortable.

Bewildered, the girl had no idea how many or if any shoes had been bought until Mrs. Wentworth said:

"I think she had better wear this pair and send the old ones home with the order. You would like to wear the dark blue ones, wouldn't you, Fraley? They go so well with your dress. They are perfectly comfortable, aren't they? Yes, you may send the rest up, Mr. Kennard. We are going to a fitting and these are a nice height of heel for that, don't you think?"

Fraley did not even have to assent, for they hadn't noticed her at all, and so she found herself standing in new dark blue kid pumps, and wondering if those were really her feet, so trim and pretty and like other people's feet.

The next store they entered was a lingerie shop, and for half an hour Violet tossed over piles of silk trifles that passed for underwear, little French importations, with exquisite hand work expended upon them. Now and then she appealed to Fraley to know which one she liked best of two, and the girl supposed she was purchasing all these things for herself. It was not until they reached home that she discovered there were dozens of things being bought for her, but by that time she was a day wiser.

They next drove to an exclusive shop and the chauffeur was told to return in an hour and a half.

The place was quiet and elegant, and Fraley who was already worn with the noise and confusion of the city sank into a chair gladly to wait. She was thinking how nice it would be to get back to the house and read some of those beautiful books, curled up in a big chair with the river outside of her window and the stillness of the house surrounding her. The shop did not look very interesting.

Violet introduced her to a large imposing woman called Madam who gave her a chair and called her "my dear," and then stood off, studying her. The shop seemed a stupid place and Fraley was not deeply interested in it. She wondered why they were there till Violet said in a low tone:

"This is the gown shop. We are going to see some models." Madam went away back across the gray-velveted aisle with mirrors on each side, and presently she returned and talked with her customer about the weather and where she had been during the winter.

Then there was a little stir down the gray-velvet aisle and a girl no larger than Fraley, with a startlingly red mouth and hard black eyes, came sauntering toward them in a daring red and black outfit.

The mountain girl watched her come, and turned away. She did not like the bold black eyes and the red mouth.

"It's hardly her type," said Violet scanning the model carefully. "Very clever cut, of course, but I scarcely think I'd care for it."

"Well, perhaps," said Madam, "but it's a useful little frock for in between you know."

Another young thing had entered the gray aisle and was lingering for a signal to come on. Madam gave it, and there arrived a girl in green. She had deep red hair and brown eyes, and Fraley liked her better, but she too had that terrible red mouth that looked like a wound.

"That's not bad," said Violet. "I'm not sure but it would do. Of course she's a different coloring, but green and gold are lovely. You might have that laid aside and we'll let her try it on."

The procession seemed endless and amounted to little or nothing so far as a fashion show was concerned, to the girl from the mountain. She continued to look at the faces of the models, and to regret their red, red mouths. How did all these girls of New York get such red lips? She had noticed it just the least bit in her beloved Violet's lips, too, this morning. It must be something in the climate or the water. Perhaps her own would grow that way after a time, but she did not like it.

When a number of street dresses had been selected for further consideration, and several afternoon costumes added to their number, the various models returned, garbed now in evening wear, the first in an evening cloak of gold cloth trimmed with ermine, which when removed revealed an elaborate affair of turquoise malines cut in myriads of points, and standing out like blue spray about the frail ankles of the slim thing that wore it, but scarcely draping the upper part of her anatomy at all. It was held in place by a garland of silver roses over one shoulder.

"That! Now, that would go with her eyes," said Violet, interested. "Don't you like that, Fraley dear?"

Fraley responded instantly to the "dear," and turned her smile toward the matter in hand.

"It's a pretty color," she said, "but there isn't any top to it. It looks as if those roses were going to break and let it all down."

The models looked at one another and grinned contemptuously. The Madam said: "Oh, my dear!" and laughed affectedly, then turning to Violet Wentworth she said, "She's witty, isn't she? A clever remark!"

Fraley could see that her Violet was vexed with her, and she felt mortified, though she did not know exactly what she had done.

"Do you wear a coat over it?" she asked in a low voice, but Violet did not answer.

"I think," she said crossly, "that it's getting late and we will not bother with evening dresses this morning. We'll just let her try on the green frock, and possibly that little brown model."

Then Madam rose suavely to the occasion. A customer like this was not to be lost if anything could keep her.

"I think," said she, "if you will just have patience for one more, I would like to try something. There is a little model,—it has just occurred to me, and pardon me, but perhaps the young lady is right. The ingénue. That is the type. I have a lovely thing here in white velvet I would just like you to see—!"

There was not a model in that establishment that had the make up for wearing that white velvet, but Madame chose her most demure maiden, and bade her wash off the rouge, and hurry. By all means hurry.

In the end Violet bought the white velvet, of course. Fraley, robed in it, looked like a saint from some old castle retreat. Its draperies fell from the shoulders and came around to tie in front in long sash-like ends, clasped with a knot of yellow gold.

"There is jewelry to go with this," and Madam slung a rope of gold about the girl's neck, clasped bracelets on her arms, and brought forth earrings.

Fraley shrank back when she saw what Madam was intending to do to her, and put her hands to her ears.

"Please no," she said, and looked pleadingly toward her lady.

"She is right," said Violet, "they do not belong to the type. A saint wouldn't wear long dangling things in her ears. And you may keep the chain and armlets too. I think pearls would be better. These are too noisy. She needs something quieter. The clasp is good perhaps. I'll take the dress."

Fraley looked at herself in the mirrors dubiously. She was not sure of herself. But it was better than some. The draperies covered her arms partially at least, and the neck was modest in its cut, so she said nothing.

A blue taffeta was next forthcoming, with tiny sweetheart rosebuds on long wisps of silver cord hanging from a rosette of rosebuds at the little round waist, a full long skirt of bound scallops drawn into the round waist gave it a childish charm. Fraley could see that her lady liked it, so when asked if she liked it she said:

"All but the arms. I'd like some sleeves!"

The Madam laughed.

"It's an evening dress you know, Fraley," said Violet, "everybody wears them that way. You mustn't be a silly!"

"Wait!" said Madam seeing another sale in the offing. "I've an idea. Clotilde, go bring that lace bertha, the very thing. It's on that new model that just came in."

Clotilde brought the lace, fine as a cobweb, and the Madam flung it over Fraley's head, and adjusted it.

"The very thing!" she cried. "She's a clever girl. She knows what she needs to bring out her best style."

The lace hung in soft cobwebby folds from the round neck, deep as the waist line in the back, a little shorter in front, but covering the sweet round arms to the elbow. Violet was vexed with her charge but she could not but admit that the little mountain girl dressed thus looked very sweet and modest, and that the lace brought out the charm by which she had been attracted at the first.

So they bought the blue taffeta.

"But I can't work in any of those," said Fraley when at last they left the place.

"No, of course not, you silly! Did you think we were buying working clothes? We'll get some plain tailored things, and some sports clothes for that. We're going to lunch now, but after lunch we'll go to some of the big department stores and look around. There are several more of these little exclusive shops, too, where you can pick up really original clothes quite reasonably if you know how to look for them. I want to look around and send some more things home for you to try on. There's nothing like trying a garment in the environment in which it is to be worn to find out its defects and its good points. Of course if I find something better than these I can return them. But I'm sure the white velvet is good, and the blue taffeta is darling! We must keep that in any event."

Fraley got back into the car feeling far more worn than from a day of her pilgrimage. Such a lot of work just to get something to put on! There seemed to be a great many pretty things in the shop windows they passed. Why wouldn't any of them do? But she said nothing more. She saw that Violet was happy in this thing that she was doing.

After a frugal but costly lunch of salads and ices they went on their way again hunting more clothes.

"I don't see when I can possibly use all these," said Fraley wearily when at last they were in the car on their way back home, "I can't ever wear out so many."

"You don't wear them out, child," said Violet complacently, "you give them away when you are tired of them—or sell them. Many people sell them, but it's a lot of bother, and you have to give a maid things anyway or she gets dissatisfied."

Safe in her quiet room that night, with Violet entertaining callers downstairs, Fraley pondered on the strange ways of this new world into which she had come.

18

THE days that followed were full of shopping, and while she gradually grew more intelligent in the matter of choosing garments suitable for the occasions in which she was supposed to wear them, and acquired a certain simplicity in taste that was surprising, considering the contrast in her present circumstances from those that had surrounded her in her childhood, still Fraley was more or less bored with it all. She wanted to be doing so many other things in this wonderful city.

There was the river with its endless procession of boats going back and forth. She wanted to ride on all those boats. She wanted to climb the palisades and find out how far she could see from the top. She wanted to tramp the length of the river and then cross over and tramp back. Sometimes she wanted to get out and away from all the strange, cramping, hindering clutter of sights and sounds into her own native wilderness and beauty.

Then there were the great buildings that she gradually learned were of historic interest. She knew very little of world history or even of the history of her own country, and when she once discovered books of history she read with eager appetite. The local landmarks and great buildings that commemorated some discovery or victory or happening took on new interest, and seemed to stand out from their neighbors on the street almost as if they had been painted a different noble color.

But gradually the two great closets connected with her lovely room began to be filled with charming clothes, for morning and afternoon and evening, for hot, for cold, and for medium weather, and she began to hope that the days of toil in the shops were almost over.

To say she had not enjoyed it would be wrong, because she loved beauty, but to get it entirely out of its relation to other things in life wearied her. After the first few days, when she entered a shop, her quick eyes would rove about and search out one or two distinguished garments or articles from all the other commonplace ones, and Violet soon learned that she could trust her selection almost every time. Simplicity of line and color were her keynote, and she went unerringly to the few things in each shop that bore those distinctions.

So the first month passed, the month of April, and Fraley felt that she had worked hard for her first month's salary, even though she had done little else for her lady but select the clothes she felt were so necessary for the job. Not until she was earning some real money did she intend to write the letter she had promised to her friend—the raven of the wilderness as he had called himself. She wanted to have something real to tell him about how she was getting on. So far she had done nothing but get ready to live. As soon as the shopping tours were over she meant to begin to look around and get acquainted with New York.

But lo! when the shopping was completed, Violet began to talk of going away for the summer. Mountains, or seashore, or a water trip. She couldn't decide which to take.

"Why, you have just got home," said Fraley in dismay. "It is so lovely here. We can take our books and go out there in the park and sit on a bench and read when the hot weather comes."

Violet smiled at her simplicity.

"Nobody stays in the city in the summer, unless they are absolutely tied," she told her.

"But why?"

"It is very hot here! All the best houses are closed, and people go away to get rested from the winter and enjoy themselves."

It was of no use to talk. Going was the order of the day, so Fraley submitted, marveling over the change in her circumstances since she had started from the old cabin through her bedroom window, with only her father's coat and neckerchief for outfit, and the old gray bag containing the Bible for baggage.

Bags and suitcases and hatboxes! There seemed no end to the number that had to be packed. All those pretty dresses shut away in wardrobe trunks! She had no faith that she would ever have use for more than one or two.

And so began a round of gaiety in strange hotels, utterly foreign to the child whose life had hitherto been so quiet and isolated.

There were many people whom Violet Wentworth knew at these hotels where they stopped for a week, sometimes two or three weeks, before moving on else-where. The days passed in a round of sea bathing, automobile riding, teas, bazaars, and the like. Fraley learned to play tennis and golf, and, being the free little athlete that she was, it did not take her long to become fairly proficient in both. Her arms were strong and sinewy, her eye was true, her brain was keen, and she was as lithe as a young sapling. Presently she began to be in demand to play these games because she could play well and she really enjoyed it hugely.

Violet insisted on teaching her to dance, but she balked at the first dance she attended.

"It would be lovely if I could do it alone," she said, "but I don't like strange men, or any men, getting so familiar. My mother taught me—"

"There!" said Violet, "it's time you learned that your mother was so far out of the world for so long that she was no guide for what you should do now. You have a right to choose your own life."

Fraley was silent a moment, then she said:

"Then I do choose. And I choose not to dance. I do not want any man to put his arm around me the way they do. I watched you dancing last night and I didn't like the way your partner touched you and looked at you. You are too dear and lovely. You—! He—! He reminded me of a bad man I knew out on the mountains!"

"Stop!" said Violet flushing angrily. "You are getting impudent. You should dance of course. But I don't want to hurry you into things you don't understand. You must get over labeling everything either good or bad. That's ridiculous! You just watch, this summer, and by fall you'll feel differently about it. Come, let's go and dress for dinner."

So the days went by, and the evenings. Fraley in blue taffeta with sweetheart roses, or in white velvet with gold clasps and pearls, or in some other richly simple costume would hover on the outer edge of the things her patroness enjoyed and watch sorrowfully. But sometimes she would wander off by herself for a while and watch the sea in the darkness.

The work she was supposed to be doing for Mrs.

Wentworth seemed so indefinite and desultory that it often troubled her. It seemed to her that she was not giving enough service for all she was receiving. Of course there were always a few letters to be answered every day, and she had learned to answer them in a manner apparently quite satisfactory to her employer; at least she never found fault with her, beyond correcting a few trifling mistakes. She seemed entirely content with this slight service, and a few small errands occasionally. Her main desire seemed to be to have Fraley on call at any hour of the day or night. A less humble girl would have found out before many weeks had passed that Violet Wentworth wanted her to show her off, that she looked upon her as a sort of possession wherewith to wield her social scepter. But Fraley was never thinking of herself. It never entered her head that she was wanted for anything except the work that she could do, and she was most grateful always.

But one night she decided the time had come to write to her friend of the desert, the "Raven," as she still called him.

In her rosy tulle she sat down to the pleasant task, and she made a lovely picture indeed, with a smile on her lips and her eyes starry with memory.

It was a charming letter she wrote, frank and true, opening her heart concerning her many perplexities in the new life which she could not tell to anyone else. The writing of it gave her great content. But, she forgot to put in her New York address and they were leaving for the mountains the next day. She had not even thought to write on hotel paper to give a clue to her whereabouts. This letter did not seem to her like other letters. It was almost like sending out a little prayer. She scarcely expected an answer.

The fall was coming on and the mountains were

touched with crimson and gold, the woodbine on the rocks like flaming embroidery.

The hotel was swarming with people. Many of Mrs. Wentworth's friends were there.

There was one tall gentleman at the next table in the dining room who troubled her greatly because he was constantly reminding her of someone, yet she could not think who it was. He had a great head of wavy white hair, and keen, blue, rather unhappy eyes. His mouth was drawn down at the corners as if he wanted everybody to get out of his way and Fraley always got out of it if she possibly could.

He had a wife who never came down to breakfast, but neither did a lot of the other women there. This woman was wrinkled and painted and wore her hair marcelled so smoothly that it looked as if the waves were painted on a piece of white satin and fitted smoothly over her head. They had a grandson about fourteen who was always at odds with his grandfather and grandmother, particularly his grandfather.

One day Fraley found this boy out at the golf links, with no one to play with and she scraped an acquaintance with him and played nine holes. They got along very well together, and walked back to the hotel quite chummily. Just as they reached the steps the boy told her his name was James MacPherson, and he was being sent off to school the next day, and he didn't want to go.

"Why, isn't that funny!" said Fraley, "So is my name MacPherson. Perhaps we are distant relatives somewhere back, who knows?"

"No such luck," said the boy, "Gee, I wish I had a relative like you. You're all right!"

She played tennis with him that afternoon, and they went down to the game room in the evening and played pingpong in the hotel in the evening. He was a nice boy.

She felt sorry for him. He said his father and mother were in Europe for a year, and his sister was in California, and he hated boarding school. He said he'd like to stay at home, but "Gramp had a grouch on and couldn't see it." Fraley got up the next morning early and played nine more holes of golf with him before he had to go, and then felt forlorn and lonely as she saw him grinning good-by to her as he drove off in the hotel bus down the mountain to the station.

After that she used to watch the grandfather and grandmother every day just because they belonged to the boy. She was sorry for them, they looked so discontented.

Looking at them and knowing they bore the same name, made her think of her own father's father, and wonder if he was living.

She resolved to hunt him up as soon as she got back to New York, and not delay any longer. No matter who he was or in what circumstances, she ought to look him up. Whether she revealed her identity or not would depend on conditions, but she must find him and know what sort of person he was. Her mother evidently had wished that.

That very evening when they both came up to go to bed Violet called her into her room and talked with her awhile. She asked her more about her own home, and who her father and mother had been, and Fraley, naturally reticent, and anxious to keep the secrets of her family, told very little. Her mother and father had married against the wishes of their parents and gone west and lost sight of their respective families. That was all. She acknowledged that she knew nothing of her relatives' financial standing, though she supposed they would be comfortably off. Her mother had always spoken of having a good home, and she had spoken as if the

MacPhersons were rather proud people. That was all she knew.

Violet Wentworth narrowed her eyes as she watched Fraley under their lashes.

"Fraley," she said, "if you should find out that any of these relatives are well off and want you, would you wish to leave me and go to them?"

"I would not want to leave you," said Fraley with a wistful look, "but I could not tell what I ought to do until I knew all about it. Their being well off would not make any difference. I would go to them sooner if they were poor for they might need me to help them some way."

"You're a dear child," said Violet Wentworth with a sudden unusual gust of emotion, and kissed her for the second time.

"Now, run off to bed, or you'll lose your complexion and be just as bad as I am."

It was a great day for Fraley when they got back to New York. She settled all her beautiful fineries in the two great closets, fineries that she had grown accustomed to, now, and took for granted as she did her golden hair, and the slimness of her ankles. That slimness was the envy of all the women in the hotel, though Fraley didn't even know it.

Two days after they got home, she happened to overhear Violet answering a call on the telephone.

"Oh, is that you, Alison? I thought you weren't coming back till next week. I'm so glad you are here. Listen, Alison, I've got a young girl staying with me this winter—brought her back from my western trip. She's a girl I'm very fond of indeed and I want to show her a good time. I'm depending on you to take her to the country club and introduce her to all our young friends, and I wish you'd run over and take tea with us this afternoon informally. I want you two to know each other at once. She's charming. I'm sure you will like her."

Fraley stood still by the window in her own room and heard the receiver click as it was hung up. So, that was the way that Violet was introducing her. A friend from the west who was staying there! Not a social secretary at all! There was something disturbing in the knowledge, though Fraley could not just tell why. It did not seem wholly honest to her truth-loving soul.

And so Alison Fraley was coming to see her!

She shrank from meeting this other girl who bore her mother's dear name. Perhaps it was what Jeanne had said that had prejudiced her, and that was not right of course. So she tried to put such thoughts out of her mind, and sitting down she wrote to Seagrave the letter she had promised to write as soon as she was back in New York.

It was only a few sentences, but even that contact of the mind with the fine, true spirit who had been so wonderful to her on her journey, seemed to give her new courage. She wrote:

> *Dear Raven:*
> *We are at home at last and I am glad. I am sending you the address as I promised. I hope you will write me about the services in the log schoolhouse. I have never forgotten about that meeting.*
> *Your friend,*
>
> *Fraley MacPherson.*

With the letter in her hand she was starting out to mail it as Violet came out of her room.

"Where are you going, child? Not away I hope. I have a friend coming in to have tea with us in a few minutes, and I want you to meet her. She's the natural friend for you at this stage of the game and will do you a lot of good. Is that one of my letters?" and Violet took the letter out of Fraley's unresisting hand.

There it was, George Rivington Seagrave! There simply couldn't be two of that name, not with Rivington in it!

"What are you doing writing to Rivie Seagrave?" Violet asked in wide astonishment, searching Fraley's face suspiciously. "Wherever in the world did you meet him?"

"Out on the prairie somewhere, under a tree. I told you about it on the train. He's the man I sent the Bible to."

"Yes, you said his name was Seagrave, I remember, but you didn't say it was Rivington. How could that possibly be? I couldn't think of any man less likely to want a Bible than Rivington Seagrave, yet you said, didn't you, that he was preaching or something like that. It certainly must have been a practical joke of some kind. Of course, it can't be Riv. He would no more know how to preach than I would."

"He said he didn't know how," said Fraley gravely. "He was doing it for some poor fellow that was taken to the hospital just before train time. The other man was afraid he would lose his job if somebody didn't hold it down for him."

"Well, that sounds more like him. He's always been kind hearted, but dear me! Riv Seagrave. That's rich!"

Something in Fraley's heart rose in defense.

"He had a wonderful meeting," she said, "I went to it. He read the Bible, and he sang like the heavenly choirs."

"Yes, I'll admit he can sing like an angel, but Riv Seagrave reading the Bible! That's too good a joke!"

Fraley froze.

"He did not make a joke out of it," she said quietly, and in her voice was a gentle rebuke.

"Well, that may be so," said Violet, "but he certainly must have met with a change of heart, then."

"I think he has," Fraley said quietly.

"Well, I advise you to lay off that young man, Fraley," said Violet good naturedly as she handed back the letter. "You see he's almost as good as engaged to Alison Fraley, and I want you two to be friends. I wouldn't mention him to her if I were you."

Fraley went quietly on down the stairs, out the door and down to the corner where she mailed her letter, but she no longer smiled.

She dropped her letter in the post office box at the corner and turned to go back to the house, when suddenly it came to her that she ought not to have mailed that letter. Her raven was engaged to another girl, and she had no right to be writing him letters, even such simple friendly letters as this. There was no longer need for her to write him, because he had a Bible and that would give him all the light he needed for his work. She had been crazy to think she needed to write him any more. He had probably forgotten all about her anyway by this time.

Of course, she had promised to let him know where she was, but—well the letter was gone now, unless she stayed out there and asked the postman to give it back to her, which he wouldn't likely do.

Well, never mind, it could do no harm, and if he ever came back to New York or if he wrote her a nice little note thanking her for anything, she would let him understand that she knew it was all in friendliness. She would simply drop the thought of him out of her heart. But oh, how was she going to do it? Her one friend! And that kiss! What was she going to do with the memory of that kiss? She could not bury it as if it were dead. She could not extract it as if it were a thorn. It was there on her brow forever, and it was hers, rightfully or no, it was hers and did not belong to another.

Then she remembered that he had called her an angel. That was it! That made it all right on his part to have kissed her. He had not looked upon her as a young girl, not as he would have thought of the girl to whom he was engaged, but as a dear little girl, a sort of angel. Angels were holy beings and he had simply given her a high tribute with that kiss as if she were someone set above himself. He was a raven and she was an angel, and there was nothing meant by that kiss but a kind of homage.

So she reasoned it over and over, trying to make the situation assume a different aspect in her mind.

She walked up and down the block several times trying to get adjusted so that that kiss would not be a thorn in her heart. Trying to tell herself that she had never taken it to have any special meaning other than tenderness for a lost child.

When she went back to the house there was a sad little smile on her face, and she held her head up proudly.

Back in her room she tried to face the immediate present.

"She is coming!" she told herself, "the girl he loves! I must go down and meet her pretty soon. I must not think of that kiss as anything that ever belonged to me."

Then Jeanne tapped at the door.

"Miss Fraley, Madam would like you to come down. Tea is served in the library and Miss Alison Fraley is there."

Fraley smoothed her hair, dashed cold water in her face, dabbed it with a soft towel, and went downstairs with a look of peace upon her brow.

19

ALISON Fraley was lounging in a corner of a couch, her long slim legs crossed and stretched out to their fullest extent. She was smoking a cigarette.

Fraley had of course not been away all summer in fashionable hotels and restaurants without knowing that women nowadays smoked, but she had a strange aversion to it which, so far, Violet Wentworth had been unable to break down, though Violet herself had never yet smoked in the presence of the mountain girl.

Fraley came into the room, with an air of sweet aloofness. Her fine patrician chin was lifted just the least bit but not haughtily, her lips made a firm little line of courage and in her eyes was a look that puzzled the two women who awaited her.

Fraley had a lack of self-consciousness in the presence of strangers that constantly astonished her benefactress. Violet called it poise, though one usually thinks of poise as a thing that is acquired, not inherited. If this girl had acquired her poise she had got it from her mountain distances, and her close touch with holy things. The world troubled her, but it did not embarrass her.

She came forward quite easily and acknowledged the introduction, but there was a reservation in her attitude, a lack of response—save by a distant little smile—when Violet said she hoped these two girls would be friends. It was as if she held her friendship in abeyance until she should find out whether the other girl were such as she could take into the innermost citadel of her heart.

The other girl showed her lack of poise by her rudeness. She did not rise from her slouching attitude, nor show any courtesy of tone as she spoke, and she puffed a stream of smoke into the air even before she nodded.

"Well, it seems we're booked to have a crush on each other," she flung out almost insolently, "I can't imagine either of us picking out the other for a pal, but Vi seems to think we should, so I suppose we shall. How about Thursday morning? We'll go to the country club and have some golf. Vi says you play."

"Thank you," said Fraley simply and tried to smile.

She was studying this other girl, with her long slim legs slung out before her, the cigarette drooping from her listless fingers, with her sullen discontented eyes. She was wondering how a girl like this came to be a friend of the breezy, healthy, vivid man of the wilderness. She saw him now in memory as he stood in the dim shadows of the old log schoolhouse reading from her mother's cotton-covered Bible, the candle light flickering on his earnest face and putting glints into the crispness of the wave of hair over his forehead. She heard his voice again, reading the Bible, groping his way to the truth as if he meant it, and she could not think of this girl as having been present, or entering into the spirit of the gathering.

Violet was busying herself with the tea things, making sharp, clinking little sounds with the spoons as she laid them down in the egg-shell saucers. Fraley could see that she was watching her furtively, and presently she spoke, but it was to the other girl she directed her conversation.

"What do you hear from Riv?" she asked casually. But suddenly Fraley understood why she had asked the question. Riv was the strange name she had called Mr. Seagrave. That was what she must call him now, *Mr.* Seagrave. Even "raven" that he had asked her to use would be too intimate, now that she knew he was to marry someone else. Of course she had never expected him to marry *her*. She had not thought anything at all about it except that he was her friend, and as long as he had a perfect right to be that nothing more had occurred to her. But now that she knew he belonged to another, she felt that she had no right to a special friendship like that with him. There was an inborn fineness in her soul which her mother had, perhaps almost unconsciously, fostered.

It occurred to Fraley suddenly as she tried not to start at Violet's question, that perhaps Mr. Seagrave had written to this other girl all about finding her in the desert in a tree, and a wave of color swept up softly into her cheeks as she turned her grave eyes to hear the answer to Violet's question.

"Riv? Oh, I'm off him for life," said the slow insolent voice, as the slim arm went lazily out to accept the cup of tea her hostess was passing her. "He's off on a trip somewhere. I haven't heard a word from him all summer. He got one of his stubborn fits, insisted he had to go somewhere else when Gwen had a house party at the shore and particularly wanted him, and he hasn't turned up since. But he'll come soon now I suppose. He's always on deck when things begin. He'll be back in time for the tournaments. He never misses those. I suppose he thinks he's been giving me a much needed lesson, staying away all summer without a word, but I've been having the time of my life with Dicky Whitehead. You know he's just got a divorce and he's like a bird let loose."

Something fiery glowed in Fraley's eyes, but she busied her gaze with the little cakes on her plate, and gave the two women who were watching her no satisfaction. She wondered if Violet had said anything to her guest about the letter before she came down, but she maintained a discreet silence, and got over the hard place.

Alison Fraley presently turned to her and began to talk golf and tennis, putting Fraley through a catechism to see if she knew anything at all. Finding her quite intelligent, she decided she would make it a point to be at the golf links on Thursday.

The conversation touched on books. Alison wanted to borrow a new book that Violet had just bought.

"That is, when you both have read it of course," she added with unusual politeness.

"Oh, you can have it now," said Violet ringing for the maid, "I finished it last night, read till half past two. Fraley would not care for it."

"Fraley?" said the other girl with a sudden startled survey of the mountain girl, and a sharp look toward her hostess, "Is that your name?"

Fraley nodded.

"Where on earth did you get that name? It's mine, you know."

"Yes," said Fraley, "I know. Mine is a family name." She felt oddly averse to telling this girl that the whole name she bore had belonged to her mother.

"It would be odd, wouldn't it, if you and I should turn out to be relatives," said the other girl, again with that startled look in her bold eyes, and another swift survey of Fraley, from correct shoe tip to beautifully arranged coiffure. Well, if it should be that way of course she was nothing to be ashamed of. But, how odd!

"Did you get us here just to spring this on us, Vi?" asked Alison.

"Well, why not?" answered Violet enigmatically, but did not seem disposed to talk further about it. "When did you say your people are returning?" she asked, as if weary of the other subject.

"Dad is crossing this week, but mother is waiting to come till Aunt Greta is ready. It may be a fortnight yet. Aunt Greta is afraid of the September storms, and made such a fuss mother had to give in."

Violet's eyes narrowed.

"Bring your father over some evening when he gets back. We'll have a little bridge. But you'll have to get somebody else to make a fourth. Fraley won't learn. Perhaps Rivington will be back by that time."

"Perhaps—" said the girl yawning indifferently, "or I'll bring Dicky. He is simply great at bridge you know. But why don't you play?" she asked turning suddenly to Fraley.

"It bores her," said Violet sharply answering for the girl.

Alison took out a little gold case and handed it over to the other girl.

"Have a smoke with me," she said watching her narrowly.

Fraley drew back. She felt as if she were being put through a series of tests.

"Thank you, no," she said summoning a withdrawing smile.

But the other girl still held out the gold case.

"Oh, cut it," she said, "this is as good a time as any to begin if you don't like it. You'll soon get over that. You know you'll never get anywhere if you don't smoke or play bridge."

Fraley turned wide, amused eyes upon her.

"That depends on where you want to get," she said.

"What's the matter, does your mother object?" asked Alison with scorn in her voice, "you know that doesn't cut any ice in the world to-day."

"My mother," said Fraley with a slight lift of her lovely head, "is in heaven," and there was a look of sudden tears suppressed in the shining eyes with which she looked straight at the other girl.

It may be that Alison was embarrassed, but if she was it took the form of rudeness again:

"That must be comfortable," she said with a half sneer. "It must leave you pretty free! But of course," she added as she saw a dangerous look in the stranger's eyes, "if you don't feel that way it's rather rotten."

"I don't feel that way," said Fraley briefly, struggling to hide the desire to rush from the room and cry.

"She doesn't care for me, Vi," said Alison amusedly, turning to the older woman, "I haven't got on at all, and here I have been doing my best to be amusing."

"You're all right," said the lady, pouring another cup of tea for herself, "you don't understand each other yet. You have to find the keynote first before you can play harmoniously you know. Fraley's a dear if you just know how to take her, and when to let her have her own way."

Fraley twinkled into an appreciative smile. If Violet was pleased, and cared enough to defend her, what did it matter what this other girl said or thought?

But though the atmosphere was not quite so electrically charged after that, and the talk went on for perhaps a half hour more before the visitor took her languid leave, Fraley said very little. She could not get away from her own thoughts enough to think of something to say in this strange new environment. Hitherto this kind of thing had only revolved in a wide circle about the place where she was, but now she had been pushed intimately into it and she felt like a fish out of water.

When Alison left, Violet went to lie down for a little while and Fraley put on her hat and went out. She wanted to be in the great out-of-doors, and get the cobwebs swept out of her brain, and the tired feeling out of her heart. Nothing else could do it but the open, even though it was but a city street.

She longed for the great wide spaces of the west, for her mountain and its distant vision, for the sense of being near to God's sky. Even the river and the palisades seemed too small and near to-day.

The wind was blowing wildly as it sometimes does on Riverside Drive, and when she came to the corner where she usually turned off to go across to the little park where she loved to sit and watch the boats, she had to stop and bend forward to keep her footing. The wind swept down the side street, and almost took her with it across the street. As she lifted her head to go forward again something dark and soft swept by her face and out into the street.

In an instant she saw that it was a man's soft hat, and that it was bound across the street and down toward the river as fast as wind could carry it.

Ignoring the oncoming cars, she darted across the street after it, threading her way between traffic, almost putting her hand upon the hat only to have the wind snatch it once more and hurl it a little farther down the bank. Nimbly she darted after it again, though it evaded her several times, till in a sudden lull she pounced upon it and held it tight.

When she rose and turned around to see where it belonged she saw a tall hatless figure standing above her on the pavement, his white hair blowing wildly in the wind, his glasses dancing at the end of a long black ribbon, and his long arm and gloved hand that held a correct walking stick, waving dignifiedly at her. There was something strangely familiar about the man, but she did not stop to identify it then. She hurried up the steep bank, all out of breath from her chase, her cheeks rosy with the exercise, and her eyes bright at her success in getting the hat. She was smiling like a child when she handed it to him, and then she saw that he had put his hand in his pocket and was bringing out some money. Her laugh rang out happily as she ignored his out-stretched hand.

"I just loved getting it," she said gaily, and at her cultured voice he perceived his mistake and stared.

"I beg your pardon," he said hurrying the money back into his pocket and putting on his glasses. "I thought—" and then he perceived that he did not want to tell her what he thought. "You are very kind I'm sure," he blustered. "Not many young girls to-day would want to take the trouble to run after a passing hat. Why—why— haven't I seen you somewhere, my child? Your face looks familiar. Perhaps I ought to have known you at first, but my eyes are not so good as they were. You live somewhere along here? Perhaps I have seen you passing."

"You are Mr. MacPherson," laughed Fraley, "you saw me up at the mountain house. I used to play tennis and golf with your grandson."

"Oh, you don't say so! That must be it then. I'm sure I am deeply grateful to you. You are a nice girl. I wish there were more like you—"

Fraley laughingly protested that it was nothing and hurried away down the path to the river, leaving the old man looking after her, half perplexed lest he ought to have given her something after all. She looked such a child in the little trim knit suit she had donned before going out for her walk, and she ran so lightly down the steep incline as if she had wings on her feet. He stood for sometime looking after her, and then turned sighing away, wondering what it was in the past that stirred his memory when he looked at her. Something sweet and painful that was gone.

That night at dinner Fraley's face was bright and peaceful. She had walked off her depression, and there was peace in her eyes and soul; she could smile.

Violet watched her in admiration, for she had seen the struggle the girl had gone through while the visitor put her through her paces, and she knew she had been deeply stirred. There was something in this sweet young soul that others surely did not have, to be able to come out of it sunny and strong and wholesome.

"Well, how did you like your cousin?" asked Violet at length when the main course had been served and the butler had withdrawn for a few minutes and left them alone.

Fraley looked up with startled eyes. Their deep blue seemed almost to change to black as she looked. She went white about her lips.

"My cousin!" she exclaimed, "oh, what do you mean? Do you know something about my people that I do not know?"

"Well, I haven't quite proved it yet," admitted Violet, "but I'm rather reasonably sure."

"Did she—? Have you asked her? Did she know that I—?"

"No, she knows nothing about it yet," said Violet crossly. She was vexed that this child of the wilds was not apparently pleased at her prospect of a high connection. "You heard all she knows. I've merely put the idea to working in her mind. She's clever and she'll probably work it out after a while, and question you. You didn't think I would give you away to her without letting you know first, did you?"

"No," said the girl slowly, "I hoped you wouldn't. I trusted—that you wouldn't. Please don't say anything more to her—if you can help it."

"Well, I can help it of course if I think it is wise. But why on earth don't you want her to know? It puts you on a level with her. It gives you social standing, don't you see?"

"No," said Fraley, "I'm not sure I want that. I am not sure I want her ever to know. If I had been I would have hunted up my people right away. You see, I am—myself, and she is—herself—"

"Obviously," said Violet dryly.

Fraley smiled wanly.

"I know that sounds silly," she admitted, "but you don't understand."

"I understand perfectly," said the woman. "You don't care a little bit about social position, or wealth or anything in this world. But that is silly, and you've got to get over it. You have a right to take your own place in the world."

"I'm not sure that I have any place in the world," said the girl thoughtfully. "If I have it is not dependent on other people. God puts people up or down, where He wants them. But that isn't what I'm thinking about at all."

"No, of course not!" interrupted Violet a trifle bitterly.

"Please," said Fraley, "you don't understand. My mother went away and married my father, and I'm not sure how they feel toward her, if they even remember her at all. I don't want anybody to think that my mother's child has come back to be a burden on any-body!"

"Fiddlesticks and nonsense!" said Violet crossly. "There is no talk of that. You are here, looking after yourself, aren't you? You are not asking to be a burden on anybody. You are supporting yourself."

"You mean, you are supporting me," said Fraley, looking at the woman with honest eyes. "I don't know why you do it this way. I know I'm doing nothing in payment for a home like this."

"You're doing more than you know," was the crab-bed response. "Now, let's talk about something else. Have you got that list addressed that I gave you? I want those invitations to go out to-morrow afternoon with-out fail or I shall have to change the date. It is not correct to send invitations any later."

"They are all ready. I stamped them just after lunch," said Fraley happily.

"And yet you say that you don't do anything for me!" snapped the woman. "I never had my invitations done so quickly and so entirely without mistakes before, not even when I had a trained secretary!"

The girl smiled her shy pleasure.

After the dessert had been brought in and they were alone once more the girl looked up.

"I would like you to tell me please what makes you think that girl may be my cousin."

Violet eyed her for a moment speculatively and then answered:

"Because I went and hunted up the addresses you gave me when we first got here, and found that the people had moved. I had them traced by a detective, and found that the Mr. Robert Fraley who used to live downtown at the address your mother gave you was the father of Alison Fraley who lives on the drive."

"But isn't he a very rich man?" asked the girl after a moment's thoughtful wonder.

"Yes. He's counted one of the very rich men of the city now."

"But he used to be poor. That is, he was just a clerk somewhere."

"Well, he didn't stay a clerk," said Violet. "Sometimes they don't. He probably learned to play the market. Most people up here do."

"What's that?"

"Oh, investing their money well, even if it isn't but a little, and selling when it is at a good price and then doing it over again."

"Is—that—quite—right? Doesn't somebody have to lose?"

"I'm sure I don't know!" snapped Violet, "that hasn't anything to do with the case. I suppose it depends on how you do it. Your idea I suppose is to find out if your uncle is honest. But you really have nothing to do with that. You can't make everybody over to suit your ideas, not even if they are relatives. However, for your comfort, I can tell you that Robert Fraley is quite the correct thing in every way so far as I know. I have never heard a breath of suspicion against his morals or the way he got his fortune. He's one of those "honest Scotchmen" who are clever enough to turn a penny, and keep in with religion too. He's very prominent in one of the big Fifth Avenue churches."

"Oh," said Fraley, and watched the varying changes of her informer's face as she said these half sarcastic things about the newly discovered uncle.

Violet was going out that evening, and disappeared into her room almost immediately after the evening meal. There was no further chance to question her that night. Fraley went up to her room with much to think about. She sat down in the window where she could see the lights on the river, with her Bible in her lap. There was a reading lamp close by that she would turn on presently when she had thought her way through. But now she loved to sit with her hand on the dear old Bible, while she thought. It was more as if her mother were talking it all over with her! Oh, if she could but hear her voice, and could lay her head in her lap as she used to do and tell all that was in her heart, and see what the mother thought about it!

Fraley had long ago purchased with the money left over from Seagrave's Bible a Scofield Bible, such as she had bought for the young missionary, for after much deliberation she had decided that she would rather have that for a keepsake of him than anything else. She wanted to see what she had sent him, and she enjoyed the thought that perhaps she was reading the same things that he was reading, because she had the same kind of a copy. So she was devouring the Book again as if it were a new book, looking up all the marginal references, and reading all the enlightening footnotes, and getting daily new light on the Word. It was all very precious. But to-night, she had unlocked her treasure drawer and taken out the old cotton-covered Book because she felt that she needed the comfort of her mother's presence and guidance, and because, too, she felt that perhaps her reading of the other copy with the thought of the young man in mind, had been a thing she ought not to have done, at least, in the light of her present knowledge that he was as good as engaged to her cousin. She must get out of that habit.

So she sat there in the dusk of the city in her darkened room, and thought.

It seemed to her as if everything had been turned upside down again in her life. Her friend was gone, and

she had in his place an unwanted cousin and an unknown uncle—and there would be an aunt too, of
course, who was a still more unknown quantity. Silently,
in the darkness, the tears began to slip down her cheeks.
She longed inexpressibly to run away and get back to her
mountain. If only those men could be taken away from
there and she might have the place in quietness and
peace, she thought it would be a wonderful refuge. She
believed at that moment that she would be content to
stay there alone for the rest of her days, if she need not
fear those enemies of hers. But it seemed there were
enemies of one kind or another in the world whichever
way one turned.

Presently, as her fingers slipped between the worn
precious leaves, she felt two that seemed to stick together, and idly her fingers sought to free the soft jagged
edges from each other. But they would not come apart.
She began to realize that there seemed to be a soft layer
of paper or something between them.

Curious, she snapped on the light, and began to
examine them.

She had not read much in this book since she purchased her new one. In fact she had only used it that first
night or two in reading to Jeanne, because she had
bought the new one the second or third day she was out
shopping. She had put this one away for safekeeping, not
only lest its leaves should become more worn, but also
to protect it from the amused and curious glances of
anyone who might enter her room, for she had been
quick to see that they thought it very queer in its cotton
covering. To have it viewed by unsympathetic eyes was
like laying bare her heart.

She found that the two pages that were stuck together
were in between the Old and New Testaments. Perhaps
that was why she had not noticed them when she read

to Jeanne, because she had not had to open between them.

And now she saw that "For Fraley, dear" was scrawled in pencil in her mother's hand as if she had written it in her last hours when she was too sick and weak to write her best.

Eagerly, carefully, the girl sought a paper knife that was a part of the outfitting of the beautiful desk that adorned her room. The pages were pasted together most carefully so that the torn edges fitted each other, and it hurt her to separate them, because they kept tearing in little jagged fringes. But when she finally got them apart she found a letter within written by her mother on an old piece of paper bag. It was folded small, and addressed to her.

As if she had heard a voice from another world, she laid her hand on her heart and looked at it, smiling through the sudden tears that came. A letter from her dear mother! And that it should come just now when she was particularly sorrowful and in great doubt! Perhaps God had sent it to help her to know what to do.

20

Mother's dear little girl: [the letter began]

Some day you will find this letter between two pages in the old Bible, and it will be like me speaking to you again.

It's terribly hard for me to leave you all alone, but I feel that God is going to take care of you and when you read this you will I hope be far away from here with good people somewhere who will help you find a way to earn your living.

But there will be times when things all look black, for life is like that. And perhaps this letter will help you then, and you will remember that your mother thought ahead and wished she could bear all the hard things for you. But I suppose you have to have your hard testings like everybody else, to get you ready for the life everlasting. Remember you don't have to do it all alone. If you ever get where you don't know what to do go to God, and tell Him just as you used to tell me everything.

I can't write any more. My strength is almost gone, and this is all the paper there is, but you know I love you and I'll be waiting for you when you come home.

> *If, where I am going, they let mothers like me be*
> *guardian angels, I'll ask to be allowed to guard you,*
> *precious child, till we meet in heaven.*
> > *Your loving mother,*
> > *Alison Fraley MacPherson.*

For a long time Fraley sat reading this letter over and over until she had each line by heart. It seemed so wonderful to hear her mother's words spoken out of the grave, and to have the letter come just now when her soul was tried. It seemed to make all the things that had troubled her sink into insignificance before the fact that she was in this world being tested, and that if anything that she desired was not the Father's will she must not want it, that was all. It might seem to her that she could not live without it, but that would not be so, for the Lord knew best, and He was able to bring her through a thing of the Spirit as well as He had brought her through the perils of her pilgrimage.

She went to bed that night with her mother's letter under her cheek, and a more peaceful look upon her brow than she had worn for several days.

Violet Wentworth did not arise early, and it was understood that the mornings were Fraley's to do with as she pleased, unless there were letters to be written.

Fraley had planned to go downtown this morning, so she started out early, intending to walk until she was tired and then take the bus.

As she came out to the pavement she saw old Mr. MacPherson coming down the street with his stately tread, looking keenly at her, evidently recognizing her. The smile that lit his crabbed old face gave her a new view of what the man might have been.

Fraley smiled up at him, and would have let him pass, but he halted and spoke to her.

"Good morning, little maid," he said with a somewhat courtly manner. "Are you feeling any the worse for your sprint after my hat yesterday?"

"Oh no," laughed Fraley, "I was glad to have a good run. There isn't often so good an excuse for running in the city you know, and I'm supposed to be grown up."

"Are you, indeed!" smiled the old man watching her sparkling beauty with admiration. "And is this where you live?"

He glanced up sharply at the house.

Fraley said it was.

"And are you going out to walk? May I walk with you a little way? We are neighbors, we ought to be acquainted."

Fraley said she was and would be glad of his company, and they fell into step along the pavement.

"I suppose I ought to know you," said the old man smiling down at her scrutinizingly. "But I'm not very good at remembering names and faces. Your face however is not hard to remember. Whose house is that where you came out, anyway? I declare I'm not quite sure."

"Mrs. Wentworth lives there," said Fraley.

"Oh!" said the old man, and *"Oh!"* in quite a revealing tone. It was most evident that he did not approve of Mrs. Wentworth. "And—you are—her—*daughter?"* he asked and Fraley fancied his tone was now less cordial.

"No," said the girl, "I'm just staying there for a little while. I'm helping her. She calls it social secretary work."

"I see," said her companion more cordially. "Well, that's good. You are a good little girl I'm sure. Always keep yourself sweet and unspoiled the way you are now. I'm glad you don't paint your lips. It's ghastly the way the girls do that. You couldn't smile the way you do if

your lips were painted. You make me think of something sweet I lost once."

"Oh," said Fraley shyly, "I'm sorry! I wouldn't want
to trouble you."

"You don't trouble me," he said gruffly, "I like to
watch you."

They walked a long distance toward downtown till
the old man said he would have to go back, that he was
getting beyond his beat. So Fraley took the bus and went
on down, wondering at the strange friendship she had
picked up with this old man who bore the same name
that she did. There seemed to be a wistfulness about him
as if he were hungering for something he could not find.

Fraley's errand that morning was to look up the
addresses her mother had put in the old Bible. She felt
that she wanted to know for a certainty about her
mother's people before she went with Alison. She
wanted to be sure that Violet's information was correct.

She had no trouble in locating the address of Robert
Fraley, and, as Violet had experienced before her, she
was sent to an old crippled shoemaker across the street
to gain information about the former occupants of the
house.

"Yes, I been here thirty years," he informed her
eyeing her curiously. "Yes, I knowed Robert Fraley all
right; a right nice sort of feller he useta be afore he made
his pile. Always had a pleasant word. I've mended many
a shoe fer him in his younger days afore he got up in the
world. He had a pretty little wife, an' she useta wheel her
kid up an' down this street. I made the kid a pair o' shoes
outa pretty red leather oncet. Her name was Allie—little
Allie—fer a sister o' hisn who married a poor stick an'
went out west—"

Fraley sank down on the wooden chair offered her
and listened and questioned till she had no more doubt

left in her mind but that Alison Fraley was her own cousin.

"They don't talk any more," went on the garrulous old man, "they *ride*, they do, an' not in no trolley car neither. They has their limousines now, more'n one, and they resides on Riverside Drive when they ain't abroad, which they are just now. I seen it in the paper the other day. 'Mr. Robert Fraley and wife after a winter in Yorrup is sailin' fer home, an' booked to arrive in N'York about the twenty-fif'.' That's the way they write it. But I ain't seen him fer a matter of ten year now. He don't never come down this way any more. He's got too high hat fer this street—at least his wife an' kid have. He was a nice man, I will say that fer him. An' ef he were to meet me now, allowin' he knowed me after all these years, I wouldn't put it past him to speak as pleasant as ever he done. But her, now, she's another kind. And I've heard say the kid is more high steppin' than them all."

When Fraley left the dusty old shoe shop and went her way back to Riverside Drive, her heart was very heavy. She seemed to have come suddenly very close to her dear mother again, and to feel with her, the great isolation from her family. Mother had felt that her brother Robert was the salt of the earth, and would care for his niece. But Mother never knew of this rise in circumstance. Mother had not spoken much about her brother's wife, and now Fraley felt as if she knew the reason why. The sister-in-law was of another kind. This crooked old cobbler had keen little discerning eyes. Fraley felt she understood the whole situation. She was sure beyond the shadow of a doubt that Alison Fraley was her own cousin, and she felt also very sure that she did not care to claim relationship, at least not until she knew her better. But she had completely forgotten to look up the MacPherson side of the house at all.

"What is the matter with you?" asked Violet crossly at breakfast the next morning, watching the lovely, troubled face jealously. "I've asked you a question twice and you don't seem to even hear me."

"Oh, I beg your pardon," said Fraley getting pink, "I'm sorry. I was just thinking."

"Thinking about what?" asked Violet suspiciously. "Because if it's about that young man you wrote to, you better cut it out. You're much too young to be thinking about young men. You need to wait another year or two anyway."

Fraley's face was flaming now.

"I was not thinking about any young man," she said, tremulously, "I don't think you should talk to me that way. There is nothing wrong about that young man. He was just kind to me when he met me when I was lost, and couldn't find my way to anywhere. I had promised him that I would let him know when I found a place to stay."

Violet still eyed her suspiciously.

"Why should he want to know where you were? Was there anything between you? You know a young man like that doesn't mean any good to a girl he picks up on the desert."

Fraley rose, her face growing white with anger, and her eyes darkening with feeling.

"You shall not say things like that about Mr. Seagrave!" she said. "He was wonderful to me. He took care of me as if he had been my own brother. He wanted me to write so he could be sure I was safe. He was just kind."

"Oh, well, you needn't cry about it!" said Violet contemptuously, "I was just warning you. You've got a lot to learn and you may as well find it out first as last.

Well, if you weren't thinking about him who were you thinking about?"

"I was thinking about Joseph."

"Joseph who?" with new alarm in her voice.

"Joseph in the Bible," said Fraley desperately. "I was reading about him this morning how he was sold into Egypt. You don't like me to talk about the Bible or I would have told you at once."

"The Bible again," said Violet in great annoyance. "I certainly am Bibled to death. I can't teach you the things you need to know when your head is full of this Bible stuff. You know enough about that. It's time you got some worldly wisdom. Now, run along and don't bother me any more, and for pity's sake don't look so glum! I didn't ask you here to look like a tombstone!"

Sadly Fraley went up to her room to dress for the golf game with her stranger cousin. Life certainly did not look very rosy just now to her. She could not anticipate the coming ordeal with anything but dread.

As she was going out to the car where Alison Fraley awaited her the postman arrived and the butler stood in the hall with his hands full of letters.

"Here's one for you, Miss Fraley," he said as he sorted them over. "Will you have it now or shall I put it up in your room?"

"Oh, I'll take it now," said Fraley, curious to know who could possibly have written to her. But a glance at the letter flooded her face with color. She had seen that handwriting but once but she never would forget it, and it did not need the inscription in the left hand corner, "Return to G. R. Seagrave" to tell her that her friend of the wilderness had not forgotten her.

Tremulously she hid the letter in her pocket and ran down the steps to the car.

All the morning she had a guilty feeling with that

letter crackling whenever she turned, and she could not get away from the longing to run away somewhere and see what it contained. She tried her best to concentrate on what she was doing and play a good game, but her thoughts were far away.

Alison gossiped a great deal about the different people on the golf links. Also she told Fraley much about Violet Wentworth's past which she would rather not have known, and which filled her with a new dismay. Was Violet really like that? And was all this mess the reason why Mr. MacPherson had lost his cordiality when he found out where she was living—when he thought she was a relative of Violet's?

"Now," said Alison, "we're going into the club house and have a cocktail. Vi said I was to teach you to like them, and I give you fair warning there's no use trying to get out of it. Then we're going to have a smoke. It's time you learned."

Fraley walked thoughtfully toward the club house, her mouth set in a firm little line. When they reached the porch she paused.

"Come on," said Alison pointing to a group, "the gang's all here and Vi said I was to introduce you to them. This is Teddy and Rose Frelingheysen, May Ellen Montgomery, Martha Minter, Jill Rossiter, Jack Schuyler, Sam Van Rensalaer, and Dick Willoughby."

For the "gang" had thronged over to where they stood as if by preconcerted arrangement, and there was no opportunity to escape.

"And here come the drinks!" cried the one they called Dick, as if that were the end and aim of all mornings.

"I'll wait in the car, Alison, if you'll excuse me," said Fraley with sudden determination.

"Not on your life you won't!" cried Alison laughing, "I've given my word to initiate you before I go home.

Put her in a chair, boys, and let her see we mean business."

Laughingly they laid hands upon her, those maidens and elegant youths, dressed in the latest importation of fashion, children of fortune who had no need to do anything in the world but play. They literally carried her to a veranda chair with a great whorl of a back that looked like the top of a king's throne, and placed her in it. And then the youth called Jack laughingly held a glass to her lips.

Now it is well known that though you may lead a horse to water you cannot make him drink, and Fraley, though her arms were pinioned to the straw arms of the great chair, and though there were so many of her tormentors that she could not hope to get free if she tried, resolutely held her lips closed.

At last the youth who held the glass stood back and said, "Why won't you taste it? Just taste it!"

Fraley looked nim in the eyes.

"If I had no reason for not drinking it I certainly would not drink it now. I will not be *made* to eat or drink or do anything. I would not drink it if you tried to kill me for it."

There was something in her quiet tone that brought them to their senses, and they looked at one another. There were times perhaps when this group, after they had been drinking all night at a dance, would have kept up the buffoonery even under the gravest circumstances, but it was morning yet, and none of these young people had been drinking that day. They perceived that they were carrying a joke a little too far, and even Violet Wentworth might not uphold them in the torture they were putting upon this fair stranger.

"I'll tell you what we'll do," drawled Alison now, standing in front of her cousin. "If you'll tell us why you won't drink nor smoke nor play bridge, we'll let you off, but it's got to be a real honest to goodness reason, and I'm to be the judge, or else we're going to stay right here till you drink it."

"Yes, I'll tell you the reason," said Fraley, "though I don't like the way you are trying to force me to it. I don't play cards, nor smoke nor drink because I've seen criminals doing all those three things in the mountain cabin where I was born, till they were beside themselves. I've seen them lose every cent they had, and turn and curse my little sweet mother, and throw things at her, and then take my father who tried to make them pay what they owed him and drag him out and push him off the cliff and kill him!"

Fraley's lips were trembling with feeling and her eyes were flashing blue fire. And as they watched her the group gradually let go of her hands, and stepped back almost respectfully, shocked and amazed, but recognizing the girl's courage. Fraley looked at them steadily, and then turned her eyes on Alison, saw a curl of a sneer on her lips, and was stung into words again.

"And you," she said, "you who have always had everything you needed all your life, who never knew what it was to be hungry or cold or afraid, who have always been sheltered and cared for, are willing to do the same things that those vile men do. And not only that but you are trying to make me do them. Alison Fraley, my mother was your father's only sister, and she gave her life to protect me and keep me clean. Do you suppose I would let you undo what she gave her lifetime to do, even if you killed me in the attempt?"

Fraley stood up, free. They were all watching her in amazement now, and drinks were forgotten. They were looking at Alison in startled question. There was a quality, too, in their looks, of admiration, as Fraley stood forth, and faced them all, a little lovely angry thing with enraged righteousness in her eyes.

"I will go back by myself now," she said to Alison. "You need not come with me!" and she turned and walked off the piazza and down the winding drive of the country club.

"Imposter!"

The word followed her like a hissing serpent.

"So that's her game!" said the voice of Alison angrily, purposely loud so that she might hear it. "She is going to blackmail the family. She is expecting to get some money out of my father to finance herself. But she'll find my father is not so easily taken in. My father *had no* sister!"

But Fraley walked steadily on out the gate of the country club and down the road out of sight.

21

GEORGE Rivington Seagrave was taking a horseback ride by himself. He had wearied of the attention of his hostess and had pleaded a promised call on members of his parish to shake her for the day. And now he had ridden out along the way where he had found the little pilgrim in a tree on his first day in the west.

It did not take him long to find the place, and identify the tree.

"The little squirrel!" he said to himself as he stood looking up into the branches, "she must be some climber! Now to think of her going up into that tree as if she were a bird."

He threw the horse's rein over the saddle and sat down at the foot of the tree, going over that experience which was now several months away, for he lingered, week after week holding down the job for the poor fellow who was slowly recovering but was not yet able to take up his work. The pitiful letters scrawled from the hospital cot were the first thing that held him in the wilds, but later he grew to be interested in the queer gnarled people who inhabited these forlorn log cabins so far from most human habitation, and who were willing to take such long toilsome journeys just to hear him read the word of God once or twice a week. It was a continual miracle to him to see them come straggling into the schoolhouse faithfully on Sunday morning, and one evening a week.

Sitting under the tree Seagrave took out the Bible that Fraley had bought for him and after much fumbling around and referring to the paper he carried in his pocket, found the place which the girl had showed him sitting under that same tree. For a while he sat and read, chapter after chapter, thinking of the quaint comments the child had made as she told him the story, seeing again her sweet pure face, looking down at him from the tree when he first accosted her; smiling back to him from the saddle as they rode together; gleaming out at him from the shadows of the old schoolhouse as he told over the story himself. Oh, she was a sweet child, and how had she taken hold upon him even in that one short day! It was strange. He had never seen a human being who so stirred him. He was beginning to think now that it was something more than human, it was God, speaking through the lovely lips of the girl.

He wondered again as he had wondered many times since she left him, what had been the circumstances of her own life that had so perfected her sweet young womanhood even out in the wilds, with only one book for contact with the great world. That, too, must have been a miracle. But he would like to know. He would like to find the place where she was born, and see some of the people with whom she had associated. She had said they lived alone on a mountain, but of course that could not have been literally so. There must have been a settlement somewhere near by. They must have had some contacts with life. How interesting to search them out. What if he should do it some day? Of course he had no idea how far she had come from her home before he met her. She had not given him any data to go by, and it might be a wild goose chase, but on the other hand she had been walking with a rather heavy burden for such slender shoulders, and she could not have come far. He had the day on his hands, why not ride around and see if he could get any clue of her. She was far enough away now so that no harm could come to her by it, and anyhow he could be careful of whom he asked questions.

So he mounted his horse again and rode fast up the road where he had first seen Fraley that day in early spring.

He loved the soft tints of the distant mountains, and the lovely shadings of the woods. So he skirted the forest through which Fraley had come, that last long day of her pilgrimage, and eventually reached the far side of her lake near which she had camped on her last night out.

A fresh, spirited horse can quickly cover ground that a girl's weary feet had taken hours to walk, and Seagrave found himself, though he did not know it, going over almost the same ground that Fraley had trod on her way out.

He kept for the most part down in the valleys, for he had little knowledge of scaling mountains. He was amazed to find that he could ride so far without coming to human habitation. The house where Fraley had milked the cow was the only one he saw, for he had kept his course several miles south of the log house where she stayed all night with the woman.

And now, the sun began to warn him that he would better turn back, and looking at his watch he was startled to find that it was so late. He would scarcely be able to reach the ranch in time for supper unless he hurried.

But when he tried to find his way back he was

bewildered. The horse insisted on going one way when he felt sure he ought to go the other. He took his own turn and found himself winding up a trail above a steep precipice. He felt sure he had been in no such high path all day, but it seemed to be a well beaten track, and he argued that it might be a shorter cut to where he wanted to go. In fact there was likely to be human habitation at the end of this trail somewhere, and he might inquire the way, or perhaps even stay overnight if the house were reasonably clean, and go back the next day.

So, hurrying his horse onward he came to a turn in the trail, where up a little higher he could see the outlines of a cabin. Ah! He had been right in coming. Now, if it were not vacated he would be able to get direction.

The trail wound along narrowly, dizzily close to the precipice, and because he did not care to risk his horsemanship in such a straitened path he took to the woods just above the trail and circled about behind the cabin, and beyond, studying it from afar. There was no smoke coming from the chimney, but he thought he heard the cackling of hens a little distance from the house. Holding his horse in check he came slowly round the back intending to approach from the front, when all at once before him there arose a big rock, high and smooth, and on it he saw writing in a clear round hand. He paused surprised. Perhaps here was a sign to guide strangers on their way. "The angel of the Lord encampeth round about them that fear Him, and delivereth them," he read, and underneath it was signed "Fraley MacPherson."

Ah! He was on the right track. His little girl had been here. That was her name, Fraley MacPherson. Could it be possible that she used to live in that cabin?

He gazed off at the mountains in the distance, and

something of the greatness of the view impressed him. Here was beauty. Perhaps this was part of the explanation of her loveliness. This and the Book from which she had learned day after day.

So he picked his way among the rocks, and came around in front of the cabin, dismounted, and knocked. If there was anybody still living here perhaps they could tell him who the girl was and what about her people. He would be careful of course and not mention her, for she had seemed to be afraid of someone. But he could find out a great deal just by judicious questioning.

So he tapped at the cabin door.

There was a sound like hollow surprise through the place, and then a harsh movement, like a heavy bench being shoved back. Heavy boots too, dragging across the floor. A fumbling with the lock, and then the door was open a crack, and a gleaming sinister metal eye looked out, its cold menace almost in the face of the young man. Behind the gun there was a hand, gnarled and hairy, and behind the hand there appeared a face, dirty, unkempt, wild-eyed and full of hate.

"I beg your pardon," said Seagrave stepping back a pace, "I'm not an enemy; I merely stopped to inquire the way. I seem to be lost."

But the shining gun did not withdraw a hair's breadth.

"Lost! I guess ya air! In more ways 'n you know. Don't you stir now. I'm goin' to shoot around ya, just to give the rest of the gang a call!"

And the words were scarcely spoken when a bullet whistled by Seagrave's ear, almost grazing it.

The door was opened a little wider, showing more of the ugly, unshaven face, and bleared eyes. The breath of whisky came strongly out like an evil wind and struck his nostrils. It was combined with the smell of unwashed flesh and unlaundered garments.

"Now, stand still!" ordered the voice. "A fella never comes up here without intendin' and he never goes out when he gets here. Stand still!"

Seagrave measured the distance from himself to his horse which had reared and backed at the sound of the explosion. He guessed at his chance if he tried to bolt, and decided not to risk it.

"Oh, I say," he began putting on his best manner, "what's your grouch, pardner? I had no intention of getting in bad with you. I'm just a stranger from the east out riding. I lost my way, that was all. If you'll tell me which way to go I'll get out and never trouble you again. I'm just the guy that's holding down the preacher's job over at the log schoolhouse till the right man gets here."

"Oh, that's who you are, is it? I been layin' fer you. So you're the man that's stole my girl away from me."

"Your girl?" asked Seagrave guilelessly. "Who is your girl, and how could I steal her? I haven't got any girl."

"You haven't got any girl, haven't ye? You didn't take her over ta the railroad an' put her on the train didn't ya? I learnt all about it. I got watchers everywheres, I know what you was doin'. I heard how you an' she rid to the meetin', and then went off to where you was stayin' an' next mornin' you took 'er to tha train. I just ben waitin' till I got good'n ready to come over an' lay ya out, but now you've saved me the trouble, an' we'll fight it out right here an' now!"

Brand threw the cabin door open wide revealing the dreary room where Fraley had lived her young life, and where her poor mother had died without comfort.

"We got 'nother grudge agin ye, too. One of our men's got a girl, name o' Car'line. She's no good to him any more 'count o' you. You got 'er goin' on that there meetin' stuff, an' readin' the Bible, an' she's just natur'ly ruined fer his purposes. See? So I'm comin' out there an' shoot ya up. I'd like ta wait till the boys get here ta he'p enjoy it, but I ain't s' sure they wouldn't take the job from me ef I did, so I'll just leave 'em look on the corpse after the work's done. Air ya ready? When I shoot I shoot to kill!"

Seagrave had not spent nine months at the front in France for nothing.

"Well," he responded airily, "if I had known it was to be an affair of this sort of course I would have brought my gun along, but since I came in peace—just a minute—!"

Suddenly Brand's gun flew up in the air, and Brand took a blow on his jaw bone that banished from his drunken mind all knowledge of what was happening, and left him lying unconscious across the threshold of the cabin door.

Seagrave waited only to pick up the gun and unstrap the cartridge belt from Brand's waist and then he swung to his horse and was off.

Not down the trail where the narrow precipice lay, but out into the open, past Fraley's big pine, past rock and river and valley on and on as fast as his horse's flying feet could go.

He had sense enough to know that if there were a gang anywhere near, the sound of those shots would summon them and they knew better how to follow him than he knew how to run from them, therefore he must not lose a moment. He knew now that he must be within those mysterious limits that were known as Bad Man's Land, and he knew that his life depended on getting out of those limits before darkness dropped down.

This time he did not try to guide the horse. He let him take his own way, and the beast seemed to understand and picked his way with marvellous sense.

Half an hour they must have been on their way, before Seagrave heard shots behind him, very far away it is true, but still it meant serious business.

The sun was very low almost dropping behind the distant mountains when he reached a spot that he seemed to recognize, and a little later he came around the mountain and out to the lake that he had passed earlier in the day. But soon after that he heard more shots not far away now, and he thought that after all he was lost. He tried to turn the horse into the woods where he would be out of sight, but the animal knew where he was going and he fairly flew, mile after mile, over the soft earth, his hoofs making no sound, as the dusk grew deeper and the stars came out. And all at once Seagrave saw ahead of him the tree where he had found Fraley, and knew where he was. Then hope began to rise. He might be able to make it after all! There was only ominous silence behind, but once he thought he heard a bullet whistle through the air not far away.

Then, for the first time, Seagrave really prayed.

"Oh God! If you bring me out of this I'm going to serve you the rest of my days."

He said it aloud to the night as he flew by, and he set his lips. There was some glory perhaps in dying in France for the good of the whole world, but only ignominy in being shot in his tracks for a foolish blunder, because he was a tenderfoot. He wanted to come through this unharmed. But more than anything, he wanted to live to find little Fraley and guard her the rest of her life from all dangers. He had never realized before what woman-hood could go through till he saw that drunken brute, and the inside of that cheerless cabin.

It was not long after that however, that he reached the familiar road which he rode every day, and he knew that he was safe.

As he realized this he looked up, with a reverent gaze. "I guess it's a promise!" he said aloud to the stars.

And then, there came back to his memory the verse that he had found written on the rock with the girl's name signed to it, and the miracle of his escape seemed to him a direct fulfillment of its promise.

It was like Seagrave that he said nothing of this incident when he arrived at the ranch house. He merely told his hostess that he had been detained longer than he expected at a place where he had called, and couldn't get back sooner. When they asked him where he was, he said he had neglected to ask the name, and he sat down at the piano and whistled a love song, playing the accompaniment while his hostess was setting out food for him.

He ate his supper, but when he went to his room and took off his clothes, he looked hard at a spot of blood on his sleeve, then washed it carefully and bound up a nasty little wound in his arm that had been teasing and stinging him all the way home. "The angel of the Lord—the angel of the Lord—" What was the rest of the verse? He knew it must be in the Bible, and he meant to find it before he slept.

He sat down by his flaming candle, and opened the book, turning to the concordance in the back and finding the word angel. He was a bright young man and it hadn't taken him long, in this land whose main attractions were horseback riding and the unwanted attentions of one's flirtatious hostess, to find out and use the means provided for his knowledge of this hitherto unknown book. Before long he had the verse and was reading the whole psalm, hearing the little girl's voice in it all. For had he not seen her lovely name signed to the words, written high on the rock?

That night before he slept, after the candle was extinguished, he knelt beside his bed, and approached God for the first time in his life on his own behalf. He had made that promise out in the open, more as a promise to himself than a prayer. But this was a prayer. He had come before the Almighty God whom he had ignored all his life, to acknowledge that he was wrong, and to put himself into the attitude of humility before his Maker. He had many things yet to learn about sin in himself and the way of salvation, but he had taken the first step to put himself right with God.

Two days later the mail down at the station contained a crude letter for Seagrave, addressed to the preacher at the schoolhouse.

"Yu got off this tim but it ant fur long. Ile plug yo wen yo ant lukin, so wach out. Ya kant cum in bad Mans land an git awa withit. Ile blo yurbloomin branse out onles you quit this preachin, Brand."

Seagrave read this with much difficulty and then, while still in the post office, wrote an answer.

"Thanks for the warning, but you see, I'm working for God and I can't quit till He says so. If I'm worth anything to Him He'll take care of me."

Brand's answer was unprintable, but Seagrave wired east for a couple of good revolvers and some ammunition and always went armed thereafter.

The news that came from the young man in the hospital was not encouraging. There had been complications. He was promised that if he would keep quiet and not try to work for six more weeks he might be able to take up his work. Seagrave, with a wistful glance toward the east wrote him that he would stand by until he was able to come.

By this time the merry, breezy young preacher had created quite a sensation in the wide neighborhood. People rode for fifty and a hundred miles on horseback to attend one of his services. Word went out that he didn't exhort, he told stories out of the Bible, and more than one poor man came bringing a tattered dollar bill and asking if the preacher could send east for a Bible for him, that his gal or his boy "wanted to read them there stories out of it fer theirsel's."

Seagrave sent a large order east to a bookstore, and in due time Bibles enough for the whole circuit arrived and were given out to the eager applicants.

"If I never can do any good here myself," mused Seagrave as he rode home after that service, thinking of the happy faces of those who had received the Bibles, "I can at least get people to read the greatest book in the world." For by this time Seagrave had reached that conclusion about the Bible.

Then Seagrave set to work in earnest to study the Bible for himself.

He made a regular business of it, beginning at the beginning, and looking up every reference in the margin. The enlightening footnotes became a joy to him, as day by day he came to know the plan of salvation from the beginning of the universe, and the way the whole Bible fitted together like a wonderful picture puzzle.

"Not a contradiction anywhere from start to finish," he said to himself after a morning of hard study. "There seems to be a reason for every chapter and verse, for every book in the whole combination, each is a part of the other. I never saw anything like it. Just that fact ought to be enough to convince anybody of its divine origin. No man or men could have possibly done that." And he had always heard that the Bible was just full of contradictions.

Day after day he grew more interested, shutting himself in his room every morning for a couple of hours, or else going off to some quiet place out of doors where he could read.

"Yes, he's a great student," admitted the lady of the ranch to the few friends with whom she had thought it worth while in this wide land to make contacts. It was most disappointing to her that she was unable to draw him into all her interests, and make of him a gay companion. Surely if George Rivington Seagrave's friends in New York could have looked in on him at this time, they would have been amazed at his new attitude toward life. He had been known as being one of the gayest, merriest, idlest, most playful fellows in the world. With all the money he needed, and friends on every hand, he had rollicked through life thus far, with seemingly not a serious thought in the world. He had always been eager for all sorts of amusement. Now he withdrew early from the great living room where were often pleasant things going on, and went to his room to read awhile before he slept.

He was taking the Bible as a man reads an exciting novel, and he could not bear to break off the thread of the story for long. Some power had gotten hold of him that he did not understand.

Then one day he came on the doctrine of the new birth. And he came, spirit led with Nicodemus, by night to His Lord, and heard the mysterious word that a man must be born again before he can enter the kingdom of God. He searched out diligently all the references and cross-references on this subject, and in one of these he came upon the fact that one must die to self and sin and the things of this world if he would share Christ's risen life. He understood that if he accepted Christ and His death on the cross as a propitiation for his sins—he had reached the point some days back where he knew he was a sinner—he should die with Him as far as his old self was concerned. He spent hours on the sixth chapter of Romans. He read and reread the verses:

> *For he that is dead is freed from sin. Now if we be dead*
> *with Christ, we believe that we shall also live with Him.*
> *For in that He died, He died unto sin once, but in that*
> *He liveth, He liveth unto God. Likewise reckon ye also*
> *yourselves to be dead indeed unto sin, but alive unto God*
> *through Jesus Christ our Lord. Let not sin therefore reign*
> *in your mortal body, that ye should obey it in the lusts*
> *thereof. Neither yield ye your members as instruments of*
> *unrighteousness unto sin: but yield yourselves unto God,*
> *as those that are alive from the dead, and your members*
> *as instruments of righteousness unto God.*

Those last sentences got him.

He took them out in the desert and spent the day alone, trying to face God, and decide the great question for himself. One verse from his Bible study kept going over in his mind. "As many as received Him to them gave He power to become the sons of God, even to them that believe on His name." The question was, was he willing to receive Him? He had already an intellectual belief, but was it an active belief, one that went all the way, and received Christ into His life without reservation? For he knew that if he did it at all he would want to go the whole way.

All day he threshed it out in the wilderness, sitting sometimes under the very tree where he had met the little pilgrim with her guide book, and had first been introduced to the Bible.

That night he went home late, under the stars, with a new light in his eyes and a new peace on his face. He knew that he had been accepted, that he was born again, that he was a new creature in Jesus Christ, and he was happier than he ever remembered to have been in his life.

Stealing quietly into the house because everybody was in bed, he went to his room, lighted his candle, and there on his table lay Fraley's letter, telling him where she was living.

A thrill passed through him as he opened it and saw an address at the top of the page. Now he could write and tell her what a wonderful thing had come to pass that night in his soul. He was now a child of God, and she would be glad, for she was a child of God also. Of all the wide circle of his acquaintances she was the only one to whom he felt he could tell his new joy, who would understand it and be glad with him.

Before he slept he wrote the little girl a letter, and the next morning he rode to the station to mail it himself. He could not trust it to the ranch hands who were driving down; he wanted to put it in the letter box himself and be sure it went safely.

Turning away from the letter box he looked up to see a tall shadow standing in the open door, a young man with a scarred face, that might have been handsome once perhaps, but was marred not only by the scar, but by a leer of evil in the eyes.

As was his custom in this friendly country, he bowed and smiled. He was by nature friendly with all men, anyway, and he had found that in his capacity of preacher out here, it was universally expected of him to speak to everybody.

But this dark, evil young face did not break into a courteous smile as most did. Instead the man stood frowning at him, with an ugly leer in his eyes, and as he passed, there broke from him a taunting laugh.

Seagrave turned, with astonished eyes and looked the man straight in the face, and he saw a murderous challenge in the other's eyes. Well, this must be one of those men from Bad Man's Land. He looked it. Seagrave hesitated, and almost went back to speak to him, then thought better of it, and with firm set lips, walked on to where his horse stood and mounted it. But he turned and looked steadily once more at the man who was still standing in the doorway watching him with that sneer on his lips and the challenge in his eyes.

That night was the night for the evening worship in the old schoolhouse. Seagrave rode off as usual with his mind intent on what he was going to say. For the first time in his ministrations to these people he meant to preach a sermon himself. Hitherto he had been content to read them the Bible, occasionally throwing in a word or phrase of his own to make the meaning simpler—that is when he was sure he understood it himself. Now he was going to tell those people about the new birth, and how he had been born again. He was going out to witness what the Lord had done for him, and his heart was full of joy.

It was a wonderful meeting in the old log school-house. The very presence of the Lord Jesus seemed to be there, and the sorrowful lonely members who came their long journeys to get this little time of worship, were stirred to tears and prayers of longing and surrender, and one, Car'line, sitting back by the door in the shadow, having stayed the day and night with a friend so she could be present, lingered to talk with the young preacher, and ask if there was a way for one who had sinned greatly to be born again.

The old man and woman with whom she had come lingered outside in an old spring wagon, waiting for her. Seagrave and she stood beneath the smoky oil lamp, straight in view of the open door, and talked. Seagrave had then his first opportunity to really point the way of life to a seeking soul, and right there under the flare of that light they knelt together, while with unaccustomed lips he asked the Lord to accept this girl, and to forgive her.

Out in the darkness, behind the wooded roadside, a shadow lurked, still and grim, but the old man and woman in the spring wagon did not see it move, and crouch, and look, nor did the old man who lingered to put out the smoky lamp and lock the door.

The girl came out and got into the wagon and the old man drove away. Seagrave came out with a cheery goodnight to the old man as he lingered till he had locked the door, and then both mounted their horses and drove away in opposite directions.

The moon came up and made a silvery light along the way, and Seagrave was filled with joy. He felt like singing. He began to hum the tune of one of the hymns they had sung in the meeting, his clear baritone ringing far on the still stretches of the open.

Then, suddenly there came a stinging pain in his side, another an instant later through his right arm. He felt himself sliding from his horse, and the light of the moon going out.

A dark shadow stole away from a group of trees back on the road he had come, and slid along through the woods till it mounted a horse, and disappeared into the night.

But Seagrave lay where he had fallen, with the moonlight shining silver over his white face, and his horse whinnying beside him.

22

FRALEY had walked a great part of the way back to the city, her mind in such turmoil of anger and humiliation, and penitence that she could not reason. It was several hours later when she arrived at the house and walked straight up to Violet, who happened to be downstairs reading in the library.

"I've done a terrible thing," she said her face white and her eyes dark with emotion. "You won't like it at all. I lost my temper, and I've been rude to a lot of your friends at the country club. I made what you'll call a scene right before everybody! I'm very sorry if I have mortified you, but I couldn't do what they tried to make me. I wouldn't, not if they killed me!" she finished, her lips stern and set.

"What in the world do you mean, been rude? Made a scene at the country club? Why did you have to do that? For pity's sake stop being excited and explain!" said Violet coldly, at once on the defensive. Here was probably some more of the child's outrageous puritanism and it had got to be nipped in the bud. It couldn't go on any longer.

Fraley leaned back against the doorway and closed her tired eyes for an instant, drawing a deep breath, and then she gathered strength and began.

"They were trying to force me to drink liquor!" she said with a fierce little intake of breath.

"Who were?" asked Violet, her voice like an icicle.

"Alison and her friends. She said you had told her she must teach me before I came home." There was a question in Fraley's voice, almost a pleading, but Violet would not let herself respond to it. She looked steadily, coldly at the girl, and after an instant a weary little shadow passed over the sweet face, and Fraley went on.

"They caught me, all those young men, and put me in a big chair and held me! They had no right to touch me!"

She was still struggling between her sense of being wronged, and her penitence for having lost her temper.

"They said they would not let me up and they held the glass to my lips and tried to pry my lips open, and force me to take it!"

Still there was no relenting in the cold eyes of the woman who listened. The white lids fluttered down and up again bravely.

"I wouldn't. It was a long time, and I wouldn't! They hurt me holding my arms so hard, I suppose that was one thing that made me so angry. They hurt my neck, and they hurt my lips. But I shouldn't have been so angry. And then, when they said they would let me go if I would tell them why I would not play bridge, nor smoke nor drink, it seemed as though I just had to. So I told them."

"What did you tell them?" Violet's tone was tense now.

"I told them about the cabin on the mountain where I was born, and the men who used to play cards with my father and smoke and drink and curse my mother, and throw things at her; and how they got drunk and pushed my father off the cliff and killed him!" Fraley paused for a desperate breath. "Alison Fraley had been sneering at me, and I looked right at her and told her that my dear mother who had to stand all that was her father' sister, and that she had no right to try to make me do what my mother had spent her life in teaching me not to do."

"You told Alison that you were related to her!"

"Yes!" Fraley lifted brave steady eyes.

"Well," said Violet at last after a brief interval of thought in which conflicting emotions played over her face, "you certainly have made a pretty mess of things. I might have known that a young savage like you couldn't be trusted to go off alone among civilized people. Now, there has got to be an understanding between you and me and we might as well have it over with. It's been coming to you for some time. You've got to learn that if you stay here you must conform to my habits and customs. For instance, next week I'm giving that dinner and I want you to be present. That's one of the things I got you for, to help entertain my guests. That's why I bought you all those imported frocks and things. But you can't come to a dinner and act like a puritan. You've got to do your part and be a lady of the world. This matter of cocktails is most important. A lady knows how to drink in a ladylike way, and there is no reason whatever why a cocktail in a drawing room, or a glass of champagne at a dinner table among respectable men and women of society should remind you of a lot of boors in the wilderness who are too low down and sottish to be spoken of as human beings. Now, young lady, you may take your choice. You either make up your mind to drink what is set before you, and behave yourself, or you go out of my house! Do you understand that?"

Violet had grown very angry as she talked. She was incensed that this frail little girl with no background whatever should dare to stand against her. It offended her pride. She wanted Fraley to adore her and think her word was law. It was Fraley's admiration that had won her in the first place to take this child of the wilds and try to make her over. She wanted somebody who was lovely to glorify Violet Wentworth and help to make her name great, and she was filled with fury that she was not paramount in the girl's thoughts. She was jealous of her fine allegiance to God and her Bible, and the things her mother had taught her.

Fraley stood very still and looked at her, her eyes growing large and dark with sorrow, her face growing whiter. It seemed as if she could not believe that her friend, who had done so much for her, had spoken those awful words.

Violet saw how the child was stirred and pressed her advantage.

"I mean every word that I have said!" she said sternly. "You've got a whole week to decide. You can go upstairs now and think it over."

Fraley suddenly dropped her white lids like curtains drawn quickly, and two large tears rolled down her cheeks and splashed on the floor by her little dusty shoes.

There was silence in the room for a full minute while the girl struggled to gain her self-control. Then she lifted her eyes again, bright with sorrow, and spoke bravely:

"All right!" she said, with her lips quivering, "but there's something I must tell you first. You ought to know."

"Go on," said the cold voice.

"It's about that man, that Mr. Easton that comes here to see you. I've found out he's a bad man. I saw him at the country club in an alcove this morning kissing that

Lilla Hobart. He had her in his arms and was looking down into her face the way I saw him look at you the first night I came. I thought you ought to know."

"Get out!" shouted Violet in a fury, her face red and her eyes terribly angry. "You are meddling with things that are none of your business! Get out of my sight!"

Meekly, with her whole slender form drooping in sorrow, her head bent, Fraley turned and went out of the room. She walked slowly up the stairs and into her room, and locked the door. Then she dropped upon her knees and her body shook with a tempest of tears, while she tried to pray. Somehow, this seemed to her worse than anything that had come to her since her mother's death.

But she had no time for weeping, and her prayer was short, just a cry for help and guidance. Then she arose with determination in her face, and began to undress. There was no doubt in her mind what she had to do.

As she drew off the pretty sports dress that she had worn at the country club the letter that she had tucked in the pocket fell to the floor. She stooped and with a startled look picked it up. She had forgotten it. But the sight of it brought her no joy. It was only a reminder of another pleasant thing in her life lost.

She went to the bureau and put the letter safely inside her hand bag, the one that Violet had given her on the train. She had kept it carefully, and used it when she went out in the morning by herself. Somehow it had seemed to belong to her more than the elegant trifles that Violet had bought for her to go with the new costumes to be used in her capacity as social secretary.

Fraley put on the dress and hat that had been given her on the train, and selected the shoes and stockings that were bought to go with it that first day of shopping. Then she sat down at the desk and wrote two notes.

My dear lady: [the first began]

I am going away at once as you have said I must, and I cannot stand it to say good-by to you, because I have loved you so much and you have been so good to me. But I want to tell you just once more how grateful I am to you for all you have done, and for the things you have wanted to do for me. I am sorry I cannot please you by doing the things you wanted me to, but they are things I cannot do. They are things that would not be right for me to do. I think you will understand some day. I am going to pray God to make you understand why I could not do it. I am going to pray to Him to help you to love Him and His Bible, and then you will be very happy.

I am wearing away the first things you gave me, because it might shame you if I went out of your house in the things I wore from the mountain, but they were things you said you were going to give away anyway, and some day I hope I will earn money enough to pay you for the beautiful shoes and other things.

I ask your pardon for anything I may have done to trouble you, and I shall never forget how good you were to me,

> *Lovingly,*
> *Fraley MacPherson*

The other note was to Jeanne, and read as follows:

Dear Jeanne:

I am so sorry but I find I have to go away quite suddenly and unexpectedly. I shall miss the Bible readings with you, and I hope you will keep on reading by yourself. I shall always pray for you. Sometime, perhaps, I can see you again, and I shall not forget you.

> *In haste, and very lovingly,*
> *Fraley MacPherson*

When she had addressed these notes she laid them on the desk where she was sure they would be noticed. Then she went to the treasure drawer and unlocked it, taking out the old woolen bag her mother had made, and the little garments made of salt bags, and all the things she had brought with her from the mountain. She packed them carefully, putting the old Bible in first, and tucking the other things around it. She hesitated with her own little Scofield Bible as she was about to put it in, and then with a sigh laid it out on her bureau. She had bought it with her own money, and had loved it and marked some of the verses in it that she loved the best, but now it occurred to her that she was leaving this house without a Bible. If she left it here perhaps Violet would some-times open it and read, or Jeanne would come in when nobody was about. She would not dare give the Bible to Violet, but if she left it there as if she had forgotten it God might let it do its work somehow. Of course she had the old Bible, and it wouldn't matter so much now how it looked, there would be no one but herself to mind the cotton covers. By and by when she was earning something she would dare to spend the money for another one, and until then she could do with the old one.

So she left her new Bible on the bureau.

She found a large piece of wrapping paper in the hall closet and wrapped up her bag carefully. Then with a sorrowful look about the room that would be hers no more she turned and went slowly, softly, down the stairs, and let herself out of the door. There was no one about, and though she looked back for a last good-by to the spot that had grown so dear, she saw nobody at the windows.

Then she knew that till this last minute she had somehow hoped that Violet would relent and call her back, and tell her she did not mean that awful sentence of exile she had pronounced upon her.

With tears blinding her eyes she stumbled on down the street, block after block, narrowly escaping being run over as she heedlessly crossed the side streets.

At last, when she had gone a long distance from the house, and knew that she was beyond the sight of any one who knew her, she went across to the strip of park and sat down on a bench. She had often sat here before, when she was taking walks by herself, and watched the river in its varying moods, but now it only looked sad to her, for she was leaving this neighborhood forever and would not feel like going back to it again.

Then she remembered her letter, and a sharp pang came at the thought that this friend, too, must be renounced because he belonged to someone else. Nevertheless, she must read that letter.

She opened it with fingers that trembled with the excitement of actually hearing from him again, but at the first words a beautiful light broke over her face.

> *Dear Ladybird: [it read]*
>
> *At last you have sent me your address and I can write to you. I have been very anxious about you all these months of silence for many reasons, but now I am glad to get your letter. And glad it came just this night too, for I have something to tell you that I think will make you glad.*
>
> *I have this night given my old self over to your Jesus Christ, and I feel that I am born again. You probably know more than I do about that wonderful miracle, so I do not need to tell you, but I want you to know that it is because of you that I have found out that I was a sinner and needed to be born again. I can't think of words great enough to thank you for what you have done little*

Ladybird, and now I am no more just a raven, nor an angel either, thank God, for I can sign myself a child of God, and I guess that is better than being an angel. Anyhow it looks good to me.

I've been a bit worried about you though, since you told me you had been picked up by Violet Wentworth. I know her well, but she isn't your kind, little girl, she's a woman of the world, and a hard-boiled one I'm afraid, and although I'm deeply grateful to her for having helped you over a hard place, I don't want you to stay too long with her. She might somehow make you forget the wonderful things God has taught you out of His book. She doesn't know anything about such things, and I don't want you spoiled, Ladybird.

My sick man is about well now. He's coming out of the hospital next week, and then very soon he'll come on and take his work, and I'll come home. There are a great many things I mean to do when I get there, for my whole life is changed now, and I'm a new man in Christ Jesus, but the first thing I am going to do is to see that you are safe and happy.

So write to me, little friend, for we are going to be friends always you know, and tell me all about yourself, and soon I'll be home and come at once to see you.

Your friend who is more grateful to you than you can ever understand, for leading him to Jesus,

> Sincerely,
> George R. Seagrave.

With heart almost bursting with joy and renunciation, Fraley read this letter twice and three times before she folded it and put it away. Then she gathered up her bundle and started out into a new world, and a new life again. As before she was leaving all behind but her Bible, but God was with her, and she could trust Him to bring her where He wanted her. That ought to be enough.

About that time, Violet, who had gone to her room after Fraley left her, and had failed to be able to get to sleep as usual because she was strangely disturbed, came down the stairs to the library to get her book. She could not get away from the thought of the great distressed eyes, the pitiful white face, and the glint of the two tears that had rolled down and splashed on the floor. She wanted to absorb herself in her book again to drive the vision from her. This was going to be excellent discipline for Fraley and she must not be soft-hearted and relent just because of two tears.

She had just settled herself in her favorite chair again when the bell rang and Alison walked in, unannounced, her face dark and angry.

"I thought I'd find you here!" she said as she flung herself into another chair, and took out her cigarette case. "Such a day as I've had! I just thought I'd run in and tell you how well I succeeded in carrying out your orders. Where is that little viper? Is she anywhere around? I'd like to tell you before her what she said to me."

Violet looked up, her eyes fully as cold as they had been when talking with Fraley.

"You certainly don't seem to have exercised much common sense or taste in doing it," she remarked coolly. "You ought to have known you couldn't get anywhere by force with a girl of as strong character as that one."

"Strong character!" sneered Alison, "I'll say so! The way she slung words around. Wait till I tell you what she did!"

"She has told me," said Violet, again strangely drawn to defend her protégée.

"She *told* you!" exclaimed Alison incredulously. "I'll bet she told you a good story for herself!"

"She always tells the truth," said Violet, almost against her will.

"Well, she didn't this time. Wait till I tell you what she said about her mother and my father."

"But that happens to be true too."

"Vi! What can you mean?"

"I mean just what I said. I've known it for a long time, but I didn't mean to tell it till you two got to be friends, and you knew what a really rare character she has."

"Rare temper, I'd say! But Vi, it can't be true? Daddy never had a sister."

"Yes, he did. I have proof. There's an old man living downtown now, unless he has died in the last three months, who remembers her. Her name was Alison Fraley and you must be named after her. He told me that he remembered the look on your grandfather Fraley's face the day he discovered that his only daughter had run away with the good-for-nothing son of James MacPherson. He never smiled after that, he said, and died not many months later. That was when your people lived down in that row of little houses just off—"

"Oh, for Pete's sake don't bring all that up, Vi. Of course I knew Dad used to be poor, but there's no advantage in raking out old things like that. He isn't poor now. And so the little snake has got the MacPhersons mixed up with it too, has she? Well, but I don't see how she has put it over on you. I thought you were keen and knew a fraud when you saw one. Coming around here with her soft pretty ways and her big eyes and pretending to be good, and all the while a suit for blackmail up her sleeve. She's probably under the direction of some bold western lover who has sent her on here to play the game and get a lot of money out of two respectable old families, for them to go to housekeeping on. I didn't think you'd be fooled by a little sly thing like that."

"I tell you I have the proof, Alison," said Violet coldly. "I went and got all her papers that her mother gave her before she died. I copied them one day when she was out of the house for the morning, and then I went to the addresses given and looked up everything. I even got an expert detective on the job and had him hunt out a lot of old records and things, till I knew all the two families had done since away back. And Fraley herself doesn't even know yet that she belongs to the MacPhersons."

"But I've seen her out walking with old Mr. Mac-Pherson, several times, in the mornings."

"Oh, she met him at the mountain house this summer. He was a guest there and she played tennis with the kid grandson. But she hasn't an idea he is any connection of hers."

"Don't you fool yourself!" said Alison. "She's working a deep game, that girl is. I'd like to put her in jail. She's the most contemptible little piece I've ever seen. Just you wait till dad gets home. He'll fix her! He wouldn't stand for anybody treating me the way she did at the club house to-day. I shouldn't be at all surprised, from what she says, but that she has drunk worse than cocktails many a time. Has she ever told you what kind of men came to the house where she lived on that mountain? It sounds to me like the worst kind of a roadhouse, and she pretends to be so terribly good! Just you question her and you'll find out a few things that will open your eyes, Vi Wentworth!"

"Very well," said Violet putting her hand out to the bell and summoning the maid. "We'll send for her and ask her a few questions. Incidentally, I'll tell her about her Grandfather MacPherson and you may watch her face and see whether you'll be satisfied that she doesn't know a thing."

"By all means send for her," said the girl contemptuously. Alison arose and began pacing up and down the room as Jeanne appeared at the door.

"Tell Miss MacPherson I want her to come down to the library at once!" ordered Violet.

Jeanne disappeared, and a silence ensued. It seemed almost a hostile silence. Violet could not quite understand her own feelings.

The door bell sounded faintly in the distance and they could hear the butler going to open the door, and letting someone in. Presently he appeared at the door.

"Mr. MacPherson to see Mrs. Wentworth," he announced. "Shall I say you are engaged?"

Violet looked up astonished.

"I told you so," said Alison pausing in her restless walk, "he's found her out too, very likely. Now you'll see I was right."

Violet's face hardened. She accepted the challenge.

"Show Mr. MacPherson in here," she said, with a glitter of daring in her eyes. "We might as well have the whole show at once and be over with it," she added with a hard little laugh, "though, of course, I hadn't planned it just in this way."

"I should hope not!" muttered Alison.

They could hear Mr. MacPherson's slow step, and the tap of his cane as he followed the butler with stately tread down the hall.

He appeared at the door and looked from one lady to the other, a trifle annoyed perhaps to find someone else present besides the person he sought.

He paused in the doorway. They noticed that he held a small package in his hand.

"Good afternoon, Mrs. Wentworth. We ought to

know one another, I suppose," he said in a rather haughty way, "neighbors of course—"

"Won't you have a chair, Mr. MacPherson?" said Violet rising and greeting him pleasantly.

"Oh, no," he said. "You have a guest. I'll not trouble you. I just wanted to ask a favor of you. It won't take a moment. I have a little trifle here—a small gift—that is—You have a young girl here, a very sweet little unspoiled thing, working for you? Social secretary I think she said she was. She was very kind one day to run after my hat and capture it when it blew away in a high wind. She ran almost down to the river after it, and she would accept nothing for her services. That is—I saw of course after I had suggested it that she was a very superior little girl, and I shouldn't maybe have offered it. But I would like to do something in recognition of her kindness. Not only because she was so pleasant and quick about it, but because she reminds me strangely of some one I loved long ago. I have met her by accident a couple of times since and walked a few blocks with her till our ways parted, but I have never got quite to the place where it seemed possible to offer it to her. She seems to have so much—what should I call it—not exactly self-respect, nor dignity. Perhaps you might call it refinement. I was afraid she might not like my offering it, and so I thought I would come to you, that perhaps you would know how to give it to her without hurting her feelings. It's just a little wrist watch. I thought it might be useful in her work. She seems a charming child. And another thing, you know I don't know her name, but you surely know who I mean. There can't be two like her working for you."

Violet was standing with her hand on the back of a chair listening, mingled emotions passing over her face like the shadow of clouds on a windy day. There was a kind of triumph in the glance she swept toward Alison.

"You mean Fraley MacPherson, I suppose," she said when the old gentleman came to a pause in his lengthy, embarrassed speech.

"What! Is that her name? MacPherson? Why—why—I wonder how—Perhaps that might explain my strange feeling that there was a likeness—I've even spoken to my wife about it. Perhaps she might be a distant connection somehow. Do you know where her people came from?"

Over Violet Wentworth's face there swept a look of sudden resolve.

"I know a little about her people, Mr. MacPherson, but she can tell you more. I have just sent for her. She will be down in a moment and will tell you what she knows. But there is one thing I can tell you before she comes, Mr. MacPherson. Fraley is your grandchild. You had a son Robert, didn't you, who married a Miss Fraley—Alison Fraley? Well, Fraley is his daughter. Won't you sit down? She will be here in a moment I think."

The old man stood stock still and looked for a moment as if he were going to fall. Then suddenly a light broke over his face.

"My grandchild? You say she is my grandchild? You say she is my lost Robert's daughter? That sounds too good to be true!" and the old man stumbled into the chair that was offered him, and took out his immaculate handkerchief, mopping his brow which was wet with cold sweat.

Jeanne appeared at the door just then. Her eyes were red with weeping which she made no effort to conceal.

"Mrs. Wentworth, Miss Fraley has gone!" she said with a woebegone look.

"Gone," said Violet sharply. "Where has she gone? How do you know?"

"She left these notes," said Jeanne, her lip beginning to tremble, "and Madam, she doesn't say where she is gone, but it seems as though she did not mean to come back."

Jeanne handed over the two notes, and Violet with sudden premonition tore open her own, her face growing white and stern as she read.

"Well, I hope you are satisfied, Alison," she said lifting her eyes to the sullen girl who stood watching her curiously. "She's gone and she hasn't left a clue behind her." There was a ring of almost triumph in her voice. "It is like her," she added in a curiously gentle voice.

"What?" asked the old man looking up, "what do you say? She is gone? You have not let my granddaughter go off without knowing her destination have you? You expect her to return, don't you?"

"I don't know," said Violet with sudden trouble in her voice, "she can't have been gone an hour. Surely we ought to be able to find her. You see, we had a little trouble. It was only a trifle of course, but I think—she must have misunderstood me. She is very sensitive—she thought she had done something that would hurt me very much, and that I would not forgive. But it was not her fault—" She darted a vindictive look at Alison. "I foolishly told her she must do something I wanted or she could leave, and she has taken me literally. I should have known—she is so gentle—and so easily hurt—" There was almost a sob in her voice now. Then with quick anxiety in her face she called:

"Jeanne, go to the phone and call my lawyer, quick. He will tell us what to do. Surely she can be found. And Jeanne, tell Saxon to go out and search the neighborhood. Tell him not to wait to change to his street things, she may be right near here somewhere. She wouldn't know where to go!"

"I have lost her, just when I had found her?" said the old man, passing a trembling hand over his cold forehead. They noticed that the little box that held the watch was shaking in his hold.

"Jeanne, as soon as you have got the lawyer you run out yourself. She likes you and maybe you can find her," Violet called distractedly.

"I will go out myself and look for her," said the old gentleman rising tremulously and starting toward the door. "I—I—don't know who this young lady is, but perhaps she will go with me. You are—perhaps—her friend?"

"This is Alison Fraley, her cousin, Mr. MacPherson," said Violet pausing in her mad rush of issuing commands. "Certainly she will go out and help to hunt her cousin. The whole world will soon know it if she doesn't," and Violet gave Alison a look that made her open her eyes in astonishment.

That was the beginning of the long search, that lasted all the fall, and into the early winter, and still no trace had been found of Fraley.

Old Mr. MacPherson aged visibly, Violet Wentworth canceled all her social engagements and gave herself to the search. She even sent a telegram out to George Rivington Seagrave at the strange, brief address in the west that she remembered to have read on Fraley's letter, asking if he knew Fraley's present address, but a reply came back the next day. "Seagrave too ill to read your telegram." And signed with a name she had never heard.

The best skilled service of the great city was employed, at first quietly, and by and by using every means, even the radio, to find the lost girl. But none of them came anywhere near little Fraley, hid away safely in the hollow of His hand, till His time had come to reveal her hiding place.

Even Alison had become depressed with the terrible mystery that hung over her unknown cousin. Her father and mother had returned, and of course had been called upon to help in the search. Her father's keen anxiety when he heard of the unknown niece at once convinced Alison that she had been wrong, and she dared not let her father know what part she had played in this tragedy. Even her mother who had never known the beloved sister Alison Fraley, was warm in her sympathy and earnest in her efforts to find that sister's child. Alison's friends at the Club House also, grew interested in the girl who had so bravely and so completely defied them, and made Alison's life miserable by constant questions, until she began to stay away from her usual haunts, and became sullen and morose. The young people who had tormented Fraley that memorable day of her disappearance were fast making her into a heroine.

And then the terrible thought came creeping with sinister shadow of fear into the hearts of those who cared, that perhaps the child had been killed somewhere in the awful city. The records of the morgue were sought, but nothing anywhere gave up the secret of Fraley's disappearance.

And at last Violet Wentworth, from loss of sleep, and lack of food, for she neither ate nor slept much, and perhaps from other anxieties which only her own soul knew, fell ill with a fever.

23

IT was characteristic of Fraley that she was not deeply concerned for her own homeless condition. A bird of the wilderness, she felt that there might be a lodging tree almost anywhere, and crumbs would somehow come to her lot. She was asking no more of life.

The beautiful glimpse she had had of luxuries that others were enjoying had not spoiled her. She went on her winged way trusting in a higher power for the things needful, and she shed things worldly as if they were a foreign substance.

She had walked a good many miles before it gradually came to her consciousness that she was not getting anywhere, and she did not know where she was going.

The streets about her looked strange and foreign. Little children in scanty attire scuttled in groups here and there, and dishevelled parents hung forlornly about unattractive doors, watching her with hostile eyes. Now and then an old person hurried furtively by with a haunted look like one who had come a long way, and there were men lounging about who stared at her and reminded her of Brand and his kind. This was not the

New York she had known since she had been with Violet Wentworth. She must have wandered into some strange quarter. Many of these people were foreigners for they spoke unknown languages.

She was hungry, too, and suddenly felt that she could scarcely drag herself another step. It was growing dark and she felt afraid. She turned about and tried to retrace her steps but when she reached a corner she could not tell which way she had come, and the surroundings seemed only to grow worse.

At last she ventured up to a group of women who had been eyeing her critically and asked if they could direct her to a nice quiet place where she could get something to eat.

They looked at her dress, they looked at her shoes, and hat, all bearing an unmistakable air of refinement and money, and they laughed a mirthless meaningful laugh.

"Right acrost the street an' up them stairs!" pointed one, with a toothless upper gum and a gray bushy bob "That's where you b'long my pretty! You'll get all that's comin' to you up there!" and she laughed again. The sound of her mockery sent a shudder through Fraley; but just to get away from it if for nothing else she crossed the street and stood hesitating in the entrance, while they watched her like an evil menace.

The stairs were narrow and dirty, but a light shone up at the top and there was music. It was not the kind of music Violet made on the grand piano at Riverside Drive, but, from the unfriendly street, there was a certain jazzy cheer in it and she went up.

It was a strange scene that met her gaze. Lights and color, and crudity. Girls in flimsy bright dresses were dancing with men in the middle of the room and a mingling of cheap perfume and unwashed flesh met her nostrils. But there were little tables about the walls of the big room, and she was famished. She slipped into a chair by a table that was comparatively sheltered and gave a shy order. "Could you bring me a bowl of soup and some crackers, please?"

He laughed.

"We don't serve soup, lady. You picked the wrong dump. We just serves drinks and ices and sandriges and that like."

The waiter's intimate tone and searching look he gave her brought the quick color to Fraley's cheeks, but she said hastily:

"Oh, then please bring me a cup of coffee and a sandwich."

The waiter lingered, a dirty tray balanced above his shoulder.

"Want I should interjuce ya to some nice man?"

"Oh, no! Thank you!" said Fraley in a weak frightened voice. "I'm in—rather of a hurry!"

"I see!" said the waiter still watching her as he made slow progress to a door at the back of the room.

She noticed that he stopped at a table where four men sat drinking something in tall foamy glasses and spoke to them, and that they all turned and looked her way.

Fraley grew more frightened every instant. She turned her eyes away, as if she didn't see them, but when she looked up again one of the men was coming toward her, and he had eyes like Pierce Boyden's. Strange how many eyes like that there seemed to be in the world!

More frightened than ever now she rose to her feet, but he was beside her.

"Hello, Baby darlin'!" he addressed her. "I ben waitin' fer you all my life. Let's you and me have a dance while we're waitin' fer the drinks!" He slid his arm boldly about her waist and tried to draw her into the middle of the room.

Fraley drew back and braced herself against the wall, her face very white. She could smell the liquor on his breath.

"Oh, no!" she said. "Please don't! I don't dance! I must have made a mistake. I thought this was a restaurant—I must go!"

She was edging away as he talked. Long experience with drunken men had led her to use strategy rather than to make outcry.

"Go anywhere you shay, Baby darlin'," said the man with a silly grin.

Fraley looked about for help, but saw only the waiter back by the door, grinning, and the other three men rising and apparently coming forward eagerly to join in the discussion. Fraley, in her terror, measured the brief distance to the stairs. She must get there before the other men arrived. She gave a frantic pull and tried to get away from her captor, but he had her pretty well pinioned between the table and the wall, and she was sure now there was to be no help from anyone in that awful room. Even the band men were laughing and calling out in time to their music. Was there nothing she could do?

Then she noticed the glass half full of water standing on the sloppy table beside her, and instinct once more served her. She seized it with her free hand and flung its contents full in the face of the man who was trying to hold her. Then snatching up her little bundle she fled down the steep stairs out into the street.

Mocking laughter and angry cries followed her, and somewhere above her she thought she heard a shot. They were coming after her! She could hear loud stamping feet on the bare boards! She flew down the street past detaining hands and mocking voices, straight into the arms of a great policeman, who took hold of her firmly, and said in a gruff voice:

"Well, what are you trying to put over, kid?"

He had a hard face, scarred and unkindly, but he was knocking the crowd away with his club, as if they had been so many dogs trying to devour her.

"Oh, please!" said Fraley in a small little voice full of sobs and terror, "won't you show me the way to the Pennsylvania station? I—think—I—ammm—a little lost—!"

The man eyed her suspiciously.

"Well, if you ain't now you soon will be, if you stay long down here," he said roughly. "If you was huntin' for the Pennsylvania station what was you doin' up in a joint like that?" he asked looking her severely in the eyes. "That's the toughest joint in New York City, barrin' none—"

"Oh!" said Fraley, aghast, "those ladies across the street said it was a restaurant—"

"Ladies?" the policeman repeated lifting his eyes to the group of slatternly women pressing near, gloatingly. "Ladies! Ha-ha! Say, you better come along 'ith me, kid!"

"Oh, thank you!" breathed Fraley with relief. "If you'll just show me where I can get a bus, or a taxi. Would it be very expensive to take a taxi to the station?"

The policeman looked at her curiously. This was a new specimen. There was something in the quality of her voice that showed him that she did not belong in this quarter.

"Say, Miss," he said, "what are you anyway? Where'd you fall from?"

Fraley tried to explain.

"I'm from the west. I haven't been in the city long and I must have got turned around. If I can only get to the Pennsylvania station I shall know my way all right."

He took her by the arm and cleared a way through the

crowd, conducting her several blocks and questioning her. But by the time they reached a bus line he had somehow satisfied himself that this was no young criminal, merely a babe-in-the-woods who had strayed. Fraley never knew how very near she came to being taken to the station-house that night and locked up. Then she would have had to call for assistance from Violet Wentworth, and incidentally would have saved a great deal of trouble to those who loved her. Though it is doubtful if even under such trying circumstances her proud spirit would have been willing to trouble the woman who had sent her from her home. Fraley had strange vital ideas of self-respect and honor, and would never flinch even in the face of absolute disaster.

So the policeman of the tenderloin, who bore the title of "hard-boiled," put her carefully into a bus going stationward, and Fraley was once more saved from peril.

She spent that first night in the Pennsylvania station.

She wandered through its palatial vistas back and forth until she began to understand its various passages and windings, and finally discovered a ladies' waiting room where were rocking-chairs and a couch.

The couch was occupied by a tired-looking woman with a baby in her arms, but there was a vacant rocking-chair and Fraley sank into it gratefully. She was not at all sure she would be allowed to stay here long, but at least she would rest until someone told her to move on.

By this time the gnawing hunger had ceased to trouble her. She was only utterly weary. She let her head rest back and closed her eyes, too tired even to think of her recent horrible experiences.

The next thing she knew, someone touched her on the shoulder and she opened her eyes and started up. It seemed a long time since she had sat down, and she knew by the feeling of her eyes that she must have been asleep.

She looked around, half bewildered. Perhaps they were going to arrest her for having dared to go to sleep here.

But it was only the woman who had been lying on the couch. She was smiling at her.

"I just thought maybe you'd like to take the couch," she said in a kindly tone. "You look awfully tired, and I'm leaving in a few minutes. I take the midnight train, and if you get on here before I leave nobody else will get ahead of you."

"Oh," said Fraley relieved. "That's very kind of you. Would I be allowed to lie there the rest of the night?"

"Sure, I think you would, unless somebody was to come in real sick. Anyhow you can stay till someone puts you off."

So Fraley curled herself gratefully on the hard leather couch, watched her benefactor trudge off with her sleeping baby, and then dropped promptly off to sleep herself, too dazed to worry over her present situation, too drugged with trouble and weariness to even remember much about it.

She had two good hours of sleep on the couch before the caretaker roused her to give the couch to a woman more in need. But afterwards, dozing in another rocker, she began to come to her senses again.

Then it came to her that life in a great city with no friends was not going to be much better than life in a desert hiding from enemies. There seemed to be enemies on every hand everywhere.

As morning dawned grayly, and the time drew nearer when she would have to leave this brief haven and go out to find a new place in the world, she bethought herself of the advice her friend of the desert had given her. The Travelers' Aid! She would go to the Travelers' Aid and ask advice!

She dozed in her chair till morning was fully come and

the rush of the workaday world began to breeze through the waiting room. Then she tidied herself, picked up her little package and went to the restaurant.

A cup of coffee and some toast seemed to be about the cheapest thing she could get to eat, and after it was swallowed she felt courage rising within her.

During her morning meditations, it had occurred to her that there was still an unknown grandfather who might be applied to perhaps, for advice. But her proud young spirit shrank from going to her relatives a pauper. Not for worlds would she reveal her present condition to the family who had turned against her father for marrying her precious, saintly mother, even if she could find them. She had set her feet to walk a thorny path, and did not falter.

The Travelers' Aid asked several questions; where she had come from and where she was going. Fraley was not fond of giving information about herself, but she managed to evade the main issue, very cleverly.

"I'm from the west and my parents are dead," she stated quietly. This in answer to a query, why she had come to the city. "Yes, I had work but the lady wanted me to do some things that I did not think were right and I had to leave her. No, I would not feel like asking for a reference. I would rather find something for myself. Yes, I have some relatives in the city but—they are not in a position—that is I do not wish to ask help from them. I have a very little money, and I want to get a decent room where I will not be afraid, and something to do. I was told you could direct me."

There was a grave sweet dignity about the child that stopped further questions, and the Travelers' Aid with secret admiration began to look over her list of rooms.

"There are rooms of course as low as twenty-five cents a night, but they are not very nice. They are clean, but they are small and dark, and up several flights of stairs."

"Oh, that's all right," said Fraley with relief. "I can climb stairs. I'll take one, if you please."

"They are not in a very pleasant neighborhood, and there is very little furniture, only a cot and a table, perhaps a chair," said the woman eyeing the rich material of Fraley's imported frock, trim slippers and chic hat.

"Do you mean there would be bad men in the neighborhood?" asked Fraley, a frightened look coming in her eyes.

"Oh, no!" said the woman kindly. "We only recommend rooms in a respectable neighborhood of course. I mean the houses are not very attractive and the rooms are quite bare."

"I don't mind that!" said Fraley with a relieved sigh. "Now, do you know how I should go about getting a job? I'm willing to do anything."

"But you know you can't get a really good job without a reference, my dear."

The fright came back to the girl's eyes.

"Not *anything*?" she asked pathetically.

"Well, not anything that pays very well. There are a few places, of course, that are not so very particular. I'll give you a list and you can try."

Armed with the list and promising to come back if she got into difficulties, Fraley went on her way, full of good advice and directions.

The first three places on the list were filled, but the fourth turned out to be still vacant. Fraley shrank from the eyes of the proprietor, who looked her over as if she were a piece of merchandise, and finally hired her at an exceedingly small wage, so small that she knew that she must take the very cheapest room that was to be had in the city, and then scrimp at every turn. Even then she must eke out her needs with the few dollars left from her store brought from the west.

Her duties began that afternoon. She was to pull bastings from coarse finished garments that a dozen other women in the grimy room were making, on a dozen noisy sewing machines.

The room she finally took after a long search, was on the fourth floor overlooking chimney roofs and chimney pots through its tiny grimy window. It contained a gaunt cot scantily furnished, and absolutely nothing else. There were lavatory privileges on the floor below, all very dismal and utterly repelling. But the sad, sharp-faced, sick-looking proprietress looked decent at least and Fraley took the room because it was cheap.

In a cheap little shop not far away she purchased a dark cotton dress for a dollar, paid ten cents at a grocery for an empty orange box, purchased a box of crackers, some cheese and a bottle of milk, and set up housekeeping. The orange box she set on end for a combined table and pantry, put her Bible on the top, and her supplies on the shelf below. Then she changed into the cotton dress, ate a hasty lunch and hurried off to her work.

The atmosphere of the first workroom was almost unbearable, both morally, and physically. The air was bad, reeking of the unwashed, the language which her fellow workwomen used was worse, and their hostile manner reminded her of the women who had sent her into the dance hall the night before. Moreover, the proprietor was half drunk most of the time, and so cross that one could never please him, though Fraley tried with all her might. Her fingers were cut with the threads, and sore from contact with the rough goods, and her spirit was sore with the alien atmosphere about her.

When, at the end of a week, the proprietor refused to pay her but half the scanty wage promised her because he said that was all she was worth to him while she had been learning her job, she turned aghast and walked out of the shop.

Her next employment was in a small forlorn shop where derelict furniture found harbor and changed hands occasionally. The wages were a few cents more than in the tailor shop, but the proprietor required her to lie about the furniture, producing all sorts of fairy tales concerning articles on display, stories about former owners of renown, and finally dismissing her without pay because she had refused to lie about a chair with a broken leg when a customer asked if it hadn't been mended.

She grew thin and sorrowful as one experience of this sort after another met her. Her rounded cheeks lost their curves and rose tints, her eyes wore no more glints of happiness. Yet it never once entered her mind to go back to Violet Wentworth and give in to her conditions.

At last Fraley got a position as a waitress in a restaurant. It was not a high-class restaurant. In fact Fraley did not know how very low-class it was. A girl who roomed in the same house with her had told her of it. Her predecessor had died the night before of pneumonia, and the restaurant needed someone at once. The wages were better than any she had had so far, and though the hours were long and the duties heavy she started in happily.

Just one small pleasure she permitted herself. She did answer Jimmie MacPherson's letter, and his breezy reply gave her much comfort.

But a new trouble arose on the horizon when the proprietor began to grow fond of her, and insisted on making love to her.

She avoided him as much as possible at first, and went on her sweet impersonal way, keeping to herself, doing her hard work well and quickly, moving among her sordid surroundings like a young queen, and breaking her heart at night when she crept to her cot, too weary to even grieve long over the situation. Like her mother before her, she seemed to be caught on the wheel of circumstance, and to be condemned to go on because there was no way of getting off.

But a crisis arose late in November when Max, the dark-browed Russian proprietor, asked her to go to a movie with him that night.

It was during the six o'clock supper rush that it occurred. The headwaiter told her to go up to the desk, that Max wanted to see her.

With fear and trembling she obeyed, thinking perhaps she was to be dismissed, for she had broken some dishes that morning when the cook ran against her full tray. Also, she knew that he had been cross at her ever since she had refused to go to a dance with him the week before. But she had tried to be smiling and pleasant about it, and not anger him. She had told him that time that she did not feel well, and wanted to get straight home to bed. Now, she watched him anxiously as she threaded her way among the tables toward the desk. It was not that she dreaded leaving, for the work was terrible and the hours almost unbearable, but even such work was better than none at all, and the cold weather was at hand. She needed a warm coat. She had nothing but a thin sweater for a wrap, that she had bought at a second hand store for fifty cents, and carefully washed and mended.

So, when Max spoke in his most winning tones and asked her how she was feeling that night, she gave him a relieved smile. She did not see a dark fellow with lowering eyes across the room at a table in her own territory, who watched her narrowly with an evil gaze.

"Well, how about a picture tonight?" smiled Max wetting his voluptuous red lips, and watching the pretty color drain out of the smooth cheeks. "You and me has gotta get tagether, Birdie. I let you off tonight at seven, see? You can get dolled up and I meet you here at ten ta eight. See?"

Fraley's face was white now and her eyes troubled and earnest.

"Oh, Mr. Kirschmann, I couldn't. I really couldn't. I have some work I have to do this evening, and I really can't do my work here well if I stay up late nights—"

But she could see that her excuses were not getting her anywhere, and she drew back in dismayed protest.

"I ain't takin' no excuses. See?" went on Max, and reaching out his great grimy paw he caught both her hands and held them like a vise. "What I say goes. If you've gotta date with some other guy, break it. See? You're goin' out with me tonight an' that's straight. We're mebbe takin' dinner in a cabaret afterwards too, so put on yer best rags an' do me proud."

"But—" said Fraley wide-eyed and struggling to get free, aware of the hostile glances of her fellow laborers.

"Ain't no buts," said Max gruffly. "You gotta date 'ith me tonight. Ef you're to high hat ta go with Max you c'n leave the job *tanight!* See? But ef you do the right thing by me I'll see you sit pretty, my cherry! Now, run back ta yer table. There's a bird ben waitin' there five minutes an' he looks mad enough ta shoot. Run!"

Fraley ran, a great fear growing in her soul. Trouble was looming ahead of her. She could see that plainly. She must either go with this wild Russian fellow or she must give up her job. There was no use trying to get out of it. She could see that he was quite determined. She had seen enough men of this type to know and fear.

She was so concerned with her own thoughts that she scarcely noticed where she was going, and arriving at her table handed a grubby-looking menu card to her customer without noticing him.

But when he spoke:

"Get me a beef stew and make it snappy!" her eyes came about to look into his with horror, and he looked up and met her gaze with a dark insolence that searched her to the soul. It was Pierce Boyden himself sitting before her at the table!

For an instant it seemed to Fraley that she hung suspended between life and death. This surely was the end! He had searched her out forlorn and helpless! There was no one in the world to whom she could turn for protection unless she chose to appeal to her employer and accept his repulsive attentions. Perhaps he might be strong enough to outwit even Pierce Boyden, though she doubted it.

All this flew through her consciousness while she stood for that instant wondering if she were about to fall, and then to her surprise she turned and walked away from the table with the menu card in her hand, back to the kitchen. She was perfectly conscious, every step she took, that Pierce Boyden's eyes were upon her as she walked, and yet she was able to go steadily as if nothing unusual had happened. She felt that some power beyond herself was enabling her to do this, for in herself she had only awful weakness.

Back in the kitchen out of sight for the moment she seized the arm of a waitress just returning with a tray laden with soiled dishes.

"Anna! Take my customer! I don't feel well! He wants a beef stew in a hurry. You may have my tip."

She did not wait for the other girl to answer. She did not even wait to get her old grey sweater. She slipped out the back door into the dark alley, and was gone into the night. How many minutes would it be before Pierce would be after her? Perhaps even now he was on her track. Perhaps Max, too, had been watching her!

Her feet seemed to be made of lead, her arms weighed heavily at her sides, and although she did not seem to be making much progress, she was panting wildly. She longed for the wilds of the desert, and a friendly place to hide. She was afraid of every nook and corner of this alley, afraid of the streets she had to pass through, afraid of the whole awful city.

Though it seemed like ages, she did finally arrive at her stopping place, climb step by step up to the fourth floor, and was locked at last into her room. Then she fell upon her knees beside the bed, panting, breathless, her heart breathing an inarticulate prayer for help.

In a moment or two when the wild beating of her heart was somewhat quieted she sprang into action.

Quickly tearing off her work dress she put on her one good frock, threw her few possessions together into the old faithful gray bag her mother had made, put on her hat and hurried out of the room and down the stairs. She must get out of this place before any one came after her! She felt certain that Max would come even if Pierce was not able to find her at once. Some of the girls in the restaurant knew where she roomed, and Max would lose no time in finding her. She must get away at once and she must get away from this part of the world forever. She would go north or south or somewhere that Pierce Boyden could never find her! Perhaps she would even be able to find something to do on a ship and get away from the country altogether!

And how fortunate it was that she did not have to stop and talk with her landlady! She had paid her week's rent in advance three days ago, so that poor creature would not be out anything by her sudden flight.

This was her thought as she rounded the stair railing on the third floor and started down the dark narrow stairs to the second; and then suddenly she came face to face with a tall form, and would have fallen if strong arms had not caught her.

It was very dark in that upper hall, for the screaming uncertain gas jet had gone out, and as she struggled with her unknown adversary she felt herself falling. When she lost her footing her senses seemed to swim and swing in the balance, and she wondered if this might be what they called fainting, and then she felt herself lifted firmly and carried down to the floor below.

He had found her then, her enemy! Pierce or Max. It did not seem to matter; they were all one to her tired heart and brain. It was no use to struggle. This was the end!

24

FROM the start Violet's illness was desperate, and the physician and nurses and friends looked gravely at one another. And then she began in her delirium to call for Fraley. Night and day she tossed, and asked everyone who came in the room if they had found her yet.

They tried to pacify her with lies, but she paid no heed to them, only kept looking toward the door, and calling out to her to come. And the cry grew into a strange sentence.

"Come here! I'm going to die. I've got to see you about my sins! I don't know what to do!"

Over and over she would call it, till in desperation they sent for a minister of the fashionable church she had attended occasionally.

He tried to soothe her, to tell her she had no sins worth speaking of, to tell her it was all right, and he prayed a worthy and happy prayer to pave the way straight to heaven for her worried feet. But she only stared at him bewildered, and tossed her head and moaned: "It's Fraley I want. I've got to see her about my sins. She's the only one that knows what to do. She has a Bible."

So Jeanne came one day, with fear and trembling, and Fraley's Bible she had found on the bureau, and began to read in a low voice verses that Fraley had marked for her, verses about sins.

"As far as the east is from the west so far hath He removed our transgressions from us." "He hath put thy sins behind His back." "He hath drowned them in the depths of the sea." "For God so loved the world that He gave His only begotten son that whosoever believeth in Him should not perish, but have everlasting life." "For God sent not His son into the world to condemn the world, but that the world through Him might be saved."

And then that other chapter, the fourteenth of John, the first that Fraley had read to Jeanne: "Let not your heart be troubled, ye believe in God, believe also in me—"

The weary head turned, and the sunken fevered eyes looked at Jeanne, and she seemed to listen. On and on Jeanne read, her voice low and soothing, the tears continually blinding her.

At last a weak voice that sounded almost natural said:

"But that's not for me, Fraley knows. Oh, if Fraley would come and tell me about my sins!"

Said the doctor, who had come in during the reading and was watching the patient with practiced finger on the fluttering pulse:

"Where is this Fraley person that she talks about continually? Isn't there some way to get in touch with her? She might live if she came. Such things turn the tide sometimes."

They told this to old Grandfather MacPherson when he came to inquire, and he went sadly back to his wife, and reported it.

Jimmy was home from school for Thanksgiving vacation, and was in the next room listening.

"Fraley?" he said strolling to the door, "Fraley? Do you mean Fraley MacPherson? The girl I played golf with last summer? Why I know where she is. I had a letter from her last week. I've got her address, I'm going to see her tomorrow and take her one of my school pennants. She said she would like it to put in her room. She's been writing to me all fall."

Grandfather MacPherson started up and was wanting to go right off without his hat, till his wife protested. But Jimmy said:

"Aw, Gee. Lemme have the car, Grampa, I'll bring her back in no time. Naw, you needn'ta go along. Well, have it your own way, but she's gonta sit in front with me."

That was the wildest drive that the old man ever took in the midst of the traffic of a great city, and more than one officer of the law held up a worthy hand, and cried out, but Jimmy stopped not on the order of his going. Yet if his grandfather had to pay a fine next day, Jimmy never knew it. The old gentleman had his hat in his hand. He had not thought to put it on even when it was given him, and his wavy silver hair tossed wildly in the breeze as they sailed down Fifth Avenue at a speed no one in his senses dared to go.

And so it was Jimmy who went in after her, who mounted the stairs himself because the apathetic landlady said she didn't know whether the lodger was in or not and she was too tired to go and see. It was Jimmy who caught her on the wing and kept her from falling down stairs, who carried her down to the front door.

"Oh, gee! I'm glad I found ya!" he said setting her down at last, bewildered, overjoyed to find her enemy a friend. "Just suppose you'd gone out! You *were* going out, weren't ya? Say, they wantya bad down at yer house. That Mrs. Wentworth is awful sick and she keeps calling fer ya, and the doc says she's gotta have ya! And my grandad has been carrying on something fierce. If they'd just asked me before, I coulda told 'em!"

She ran before them all when she reached the house, past the overjoyed butler who opened the door, past frightened Alison who sat in the hall at her father's command to await a possible message to him, past the doctor who stood gravely at Violet's door, and the nurse who was putting away the medicine she had just administered.

Softly she knelt beside the bed and took the hot hand that picked at the coverlet.

"I've come," she whispered softly, "Violet, did you want me?"

The moaning stopped, the restless head turned to look, and the fevered eyes lit with sanity.

"Oh, you've come, Fraley, you've come! And now, you'll forgive me, won't you? I'm sorry, Fraley, little girl, I'm sorry! And what shall I do about my sins?"

"I've nothing to forgive, dear lady," said Fraley with her soft lips against the pale fingers, "I love you and I've come back. And don't worry about the rest. Jesus loves you, and died to save you."

"But I've sinned!" moaned the woman, "it's just as you knew. I've sinned!"

"Yes, Jesus knew all that. That's what He died for," said the girl with wonderful tenderness.

"Are you sure?"

"Perfectly sure."

"How do you know?"

"He told me so in His book."

"And will you stay right here and not go away any more?"

"Yes, I'll stay right here—"

Softly the white lids dropped over the bright restless eyes, more quietly the breath began to come, while Fraley knelt and held the frail hand, and the watchers stood outside the door and waited.

Perhaps an hour passed, and the doctor tiptoed in, touched the white wrist again, and nodded, looking at his watch.

Out in the hall later, when they had motioned Fraley away to get some rest the doctor told her:

"Little sister, you have saved her life. I think she'll pull through now, if you stay around. But you came just in time. Another hour and it would have been too late."

There were others waiting for Fraley down in the hall, waiting all the time that she knelt by the sick bed, until the night nurse took charge, promising to call her if she were needed. Old Mr. MacPherson waited with white face, and eager eyes, to clasp the child of his long-lost son, waited to take her home to her grandmother, where she was eagerly anticipated. Jimmy waited grim and important, feeling that he ought to have come before. All this fuss about something he could have straightened out in a minute. Now, perhaps his grandfather would see it would be best for him to stay around home instead of going back to that old stuffy school the next semester.

Alison waited to make a sullen apology to the girl she knew she must accept.

Jeanne waited to welcome her beloved Miss Fraley back and tell her she had never forgotten to read the blessed book.

But while they all waited, Alison, and Jimmy and MacPherson in the hall near the foot of the stairs, Jeanne just behind the reception room portiere where she could not be seen, the butler back farther in the hall, the door bell rang. Its muffled peal stirred on their strained senses like the boom of a cannon.

Fraley had just started down the stairs as the butler reached the door to open it, and paused looking down to see who it was. All the others started up eagerly, even Alison, relieved that the long wait was over. Saxon opened the door. A young man with a white face and one arm in a sling entered.

"I want to see Mrs. Wentworth right away, Saxon, please," rang out a voice that Fraley never would forget, a voice that thrilled through her heart and made her forget everything except that she was hearing it again.

"I'm sorry, Mr. George," said Saxon in a low apology,—for Saxon used to work for the Seagraves in the years that were past. "Mrs. Wentworth has been very ill indeed, sir. She is very low to-night."

The young man's face was full of sympathy.

"Oh!" he said, "I'm sorry, I didn't know."

His glance went around the group in the hall without perceiving who they were, and lifted to the stairs. Then his whole face lit with a wonderful joy.

"Ladybird!" he cried and sprang up the stairs to meet her. "My Little Ladybird! Thank God!"

About the Author

Grace Livingston Hill is well known as one of the most prolific writers of romantic fiction. Her personal life was fraught with joys and sorrows not unlike those experienced by many of her fictional heroines.

Born in Wellsville, New York, Grace nearly died during the first hours of life. But her loving parents and friends turned to God in prayer. She survived miraculously, thus her thankful father named her Grace.

Grace was always close to her father, a Presbyterian minister, and her mother, a published writer. It was from them that she learned the art of storytelling. When Grace was twelve, a close aunt surprised her with a hardbound, illustrated copy of one of Grace's stories. This was the beginning of Grace's journey into being a published author.

In 1892 Grace married Fred Hill, a young minister, and they soon had two lovely young daughters. Then came 1901, a difficult year for Grace—the year when, within months of each other, both her father and husband died. Suddenly Grace had to find a new place to live (her home was owned by the church where her husband had been pastor). It was a struggle for Grace to raise her young daughters alone, but through everything she kept writing. In 1902 she produced *The Angel of His Presence*, *The Story of a Whim*, and *An Unwilling Guest*. In 1903 her two books *According to the Pattern* and *Because of Stephen* were published.

It wasn't long before Grace was a well-known author, but she wanted to go beyond just entertaining her readers. She soon included the message of God's salvation through Jesus Christ in each of her books. For Grace, the most important thing she did was not write books but share the message of salvation, a message she felt God wanted her to share through the abilities he had given her.

In all, Grace Livingston Hill wrote more than one hundred books, all of which have sold thousands of copies and have touched the lives of readers around the world with their message of "enduring love" and the true way to lasting happiness: a relationship with God through his Son, Jesus Christ.

In an interview shortly before her death, Grace's devotion to her Lord still shone clear. She commented that whatever she had accomplished had been God's doing. She was only his servant, one who had tried to follow his teaching in all her thoughts and writing.

Don't miss these Grace Livingston Hill romance novels!